THE CIRCULAR STAIRCASE

THE ORIGINAL CLASSIC MYSTERY
COMPLETE & UNABRIDGED

MARY ROBERTS RINEHART

SUMMIT CLASSIC LARGE PRINT MYSTERIES
SUMMIT CLASSIC PRESS
AKRON, OHIO

SUMMIT CLASSIC MYSTERIES

VINTAGE MYSTERIES & DETECTIVE ADVENTURES

About the Author — Mary Roberts Rinehart

Mary Roberts Rinehart (August 12, 1876-September 22, 1958) was a popular and successful American writer best known for her mysteries. Sometimes referred to as "the American Agatha Christie," Rinehart's first mystery novel actually appeared over a decade before Christie's. She is considered the originator of the "Had-I-But-Known" style of mystery, as well as the source of the phrase "The butler did it."

She was born in Allegheny City, Pennsylvania, since absorbed as a part of Pittsburgh, to Thomas and Cornelia Roberts. Of her childhood growing up in a house with her extended family, she would later recall, in her autobiography, *My Story* (1931, revised 1948), her grandmother working long hours in the dressmaking shop at the back of the house, and the fact that "There was never any money in those days." Her father was involved in the sewing machine business and had actually obtained a patent for his design for a rotary shuttle for sewing machines. But while his constant tinkering resulted in the "invention" of numerous gadgets, none were successful and his failure as an inventor led to his suicide. Years later Rinehart remembered her father taking his own life: "He went away one day and killed himself, standing in front of a mirror in a strange hotel so that the shot would not fail."

Roberts was educated in the local public schools. Left-handed at a time when it was considered a "defect," she was forced by her teachers to use her right hand. She graduated at age 16, then enrolled at the Pittsburgh Training School for Nurses at Homeopathic Hospital. She later described the experience as "all the tragedy of the world under one roof," and graduated in 1896. After graduation, she married Stanley Marshall Rinehart (1867–1932), a physician she had met at the hospital. The marriage produced three sons and one daughter, Stanley Jr., Frederick, Alan, and Elizabeth.

Roberts assisted in her husband's medical practice while raising their children and caring for her family, but when the family's savings were lost in the stock market crash of 1903 she turned to publishing her writings as a means of generating additional income. She was 27 years old at the time, and in about one year she produced 45 short stories. In 1906 *The Man in Lower Ten*, the first of her many popular mystery novels, was published, and in 1907 she wrote *The Circular Staircase*, which made her a national celebrity and launched her career as a celebrated mystery novelist. This success was quickly followed up with *The Window At The White Cat* (1908), another major success.

She soon became a regular contributor to The Saturday Evening Post, and her immensely popular stories and articles have been credited with helping to shape middle class manners and tastes. In 1909 she collaborated with Anthony Hopwood on a very successful Broadway comedy, *Seven Days*. By 1911 she had published a series of successful novels, and the family bought a large, old home in a state of considerable disrepair. The rehabilitation and renovation of the property became Mrs. Rinehart's personal project. As she later recorded in her autobiography, "The venture was mine, and I had put every dollar I possessed into the purchase. All week long I wrote wildly to meet the payroll and contractor costs."

With the outbreak of World War I, she became the first woman war correspondent in Belgium. While in Belgium she interviewed Albert I of Belgium and Winston Churchill, and of her meeting with the Queen of England she wrote; "This afternoon I am to be presented to the queen of England. I am to curtsey and to say 'Your Majesty' the first time!" Rinehart also worked in England as a war-time correspondent for The Saturday Evening Post, and was in Paris in 1918 reporting on developments to the War Department when the armistice was signed.

In the early 1920s Dr. Rinehart accepted a post in the Veterans Administration and the family moved to Washington, DC. Rinehart resumed her writing career, publishing, among other works, *The Breaking Point* (1922), *The Red Lamp* (1925), *The Door* (1930), and another Broadway play, *The Bat* (with Avery Hopwood, 1932). *The Bat* was based on a costumed supercriminal created by Rinehart, listed by Bob Kane as one of the influences which led to his creation of "Batman." This character also provided the basis for two film adaptations, The Bat (1926) and The Bat Whispers (1930), as well as a 1959 remake of The Bat. In 1933 *The Bat* also became one of the first RCA Victor "talking book" recordings.

Dr. Rinehart, a major in the Army Medical Corps, died in 1932 and was buried in Arlington National Cemetery. Rinehart remained in Washington, continuing her writing, until 1935, when she moved to New York City and helped her sons found the Farrar & Rinehart publishing company.

Rinehart continued writing and publishing, including *The Album* (1933), *The State Vs. Elinor Norton* (1933), *The Wall* (1938), *The Great Mistake* (1940), *The Yellow Room* (1945), *A Light in the Window* (1948), *The Episode of the Wandering Knife* (1950), *The Swimming Pool* (1952), and *The Frightened Wife* (1953).

In 1947, at her vacation home in Bar Harbor, Maine, Rinehart was involved in a bizarre incident that could have come from the pages of one of her books, when a chef who had worked for her for 25 years fired a shot at her and then attempted to attack her with a knife. Other household servants intervened, and the chef committed suicide in his cell the next day. Also in 1947 the interview "I Had Cancer" was published in Ladies' Home Journal. Rinehart had breast cancer, which resulted in a radical mastectomy. She became perhaps the first prominent and well-known woman to go public with her story, in an era when such matters were not discussed openly. In the interview Rinehart encouraged women to have breast examinations, in effect launching the modern era of breast cancer awareness.

Many of Rinehart's books were best-sellers, but her mysteries were her most popular works, and remain popular with mystery fans today. Rinehart was an early writer of mysteries featuring women as main characters, often an unlikely heroine thrust unexpectedly into the role of sleuth. In *The Circular Staircase* Rinehart is credited with originating the "Had-I-But-Known" mystery, in a story in which "a middle-aged spinster" rents a country house for the summer and is plunged into a murder mystery. In this type of story, the protagonist takes some action which prolongs or furthers the story, later realizing, along with the reader, that had she understood the significance of a clue, or had a certain bit of information, the further travails might have been avoided. An indication of the wide popularity of Rinehart's work is the fact that the phrase "the butler did it," which has become the ultimate mystery genre cliché, apparently originated with Rinehart's novel *The Door*, in which the butler actually did do it...but the phrase was never actually used in the book.

Mary Roberts Rinehart died at age 82 at her home on Park Avenue in New York City in 1958, having received a Mystery Writers of America Special Award for her lifetime contribution and an honorary Doctorate in Literature from George Washington University. She was buried beside her husband in Arlington National Cemetery.

The Circular Staircase
Mary Roberts Rinehart
Table of Contents

1.   I TAKE A COUNTRY HOUSE

This is the story of how a middle-aged spinster lost her mind, deserted her domestic gods in the city, took a furnished house for the summer out of town, and found herself involved in one of those mysterious crimes that keep our newspapers and detective agencies happy and prosperous. For twenty years I had been perfectly comfortable; for twenty years I had had the window-boxes filled in the spring, the carpets lifted, the awnings put up and the furniture covered with brown linen; for as many summers I had said good-by to my friends, and, after watching their perspiring hegira, had settled down to a delicious quiet in town, where the mail comes three times a day, and the water supply does not depend on a tank on the roof.

And then—the madness seized me. When I look back over the months I spent at Sunnyside, I wonder that I survived at all. As it is, I show the wear and tear of my harrowing experiences. I have turned very gray—Liddy reminded me of it, only yesterday, by saying that a little bluing in the rinse-water would make my hair silvery, instead of a yellowish white. I hate to be reminded of unpleasant things and I snapped her off.

"No," I said sharply, "I'm not going to use bluing at my time of life, or starch, either."

Liddy's nerves are gone, she says, since that awful summer, but she has enough left, goodness knows! And when she begins to go around with a lump in her throat, all I have to do is to threaten to return to Sunnyside, and she is frightened into a semblance of cheerfulness,—from which you may judge that the summer there was anything but a success.

The newspaper accounts have been so garbled and incomplete—one of them mentioned me but once, and then only as the tenant at the time the thing happened—that I feel it my due to tell what I know. Mr. Jamieson, the detective, said himself he could never have done without me, although he gave me little enough credit, in print.

I shall have to go back several years—thirteen, to be exact—to start my story. At that time my brother died, leaving me his two children. Halsey was eleven then, and Gertrude was seven. All the responsibilities of maternity were thrust upon me suddenly; to perfect the profession of motherhood requires precisely as many years as the child has lived, like the man who started to carry the calf and ended by walking along with the bull on his shoulders. However, I did the best I could. When Gertrude got past the hair-ribbon age, and Halsey asked for a scarf-pin and put on long trousers—and a wonderful help that was to the darning—I sent them away to good schools. After that, my responsibility was chiefly postal, with three months every summer in which to replenish their wardrobes, look over their lists of acquaintances, and generally to take my foster-motherhood out of its nine months' retirement in camphor.

I missed the summers with them when, somewhat later, at boarding-school and college, the children spent much of their vacations with friends. Gradually I found that my name signed to a check was even more welcome than when signed to a letter, though I wrote them at stated intervals. But when Halsey had finished his electrical course and Gertrude her boarding-school, and both came home to stay, things were suddenly changed. The winter Gertrude came out was nothing but a succession of sitting up late at night to bring her home from things, taking her to the dressmakers between naps the next day, and discouraging ineligible youths with either more money than brains, or more brains than money. Also, I acquired a great many things: to say lingerie for under-garments, "frocks" and "gowns" instead of dresses, and that beardless sophomores are not college boys, but college men. Halsey required less personal supervision, and as they both got their mother's fortune that winter, my responsibility became purely moral. Halsey bought a car, of course, and I learned how to tie over my bonnet a gray baize veil, and, after a time, never to stop to look at the dogs one has run down. People are apt to be so unpleasant about their dogs.

The additions to my education made me a properly equipped maiden aunt, and by spring I was quite tractable. So when Halsey suggested camping in the Adirondacks and Gertrude wanted Bar Harbor, we compromised on a good country house with links near, within motor distance of town and telephone distance of the doctor. That was how we went to Sunnyside.

We went out to inspect the property, and it seemed to deserve its name. Its cheerful appearance gave no indication whatever of anything out of the ordinary. Only one thing seemed unusual to me: the housekeeper, who had been left in charge, had moved from the house to the gardener's lodge, a few days before. As the lodge was far enough away from the house, it seemed to me that either fire or thieves could complete their work of destruction undisturbed. The property was an extensive one: the house on the top of a hill, which sloped away in great stretches of green lawn and clipped hedges, to the road; and across the valley, perhaps a couple of miles away, was the Greenwood Club House. Gertrude and Halsey were infatuated.

"Why, it's everything you want," Halsey said "View, air, good water and good roads. As for the house, it's big enough for a hospital, if it has a Queen Anne front and a Mary Anne back," which was ridiculous: it was pure Elizabethan.

Of course we took the place; it was not my idea of comfort, being much too large and sufficiently isolated to make the servant question serious. But I give myself credit for this: whatever has happened since, I never blamed Halsey and Gertrude for taking me there. And another thing: if the series of catastrophes there did nothing else, it taught me one thing—that somehow, somewhere, from perhaps a half-civilized ancestor who wore a sheepskin garment and trailed his food or his prey, I have in me the instinct of the chase. Were I a man I should be a trapper of criminals, trailing them as relentlessly as no doubt my sheepskin ancestor did his wild boar. But being an unmarried woman, with the handicap of my sex, my first acquaintance with crime will probably be my last. Indeed, it came near enough to being my last acquaintance with anything.

The property was owned by Paul Armstrong, the president of the Traders' Bank, who at the time we took the house was in the west with his wife and daughter, and a Doctor Walker, the Armstrong family physician. Halsey knew Louise Armstrong,—had been rather attentive to her the winter before, but as Halsey was always attentive to somebody, I had not thought of it seriously, although she was a charming girl. I knew of Mr. Armstrong only through his connection with the bank, where the children's money was largely invested, and through an ugly story about the son, Arnold Armstrong, who was reported to have forged his father's name, for a considerable amount, to some bank paper. However, the story had had no interest for me.

I cleared Halsey and Gertrude away to a house party, and moved out to Sunnyside the first of May. The roads were bad, but the trees were in leaf, and there were still tulips in the borders around the house. The arbutus was fragrant in the woods under the dead leaves, and on the way from the station, a short mile, while the car stuck in the mud, I found a bank showered with tiny forget-me-nots. The birds—don't ask me what kind; they all look alike to me, unless they have a hall mark of some bright color—the birds were chirping in the hedges, and everything breathed of peace. Liddy, who was born and bred on a brick pavement, got a little bit down-spirited when the crickets began to chirp, or scrape their legs together, or whatever it is they do, at twilight.

The first night passed quietly enough. I have always been grateful for that one night's peace; it shows what the country might be, under favorable circumstances. Never after that night did I put my head on my pillow with any assurance how long it would be there; or on my shoulders, for that matter.

On the following morning Liddy and Mrs. Ralston, my own housekeeper, had a difference of opinion, and Mrs. Ralston left on the eleven o'clock train. Just after luncheon, Burke, the butler, was taken unexpectedly with a pain in his right side, much worse when I was within hearing distance, and by afternoon he was started cityward. That night the cook's sister had a baby—the cook, seeing indecision in my face, made it twins on second thought—and, to be short, by noon the next day the household staff was down to Liddy and myself. And this in a house with twenty-two rooms and five baths!

Liddy wanted to go back to the city at once, but the milk-boy said that Thomas Johnson, the Armstrongs' colored butler, was working as a waiter at the Greenwood Club, and might come back. I have the usual scruples about coercing people's servants away, but few of us have any conscience regarding institutions or corporations—witness the way we beat railroads and street-car companies when we can—so I called up the club, and about eight o'clock Thomas Johnson came to see me. Poor Thomas!

Well, it ended by my engaging Thomas on the spot, at outrageous wages, and with permission to sleep in the gardener's lodge, empty since the house was rented. The old man—he was white-haired and a little stooped, but with an immense idea of his personal dignity—gave me his reasons hesitatingly.

"I ain't sayin' nothin', Mis' Innes," he said, with his hand on the door-knob, "but there's been goin's-on here this las' few months as ain't natchal. 'Tain't one thing an' 'tain't another—it's jest a door squealin' here, an' a winder closin' there, but when doors an' winders gets to cuttin' up capers and there's nobody nigh 'em, it's time Thomas Johnson sleeps somewhar's else."

Liddy, who seemed to be never more than ten feet away from me that night, and was afraid of her shadow in that great barn of a place, screamed a little, and turned a yellow-green. But I am not easily alarmed.

It was entirely in vain; I represented to Thomas that we were alone, and that he would have to stay in the house that night. He was politely firm, but he would come over early the next morning, and if I gave him a key, he would come in time to get some sort of breakfast. I stood on the huge veranda and watched him shuffle along down the shadowy drive, with mingled feelings—irritation at his cowardice and thankfulness at getting him at all. I am not ashamed to say that I double-locked the hall door when I went in.

"You can lock up the rest of the house and go to bed, Liddy," I said severely. "You give me the creeps standing there. A woman of your age ought to have better sense." It usually braces Liddy to mention her age: she owns to forty—which is absurd. Her mother cooked for my grandfather, and Liddy must be at least as old as I. But that night she refused to brace.

"You're not going to ask me to lock up, Miss Rachel!" she quavered. "Why, there's a dozen French windows in the drawing-room and the billiard-room wing, and every one opens on a porch. And Mary Anne said that last night there was a man standing by the stable when she locked the kitchen door."

"Mary Anne was a fool," I said sternly. "If there had been a man there, she would have had him in the kitchen and been feeding him what was left from dinner, inside of an hour, from force of habit. Now don't be ridiculous. Lock up the house and go to bed. I am going to read."

But Liddy set her lips tight and stood still.

"I'm not going to bed," she said. "I am going to pack up, and to-morrow I am going to leave."

"You'll do nothing of the sort," I snapped. Liddy and I often desire to part company, but never at the same time. "If you are afraid, I will go with you, but for goodness' sake don't try to hide behind me."

The house was a typical summer residence on an extensive scale. Wherever possible, on the first floor, the architect had done away with partitions, using arches and columns instead. The effect was cool and spacious, but scarcely cozy. As Liddy and I went from one window to another, our voices echoed back at us uncomfortably. There was plenty of light—the electric plant down in the village supplied us—but there were long vistas of polished floor, and mirrors which reflected us from unexpected corners, until I felt some of Liddy's foolishness communicate itself to me.

The house was very long, a rectangle in general form, with the main entrance in the center of the long side. The brick-paved entry opened into a short hall to the right of which, separated only by a row of pillars, was a huge living-room. Beyond that was the drawing-room, and in the end, the billiard-room. Off the billiard-room, in the extreme right wing, was a den, or card-room, with a small hall opening on the east veranda, and from there went up a narrow circular staircase. Halsey had pointed it out with delight.

"Just look, Aunt Rachel," he said with a flourish. "The architect that put up this joint was wise to a few things. Arnold Armstrong and his friends could sit here and play cards all night and stumble up to bed in the early morning, without having the family send in a police call."

Liddy and I got as far as the card-room and turned on all the lights. I tried the small entry door there, which opened on the veranda, and examined the windows. Everything was secure, and Liddy, a little less nervous now, had just pointed out to me the disgracefully dusty condition of the hard-wood floor, when suddenly the lights went out. We waited a moment; I think Liddy was stunned with fright, or she would have screamed. And then I clutched her by the arm and pointed to one of the windows opening on the porch. The sudden change threw the window into relief, an oblong of grayish light, and showed us a figure standing close, peering in. As I looked it darted across the veranda and out of sight in the darkness.

2. A LINK CUFF-BUTTON

Liddy's knees seemed to give away under her. Without a sound she sank down, leaving me staring at the window in petrified amazement. Liddy began to moan under her breath, and in my excitement I reached down and shook her.

"Stop it," I whispered. "It's only a woman—maybe a maid of the Armstrongs'. Get up and help me find the door." She groaned again. "Very well," I said, "then I'll have to leave you here. I'm going."

She moved at that, and, holding to my sleeve, we felt our way, with numerous collisions, to the billiard-room, and from there to the drawing-room. The lights came on then, and, with the long French windows unshuttered, I had a creepy feeling that each one sheltered a peering face. In fact, in the light of what happened afterward, I am pretty certain we were under surveillance during the entire ghostly evening. We hurried over the rest of the locking-up and got upstairs as quickly as we could. I left the lights all on, and our footsteps echoed cavernously. Liddy had a stiff neck the next morning, from looking back over her shoulder, and she refused to go to bed.

"Let me stay in your dressing-room, Miss Rachel," she begged. "If you don't, I'll sit in the hall outside the door. I'm not going to be murdered with my eyes shut."

"If you're going to be murdered," I retorted, "it won't make any difference whether they are shut or open. But you may stay in the dressing-room, if you will lie on the couch: when you sleep in a chair you snore."

She was too far gone to be indignant, but after a while she came to the door and looked in to where I was composing myself for sleep with *Drummond's Spiritual Life.*

"That wasn't a woman, Miss Rachel," she said, with her shoes in her hand. "It was a man in a long coat."

"What woman was a man?" I discouraged her without looking up, and she went back to the couch.

It was eleven o'clock when I finally prepared for bed. In spite of my assumption of indifference, I locked the door into the hall, and finding the transom did not catch, I put a chair cautiously before the door—it was not necessary to rouse Liddy—and climbing up put on the ledge of the transom a small dressing-mirror, so that any movement of the frame would send it crashing down. Then, secure in my precautions, I went to bed.

I did not go to sleep at once. Liddy disturbed me just as I was growing drowsy, by coming in and peering under the bed. She was afraid to speak, however, because of her previous snubbing, and went back, stopping in the doorway to sigh dismally.

Somewhere down-stairs a clock with a chime sang away the hours—eleven-thirty, forty-five, twelve. And then the lights went out to stay. The Casanova Electric Company shuts up shop and goes home to bed at midnight: when one has a party, I believe it is customary to pay a fee to the company, which will drink hot coffee and keep awake a couple of hours longer. But the lights were gone for good that night. Liddy had gone to sleep, as I knew she would. She was a very unreliable person: always awake and ready to talk when she wasn't wanted and dozing off to sleep when she was. I called her once or twice, the only result being an explosive snore that threatened her very windpipe—then I got up and lighted a bedroom candle.

My bedroom and dressing room were above the big living-room on the first floor. On the second floor a long corridor ran the length of the house, with rooms opening from both sides. In the wings were small corridors crossing the main one—the plan was simplicity itself. And just as I got back into bed, I heard a sound from the east wing, apparently, that made me stop, frozen, with one bedroom slipper half off, and listen. It was a rattling metallic sound, and it reverberated along the empty halls like the crash of doom. It was for all the world as if something heavy, perhaps a piece of steel, had rolled clattering and jangling down the hard-wood stairs leading to the card-room.

In the silence that followed Liddy stirred and snored again. I was exasperated: first she kept me awake by silly alarms, then when she was needed she slept like Joe Jefferson, or Rip—they are always the same to me. I went in and aroused her, and I give her credit for being wide awake the minute I spoke.

"Get up," I said, "if you don't want to be murdered in your bed."

"Where? How?" she yelled vociferously, and jumped up.

"There's somebody in the house," I said. "Get up. We'll have to get to the telephone."

"Not out in the hall!" she gasped; "Oh, Miss Rachel, not out in the hall!" trying to hold me back. But I am a large woman and Liddy is small. We got to the door, somehow, and Liddy held a brass andiron, which it was all she could do to lift, let alone brain anybody with. I listened, and, hearing nothing, opened the door a little and peered into the hall. It was a black void, full of terrible suggestion, and my candle only emphasized the gloom. Liddy squealed and drew me back again, and as the door slammed, the mirror I had put on the transom came down and hit her on the head. That completed our demoralization. It was some time before I could persuade her she had not been attacked from behind by a burglar, and when she found the mirror smashed on the floor she wasn't much better.

"There's going to be a death!" she wailed. "Oh, Miss Rachel, there's going to be a death!"

"There will be," I said grimly, "if you don't keep quiet, Liddy Allen."

And so we sat there until morning, wondering if the candle would last until dawn, and arranging what trains we could take back to town. If we had only stuck to that decision and gone back before it was too late!

The sun came finally, and from my window I watched the trees along the drive take shadowy form, gradually lose their ghostlike appearance, become gray and then green. The Greenwood Club showed itself a dab of white against the hill across the valley, and an early robin or two hopped around in the dew. Not until the milk-boy and the sun came, about the same time, did I dare to open the door into the hall and look around. Everything was as we had left it. Trunks were heaped here and there, ready for the trunk-room, and through an end window of stained glass came a streak of red and yellow daylight that was eminently cheerful. The milk-boy was pounding somewhere below, and the day had begun.

Thomas Johnson came ambling up the drive about half-past six, and we could hear him clattering around on the lower floor, opening shutters. I had to take Liddy to her room up-stairs, however,—she was quite sure she would find something uncanny. In fact, when she did not, having now the courage of daylight, she was actually disappointed.

Well, we did not go back to town that day.

The discovery of a small picture fallen from the wall of the drawing-room was quite sufficient to satisfy Liddy that the alarm had been a false one, but I was anything but convinced. Allowing for my nerves and the fact that small noises magnify themselves at night, there was still no possibility that the picture had made the series of sounds I heard. To prove it, however, I dropped it again. It fell with a single muffled crash of its wooden frame, and incidentally ruined itself beyond repair. I justified myself by reflecting that if the Armstrongs chose to leave pictures in unsafe positions, and to rent a house with a family ghost, the destruction of property was their responsibility, not mine.

I warned Liddy not to mention what had happened to anybody, and telephoned to town for servants. Then after a breakfast which did more credit to Thomas' heart than his head, I went on a short tour of investigation. The sounds had come from the east wing, and not without some qualms I began there. At first I found nothing. Since then I have developed my powers of observation, but at that time I was a novice. The small card-room seemed undisturbed. I looked for footprints, which is, I believe, the conventional thing to do, although my experience has been that as clues both footprints and thumb-marks are more useful in fiction than in fact. But the stairs in that wing offered something.

At the top of the flight had been placed a tall wicker hamper, packed, with linen that had come from town. It stood at the edge of the top step, almost barring passage, and on the step below it was a long fresh scratch. For three steps the scratch was repeated, gradually diminishing, as if some object had fallen, striking each one. Then for four steps nothing. On the fifth step below was a round dent in the hard wood. That was all, and it seemed little enough, except that I was positive the marks had not been there the day before.

It bore out my theory of the sound, which had been for all the world like the bumping of a metallic object down a flight of steps. The four steps had been skipped. I reasoned that an iron bar, for instance, would do something of the sort,—strike two or three steps, end down, then turn over, jumping a few stairs, and landing with a thud.

Iron bars, however, do not fall down-stairs in the middle of the night alone. Coupled with the figure on the veranda the agency by which it climbed might be assumed. But— and here was the thing that puzzled me most—the doors were all fastened that morning, the windows unmolested, and the particular door from the card-room to the veranda had a combination lock of which I held the key, and which had not been tampered with.

I fixed on an attempt at burglary, as the most natural explanation—an attempt frustrated by the falling of the object, whatever it was, that had roused me. Two things I could not understand: how the intruder had escaped with everything locked, and why he had left the small silver, which, in the absence of a butler, had remained down-stairs over night.

Under pretext of learning more about the place, Thomas Johnson led me through the house and the cellars, without result. Everything was in good order and repair; money had been spent lavishly on construction and plumbing. The house was full of conveniences, and I had no reason to repent my bargain, save the fact that, in the nature of things, night must come again. And other nights must follow—and we were a long way from a police-station.

In the afternoon a hack came up from Casanova, with a fresh relay of servants. The driver took them with a flourish to the servants' entrance, and drove around to the front of the house, where I was awaiting him.

"Two dollars," he said in reply to my question. "I don't charge full rates, because, bringin' 'em up all summer as I do, it pays to make a special price. When they got off the train, I sez, sez I, `There's another bunch for Sunnyside, cook, parlor maid and all.' Yes'm—six summers, and a new lot never less than once a month. They won't stand for the country and the lonesomeness, I reckon."

But with the presence of the "bunch" of servants my courage revived, and late in the afternoon came a message from Gertrude that she and Halsey would arrive that night at about eleven o'clock, coming in the car from Richfield. Things were looking up; and when Beulah, my cat, a most intelligent animal, found some early catnip on a bank near the house and rolled in it in a feline ecstasy, I decided that getting back to nature was the thing to do.

While I was dressing for dinner, Liddy rapped at the door. She was hardly herself yet, but privately I think she was worrying about the broken mirror and its augury, more than anything else. When she came in she was holding something in her hand, and she laid it on the dressing-table carefully.

"I found it in the linen hamper," she said. "It must be Mr. Halsey's, but it seems queer how it got there."

It was the half of a link cuff-button of unique design, and I looked at it carefully.

"Where was it? In the bottom of the hamper?" I asked.

"On the very top," she replied. "It's a mercy it didn't fall out on the way."

When Liddy had gone I examined the fragment attentively. I had never seen it before, and I was certain it was not Halsey's. It was of Italian workmanship, and consisted of a mother-of-pearl foundation, encrusted with tiny seed-pearls, strung on horsehair to hold them. In the center was a small ruby. The trinket was odd enough, but not intrinsically of great value. Its interest for me lay in this: Liddy had found it lying in the top of the hamper which had blocked the east-wing stairs.

That afternoon the Armstrongs' housekeeper, a youngish good-looking woman, applied for Mrs. Ralston's place, and I was glad enough to take her. She looked as though she might be equal to a dozen of Liddy, with her snapping black eyes and heavy jaw. Her name was Anne Watson, and I dined that evening for the first time in three days.

3. MR. JOHN BAILEY APPEARS

I had dinner served in the breakfast-room. Somehow the huge dining-room depressed me, and Thomas, cheerful enough all day, allowed his spirits to go down with the sun. He had a habit of watching the corners of the room, left shadowy by the candles on the table, and altogether it was not a festive meal.

Dinner over I went into the living-room. I had three hours before the children could possibly arrive, and I got out my knitting. I had brought along two dozen pairs of slipper soles in assorted sizes—I always send knitted slippers to the Old Ladies' Home at Christmas—and now I sorted over the wools with a grim determination not to think about the night before. But my mind was not on my work: at the end of a half-hour I found I had put a row of blue scallops on Eliza Klinefelter's lavender slippers, and I put them away.

I got out the cuff-link and went with it to the pantry. Thomas was wiping silver and the air was heavy with tobacco smoke. I sniffed and looked around, but there was no pipe to be seen.

"Thomas," I said, "you have been smoking."

"No, ma'm." He was injured innocence itself. "It's on my coat, ma'm. Over at the club the gentlemen—"

But Thomas did not finish. The pantry was suddenly filled with the odor of singeing cloth. Thomas gave a clutch at his coat, whirled to the sink, filled a tumbler with water and poured it into his right pocket with the celerity of practice.

"Thomas," I said, when he was sheepishly mopping the floor, "smoking is a filthy and injurious habit. If you must smoke, you must; but don't stick a lighted pipe in your pocket again. Your skin's your own: you can blister it if you like. But this house is not mine, and I don't want a conflagration. Did you ever see this cuff-link before?"

No, he never had, he said, but he looked at it oddly.

"I picked it up in the hall," I added indifferently. The old man's eyes were shrewd under his bushy eyebrows.

"There's strange goin's-on here, Mis' Innes," he said, shaking his head. "Somethin's goin' to happen, sure. You ain't took notice that the big clock in the hall is stopped, I reckon?"

"Nonsense," I said. "Clocks have to stop, don't they, if they're not wound?"

"It's wound up, all right, and it stopped at three o'clock last night," he answered solemnly. "More'n that, that there clock ain't stopped for fifteen years, not since Mr. Armstrong's first wife died. And that ain't all,—no *ma'm*. Last three nights I slep' in this place, after the electrics went out I had a token. My oil lamp was full of oil, but it kep' goin' out, do what I would. Minute I shet my eyes, out that lamp'd go. There ain't no surer token of death. The Bible sez, *let yer light shine!* When a hand you can't see puts yer light out, it means death, sure."

The old man's voice was full of conviction. In spite of myself I had a chilly sensation in the small of my back, and I left him mumbling over his dishes. Later on I heard a crash from the pantry, and Liddy reported that Beulah, who is coal black, had darted in front of Thomas just as he picked up a tray of dishes; that the bad omen had been too much for him, and he had dropped the tray.

The chug of the automobile as it climbed the hill was the most welcome sound I had heard for a long time, and with Gertrude and Halsey actually before me, my troubles seemed over for good. Gertrude stood smiling in the hall, with her hat quite over one ear, and her hair in every direction under her pink veil. Gertrude is a very pretty girl, no matter how her hat is, and I was not surprised when Halsey presented a good-looking young man, who bowed at me and looked at Trude—that is the ridiculous nickname Gertrude brought from school.

"I have brought a guest, Aunt Ray," Halsey said. "I want you to adopt him into your affections and your Saturday-to-Monday list. Let me present John Bailey, only you must call him Jack. In twelve hours he'll be calling you `Aunt': I know him."

We shook hands, and I got a chance to look at Mr. Bailey; he was a tall fellow, perhaps thirty, and he wore a small mustache. I remember wondering why: he seemed to have a good mouth and when he smiled his teeth were above the average. One never knows why certain men cling to a messy upper lip that must get into things, any more than one understands some women building up their hair on wire atrocities. Otherwise, he was very good to look at, stalwart and tanned, with the direct gaze that I like. I am particular about Mr. Bailey, because he was a prominent figure in what happened later.

Gertrude was tired with the trip and went up to bed very soon. I made up my mind to tell them nothing until the next day, and then to make as light of our excitement as possible. After all, what had I to tell? An inquisitive face peering in at a window; a crash in the night; a scratch or two on the stairs, and half a cuff-button! As for Thomas and his forebodings, it was always my belief that a negro is one part thief, one part pigment, and the rest superstition.

It was Saturday night. The two men went to the billiard-room, and I could hear them talking as I went up-stairs. It seemed that Halsey had stopped at the Greenwood Club for gasoline and found Jack Bailey there, with the Sunday golf crowd. Mr. Bailey had not been hard to persuade—probably Gertrude knew why—and they had carried him off triumphantly. I roused Liddy to get them something to eat—Thomas was beyond reach in the lodge—and paid no attention to her evident terror of the kitchen regions. Then I went to bed. The men were still in the billiard-room when I finally dozed off, and the last thing I remember was the howl of a dog in front of the house. It wailed a crescendo of woe that trailed off hopefully, only to break out afresh from a new point of the compass.

At three o'clock in the morning I was roused by a revolver shot. The sound seemed to come from just outside my door. For a moment I could not move. Then—I heard Gertrude stirring in her room, and the next moment she had thrown open the connecting door.

"O Aunt Ray! Aunt Ray!" she cried hysterically. "Some one has been killed, killed!"

"Thieves," I said shortly. "Thank goodness, there are some men in the house to-night." I was getting into my slippers and a bath-robe, and Gertrude with shaking hands was lighting a lamp. Then we opened the door into the hall, where, crowded on the upper landing of the stairs, the maids, white-faced and trembling, were peering down, headed by Liddy. I was greeted by a series of low screams and questions, and I tried to quiet them.

Gertrude had dropped on a chair and sat there limp and shivering.

I went at once across the hall to Halsey's room and knocked; then I pushed the door open. It was empty; the bed had not been occupied!

"He must be in Mr. Bailey's room," I said excitedly, and followed by Liddy, we went there. Like Halsey's, it had not been occupied! Gertrude was on her feet now, but she leaned against the door for support.

"They have been killed!" she gasped. Then she caught me by the arm and dragged me toward the stairs. "They may only be hurt, and we must find them," she said, her eyes dilated with excitement.

I don't remember how we got down the stairs: I do remember expecting every moment to be killed. The cook was at the telephone up-stairs, calling the Greenwood Club, and Liddy was behind me, afraid to come and not daring to stay behind. We found the living-room and the drawing-room undisturbed. Somehow I felt that whatever we found would be in the card-room or on the staircase, and nothing but the fear that Halsey was in danger drove me on; with every step my knees seemed to give way under me.

Gertrude was ahead and in the card-room she stopped, holding her candle high. Then she pointed silently to the doorway into the hall beyond. Huddled there on the floor, face down, with his arms extended, was a man.

Gertrude ran forward with a gasping sob. "Jack," she cried, "oh, Jack!"

Liddy had run, screaming, and the two of us were there alone. It was Gertrude who turned him over, finally, until we could see his white face, and then she drew a deep breath and dropped limply to her knees. It was the body of a man, a gentleman, in a dinner coat and white waistcoat, stained now with blood—the body of a man I had never seen before.

4.   WHERE IS HALSEY?

Gertrude gazed at the face in a kind of fascination. Then she put out her hands blindly, and I thought she was going to faint.

"He has killed him!" she muttered almost inarticulately; and at that, because my nerves were going, I gave her a good shake.

"What do you mean?" I said frantically. There was a depth of grief and conviction in her tone that was worse than anything she could have said. The shake braced her, anyhow, and she seemed to pull herself together. But not another word would she say: she stood gazing down at that gruesome figure on the floor, while Liddy, ashamed of her flight and afraid to come back alone, drove before her three terrified women-servants into the drawing-room, which was as near as any of them would venture.

Once in the drawing-room, Gertrude collapsed and went from one fainting spell into another. I had all I could do to keep Liddy from drowning her with cold water, and the maids huddled in a corner, as much use as so many sheep. In a short time, although it seemed hours, a car came rushing up, and Anne Watson, who had waited to dress, opened the door. Three men from the Greenwood Club, in all kinds of costumes, hurried in. I recognized a Mr. Jarvis, but the others were strangers.

"What's wrong?" the Jarvis man asked—and we made a strange picture, no doubt. "Nobody hurt, is there?" He was looking at Gertrude.

"Worse than that, Mr. Jarvis," I said. "I think it is murder."

At the word there was a commotion. The cook began to cry, and Mrs. Watson knocked over a chair. The men were visibly impressed.

"Not any member of the family?" Mr. Jarvis asked, when he had got his breath.

"No," I said; and motioning Liddy to look after Gertrude, I led the way with a lamp to the card-room door. One of the men gave an exclamation, and they all hurried across the room. Mr. Jarvis took the lamp from me—I remember that—and then, feeling myself getting dizzy and light-headed, I closed my eyes. When I opened them their brief examination was over, and Mr. Jarvis was trying to put me in a chair.

"You must get up-stairs," he said firmly, "you and Miss Gertrude, too. This has been a terrible shock. In his own home, too."

I stared at him without comprehension. "Who is it?" I asked with difficulty. There was a band drawn tight around my throat.

"It is Arnold Armstrong," he said, looking at me oddly, "and he has been murdered in his father's house."

After a minute I gathered myself together and Mr. Jarvis helped me into the living-room. Liddy had got Gertrude up-stairs, and the two strange men from the club stayed with the body. The reaction from the shock and strain was tremendous: I was collapsed—and then Mr. Jarvis asked me a question that brought back my wandering faculties.

"Where is Halsey?" he asked.

"Halsey!" Suddenly Gertrude's stricken face rose before me the empty rooms up-stairs. Where was Halsey?

"He was here, wasn't he?" Mr. Jarvis persisted. "He stopped at the club on his way over."

"I—don't know where he is," I said feebly.

One of the men from the club came in, asked for the telephone, and I could hear him excitedly talking, saying something about coroners and detectives. Mr. Jarvis leaned over to me.

"Why don't you trust me, Miss Innes?" he said. "If I can do anything I will. But tell me the whole thing."

I did, finally, from the beginning, and when I told of Jack Bailey's being in the house that night, he gave a long whistle.

"I wish they were both here," he said when I finished. "Whatever mad prank took them away, it would look better if they were here. Especially—"

"Especially what?"

"Especially since Jack Bailey and Arnold Armstrong were notoriously bad friends. It was Bailey who got Arnold into trouble last spring—something about the bank. And then, too—"

"Go on," I said. "If there is anything more, I ought to know."

"There's nothing more," he said evasively. "There's just one thing we may bank on, Miss Innes. Any court in the country will acquit a man who kills an intruder in his house, at night. If Halsey—"

"Why, you don't think Halsey did it!" I exclaimed. There was a queer feeling of physical nausea coming over me.

"No, no, not at all," he said with forced cheerfulness. "Come, Miss Innes, you're a ghost of yourself and I am going to help you up-stairs and call your maid. This has been too much for you."

Liddy helped me back to bed, and under the impression that I was in danger of freezing to death, put a hot-water bottle over my heart and another at my feet. Then she left me. It was early dawn now, and from voices under my window I surmised that Mr. Jarvis and his companions were searching the grounds. As for me, I lay in bed, with every faculty awake. Where had Halsey gone? How had he gone, and when? Before the murder, no doubt, but who would believe that? If either he or Jack Bailey had heard an intruder in the house and shot him—as they might have been justified in doing—why had they run away? The whole thing was unheard of, outrageous, and—impossible to ignore.

About six o'clock Gertrude came in. She was fully dressed, and I sat up nervously.

"Poor Aunty!" she said. "What a shocking night you have had!" She came over and sat down on the bed, and I saw she looked very tired and worn.

"Is there anything new?" I asked anxiously.

"Nothing. The car is gone, but Warner"—he is the chauffeur—"Warner is at the lodge and knows nothing about it."

"Well," I said, "if I ever get my hands on Halsey Innes, I shall not let go until I have told him a few things. When we get this cleared up, I am going back to the city to be quiet. One more night like the last two will end me. The peace of the country—fiddle sticks!"

Whereupon I told Gertrude of the noises the night before, and the figure on the veranda in the east wing. As an afterthought I brought out the pearl cuff-link.

"I have no doubt now," I said, "that it was Arnold Armstrong the night before last, too. He had a key, no doubt, but why he should steal into his father's house I can not imagine. He could have come with my permission, easily enough. Anyhow, whoever it was that night, left this little souvenir."

Gertrude took one look at the cuff-link, and went as white as the pearls in it; she clutched at the foot of the bed, and stood staring. As for me, I was quite as astonished as she was.

"Where did—you—find it?" she asked finally, with a desperate effort at calm. And while I told her she stood looking out of the window with a look I could not fathom on her face. It was a relief when Mrs. Watson tapped at the door and brought me some tea and toast. The cook was in bed, completely demoralized, she reported, and Liddy, brave with the daylight, was looking for footprints around the house. Mrs. Watson herself was a wreck; she was blue-white around the lips, and she had one hand tied up.

She said she had fallen down-stairs in her excitement. It was natural, of course, that the thing would shock her, having been the Armstrongs' housekeeper for several years, and knowing Mr. Arnold well.

Gertrude had slipped out during my talk with Mrs. Watson, and I dressed and went down-stairs. The billiard and card-rooms were locked until the coroner and the detectives got there, and the men from the club had gone back for more conventional clothing.

I could hear Thomas in the pantry, alternately wailing for Mr. Arnold, as he called him, and citing the tokens that had precursed the murder. The house seemed to choke me, and, slipping a shawl around me, I went out on the drive. At the corner by the east wing I met Liddy. Her skirts were draggled with dew to her knees, and her hair was still in crimps.

"Go right in and change your clothes," I said sharply. "You're a sight, and at your age!"

She had a golf-stick in her hand, and she said she had found it on the lawn. There was nothing unusual about it, but it occurred to me that a golf-stick with a metal end might have been the object that had scratched the stairs near the card-room. I took it from her, and sent her up for dry garments. Her daylight courage and self-importance, and her shuddering delight in the mystery, irritated me beyond words. After I left her I made a circuit of the building. Nothing seemed to be disturbed: the house looked as calm and peaceful in the morning sun as it had the day I had been coerced into taking it. There was nothing to show that inside had been mystery and violence and sudden death.

In one of the tulip beds back of the house an early blackbird was pecking viciously at something that glittered in the light. I picked my way gingerly over through the dew and stooped down: almost buried in the soft ground was a revolver! I scraped the earth off it with the tip of my shoe, and, picking it up, slipped it into my pocket. Not until I had got into my bedroom and double-locked the door did I venture to take it out and examine it. One look was all I needed. It was Halsey's revolver. I had unpacked it the day before and put it on his shaving-stand, and there could be no mistake. His name was on a small silver plate on the handle.

I seemed to see a network closing around my boy, innocent as I knew he was. The revolver—I am afraid of them, but anxiety gave me courage to look through the barrel—the revolver had still two bullets in it. I could only breathe a prayer of thankfulness that I had found the revolver before any sharp-eyed detective had come around.

I decided to keep what clues I had, the cuff-link, the golf-stick and the revolver, in a secure place until I could see some reason for displaying them. The cuff-link had been dropped into a little filigree box on my toilet table. I opened the box and felt around for it. The box was empty—the cuff-link had disappeared!

5.   GERTRUDE'S ENGAGEMENT

At ten o'clock the Casanova hack brought up three men. They introduced themselves as the coroner of the county and two detectives from the city. The coroner led the way at once to the locked wing, and with the aid of one of the detectives examined the rooms and the body. The other detective, after a short scrutiny of the dead man, busied himself with the outside of the house. It was only after they had got a fair idea of things as they were that they sent for me.

I received them in the living-room, and I had made up my mind exactly what to tell. I had taken the house for the summer, I said, while the Armstrongs were in California. In spite of a rumor among the servants about strange noises— I cited Thomas—nothing had occurred the first two nights. On the third night I believed that some one had been in the house: I had heard a crashing sound, but being alone with one maid had not investigated. The house had been locked in the morning and apparently undisturbed.

Then, as clearly as I could, I related how, the night before, a shot had roused us; that my niece and I had investigated and found a body; that I did not know who the murdered man was until Mr. Jarvis from the club informed me, and that I knew of no reason why Mr. Arnold Armstrong should steal into his father's house at night. I should have been glad to allow him entrée there at any time.

"Have you reason to believe, Miss Innes," the coroner asked, "that any member of your household, imagining Mr. Armstrong was a burglar, shot him in self-defense?"

"I have no reason for thinking so," I said quietly.

"Your theory is that Mr. Armstrong was followed here by some enemy, and shot as he entered the house?"

"I don't think I have a theory," I said. "The thing that has puzzled me is why Mr. Armstrong should enter his father's house two nights in succession, stealing in like a thief, when he needed only to ask entrance to be admitted."

The coroner was a very silent man: he took some notes after this, but he seemed anxious to make the next train back to town. He set the inquest for the following Saturday, gave Mr. Jamieson, the younger of the two detectives, and the more intelligent looking, a few instructions, and, after gravely shaking hands with me and regretting the unfortunate affair, took his departure, accompanied by the other detective.

I was just beginning to breathe freely when Mr. Jamieson, who had been standing by the window, came over to me.

"The family consists of yourself alone, Miss Innes?"

"My niece is here," I said.

"There is no one but yourself and your niece?"

"My nephew." I had to moisten my lips.

"Oh, a nephew. I should like to see him, if he is here."

"He is not here just now," I said as quietly as I could. "I expect him—at any time."

"He was here yesterday evening, I believe?"

"No—yes."

"Didn't he have a guest with him? Another man?"

"He brought a friend with him to stay over Sunday, Mr. Bailey."

"Mr. John Bailey, the cashier of the Traders' Bank I believe." And I knew that some one at the Greenwood Club had told. "When did they leave?"

"Very early—I don't know at just what time."

Mr. Jamieson turned suddenly and looked at me.

"Please try to be more explicit," he said. "You say your nephew and Mr. Bailey were in the house last night, and yet you and your niece, with some women-servants, found the body. Where was your nephew?"

I was entirely desperate by that time.

"I do not know," I cried, "but be sure of this: Halsey knows nothing of this thing, and no amount of circumstantial evidence can make an innocent man guilty."

"Sit down," he said, pushing forward a chair. "There are some things I have to tell you, and, in return, please tell me all you know. Believe me, things always come out. In the first place, Mr. Armstrong was shot from above. The bullet was fired at close range, entered below the shoulder and came out, after passing through the heart, well down the back. In other words, I believe the murderer stood on the stairs and fired down. In the second place, I found on the edge of the billiard-table a charred cigar which had burned itself partly out, and a cigarette which had consumed itself to the cork tip. Neither one had been more than lighted, then put down and forgotten. Have you any idea what it was that made your nephew and Mr. Bailey leave their cigars and their game, take out the automobile without calling the chauffeur, and all this at—let me see certainly before three o'clock in the morning?"

"I don't know," I said; "but depend on it, Mr. Jamieson, Halsey will be back himself to explain everything."

"I sincerely hope so," he said. "Miss Innes, has it occurred to you that Mr. Bailey might know something of this?"

Gertrude had come down-stairs and just as he spoke she came in. I saw her stop suddenly, as if she had been struck.

"He does not," she said in a tone that was not her own. "Mr. Bailey and my brother know nothing of this. The murder was committed at three. They left the house at a quarter before three."

"How do you know that?" Mr. Jamieson asked oddly. "Do you *know* at what time they left?"

"I do," Gertrude answered firmly. "At a quarter before three my brother and Mr. Bailey left the house, by the main entrance. I—was—there."

"Gertrude," I said excitedly, "you are dreaming! Why, at a quarter to three—"

"Listen," she said. "At half-past two the downstairs telephone rang. I had not gone to sleep, and I heard it. Then I heard Halsey answer it, and in a few minutes he came up-stairs and knocked at my door. We—we talked for a minute, then I put on my dressing-gown and slippers, and went down-stairs with him. Mr. Bailey was in the billiard-room. We—we all talked together for perhaps ten minutes. Then it was decided that—that they should both go away—"

"Can't you be more explicit?" Mr. Jamieson asked. "*Why* did they go away?"

"I am only telling you what happened, not why it happened," she said evenly. "Halsey went for the car, and instead of bringing it to the house and rousing people, he went by the lower road from the stable. Mr. Bailey was to meet him at the foot of the lawn. Mr. Bailey left—"

"Which way?" Mr. Jamieson asked sharply.

"By the main entrance. He left—it was a quarter to three. I know exactly."

"The clock in the hall is stopped, Miss Innes," said Jamieson. Nothing seemed to escape him.

"He looked at his watch," she replied, and I could see Mr. Jamieson's snap, as if he had made a discovery. As for myself, during the whole recital I had been plunged into the deepest amazement.

"Will you pardon me for a personal question?" The detective was a youngish man, and I thought he was somewhat embarrassed. "What are your—your relations with Mr. Bailey?"

Gertrude hesitated. Then she came over and put her hand lovingly in mine.

"I am engaged to marry him," she said simply.

I had grown so accustomed to surprises that I could only gasp again, and as for Gertrude, the hand that lay in mine was burning with fever.

"And—after that," Mr. Jamieson went on, "you went directly to bed?"

Gertrude hesitated.

"No," she said finally. "I—I am not nervous, and after I had extinguished the light, I remembered something I had left in the billiard-room, and I felt my way back there through the darkness."

"Will you tell me what it was you had forgotten?"

"I can not tell you," she said slowly. "I—I did not leave the billiard-room at once—"

"Why?" The detective's tone was imperative. "This is very important, Miss Innes."

"I was crying," Gertrude said in a low tone. "When the French clock in the drawing-room struck three, I got up, and then—I heard a step on the east porch, just outside the card-room. Some one with a key was working with the latch, and I thought, of course, of Halsey. When we took the house he called that his entrance, and he had carried a key for it ever since. The door opened and I was about to ask what he had forgotten, when there was a flash and a report. Some heavy body dropped, and, half crazed with terror and shock, I ran through the drawing-room and got up-stairs—I scarcely remember how."

She dropped into a chair, and I thought Mr. Jamieson must have finished. But he was not through.

"You certainly clear your brother and Mr. Bailey admirably," he said. "The testimony is invaluable, especially in view of the fact that your brother and Mr. Armstrong had, I believe, quarreled rather seriously some time ago."

"Nonsense," I broke in. "Things are bad enough, Mr. Jamieson, without inventing bad feeling where it doesn't exist. Gertrude, I don't think Halsey knew the—the murdered man, did he?"

But Mr. Jamieson was sure of his ground.

"The quarrel, I believe," he persisted, "was about Mr. Armstrong's conduct to you, Miss Gertrude. He had been paying you unwelcome attentions."

And I had never seen the man!

When she nodded a "yes" I saw the tremendous possibilities involved. If this detective could prove that Gertrude feared and disliked the murdered man, and that

Mr. Armstrong had been annoying and possibly pursuing her with hateful attentions, all that, added to Gertrude's confession of her presence in the billiard-room at the time of the crime, looked strange, to say the least. The prominence of the family assured a strenuous effort to find the murderer, and if we had nothing worse to look forward to, we were sure of a distasteful publicity.

Mr. Jamieson shut his note-book with a snap, and thanked us.

"I have an idea," he said, apropos of nothing at all, "that at any rate the ghost is laid here. Whatever the rappings have been—and the colored man says they began when the family went west three months ago—they are likely to stop now."

Which shows how much he knew about it. The ghost was not laid: with the murder of Arnold Armstrong he, or it, only seemed to take on fresh vigor.

Mr. Jamieson left then, and when Gertrude had gone upstairs, as she did at once, I sat and thought over what I had just heard. Her engagement, once so engrossing a matter, paled now beside the significance of her story. If Halsey and Jack Bailey had left before the crime, how came Halsey's revolver in the tulip bed? What was the mysterious cause of their sudden flight? What had Gertrude left in the billiard-room? What was the significance of the cuff-link, and where was it?

6.   IN THE EAST CORRIDOR

When the detective left he enjoined absolute secrecy on everybody in the household. The Greenwood Club promised the same thing, and as there are no Sunday afternoon papers, the murder was not publicly known until Monday. The coroner himself notified the Armstrong family lawyer, and early in the afternoon he came out. I had not seen Mr. Jamieson since morning, but I knew he had been interrogating the servants. Gertrude was locked in her room with a headache, and I had luncheon alone.

Mr. Harton, the lawyer, was a little, thin man, and he looked as if he did not relish his business that day.

"This is very unfortunate, Miss Innes," he said, after we had shaken hands. "Most unfortunate—and mysterious. With the father and mother in the west, I find everything devolves on me; and, as you can understand, it is an unpleasant duty."

"No doubt," I said absently. "Mr. Harton, I am going to ask you some questions, and I hope you will answer them. I feel that I am entitled to some knowledge, because I and my family are just now in a most ambiguous position."

I don't know whether he understood me or not: he took of his glasses and wiped them.

"I shall be very happy," he said with old-fashioned courtesy.

"Thank you. Mr. Harton, did Mr. Arnold Armstrong know that Sunnyside had been rented?"

"I think—yes, he did. In fact, I myself told him about it."

"And he knew who the tenants were?"

"Yes."

"He had not been living with the family for some years, I believe?"

"No. Unfortunately, there had been trouble between Arnold and his father. For two years he had lived in town."

"Then it would be unlikely that he came here last night to get possession of anything belonging to him?"

"I should think it hardly possible," he admitted.

"To be perfectly frank, Miss Innes, I can not think of any reason whatever for his coming here as he did. He had been staying at the club-house across the valley for the last week, Jarvis tells me, but that only explains how he came here, not why. It is a most unfortunate family."

He shook his head despondently, and I felt that this dried-up little man was the repository of much that he had not told me. I gave up trying to elicit any information from him, and we went together to view the body before it was taken to the city. It had been lifted on to the billiard-table and a sheet thrown over it; otherwise nothing had been touched. A soft hat lay beside it, and the collar of the dinner-coat was still turned up. The handsome, dissipated face of Arnold Armstrong, purged of its ugly lines, was now only pathetic. As we went in Mrs. Watson appeared at the card-room door.

"Come in, Mrs. Watson," the lawyer said. But she shook her head and withdrew: she was the only one in the house who seemed to regret the dead man, and even she seemed rather shocked than sorry.

I went to the door at the foot of the circular staircase and opened it. If I could only have seen Halsey coming at his usual hare-brained clip up the drive, if I could have heard the throb of the motor, I would have felt that my troubles were over.

But there was nothing to be seen. The countryside lay sunny and quiet in its peaceful Sunday afternoon calm, and far down the drive Mr. Jamieson was walking slowly, stooping now and then, as if to examine the road. When I went back, Mr. Harton was furtively wiping his eyes.

"The prodigal has come home, Miss Innes," he said. "How often the sins of the fathers are visited on the children!" Which left me pondering.

Before Mr. Harton left, he told me something of the Armstrong family. Paul Armstrong, the father, had been married twice. Arnold was a son by the first marriage. The second Mrs. Armstrong had been a widow, with a child, a little girl. This child, now perhaps twenty, was Louise Armstrong, having taken her stepfather's name, and was at present in California with the family.

"They will probably return at once," he concluded "sad part of my errand here to-day is to see if you will relinquish your lease here in their favor."

"We would better wait and see if they wish to come," I said. "It seems unlikely, and my town house is being remodeled." At that he let the matter drop, but it came up unpleasantly enough, later.

At six o'clock the body was taken away, and at seven-thirty, after an early dinner, Mr. Harton went. Gertrude had not come down, and there was no news of Halsey. Mr. Jamieson had taken a lodging in the village, and I had not seen him since mid-afternoon. It was about nine o'clock, I think, when the bell rang and he was ushered into the living-room.

"Sit down," I said grimly. "Have you found a clue that will incriminate me, Mr. Jamieson?"

He had the grace to look uncomfortable. "No," he said. "If you had killed Mr. Armstrong, you would have left no clues. You would have had too much intelligence."

After that we got along better. He was fishing in his pocket, and after a minute he brought out two scraps of paper. "I have been to the club-house," he said, "and among Mr. Armstrong's effects, I found these. One is curious; the other is puzzling."

The first was a sheet of club note-paper, on which was written, over and over, the name "Halsey B. Innes." It was Halsey's flowing signature to a dot, but it lacked Halsey's ease. The ones toward the bottom of the sheet were much better than the top ones. Mr. Jamieson smiled at my face.

"His old tricks," he said. "That one is merely curious; this one, as I said before, is puzzling."

The second scrap, folded and refolded into a compass[1] so tiny that the writing had been partly obliterated, was part of

---

[1] Somewhat outdated usage meaning area or size

a letter—the lower half of a sheet, not typed, but written in a cramped hand.

> "—by altering the plans for—rooms, may be
> possible. The best way, in my opinion, would be
> to—the plan for—in one of the—rooms—
> chimney."

That was all.

"Well?" I said, looking up. "There is nothing in that, is there? A man ought to be able to change the plan of his house without becoming an object of suspicion."

"There is little in the paper itself," he admitted; "but why should Arnold Armstrong carry that around, unless it meant something? He never built a house, you may be sure of that. If it is this house, it may mean anything, from a secret room—"

"To an extra bath-room," I said scornfully. "Haven't you a thumb-print, too?"

"I have," he said with a smile, "and the print of a foot in a tulip bed, and a number of other things. The oddest part is, Miss Innes, that the thumb-mark is probably yours and the footprint certainly."

His audacity was the only thing that saved me: his amused smile put me on my mettle, and I ripped out a perfectly good scallop before I answered.

"Why did I step into the tulip bed?" I asked with interest.

"You picked up something," he said good-humoredly, "which you are going to tell me about later."

"Am I, indeed?" I was politely curious. "With this remarkable insight of yours, I wish you would tell me where I shall find my four-thousand-dollar motor car."

"I was just coming to that," he said. "You will find it about thirty miles away, at Andrews Station, in a blacksmith shop, where it is being repaired."

I laid down my knitting then and looked at him.

"And Halsey?" I managed to say.

"We are going to exchange information," he said "I am going to tell you that, when you tell me what you picked up in the tulip bed."

We looked steadily at each other: it was not an unfriendly stare; we were only measuring weapons. Then he smiled a little and got up.

"With your permission," he said, "I am going to examine the card-room and the staircase again. You might think over my offer in the meantime."

He went on through the drawing-room, and I listened to his footsteps growing gradually fainter. I dropped my pretense at knitting and, leaning back, I thought over the last forty-eight hours. Here was I, Rachel Innes, spinster, a granddaughter of old John Innes of Revolutionary days, a D. A. R., a Colonial Dame, mixed up with a vulgar and revolting crime, and even attempting to hoodwink the law! Certainly I had left the straight and narrow way.

I was roused by hearing Mr. Jamieson coming rapidly back through the drawing-room. He stopped at the door.

"Miss Innes," he said quickly, "will you come with me and light the east corridor? I have fastened somebody in the small room at the head of the card-room stairs."

I jumped up at once.

"You mean—the murderer?" I gasped.

"Possibly," he said quietly, as we hurried together up the stairs. "Some one was lurking on the staircase when I went back. I spoke; instead of an answer, whoever it was turned and ran up. I followed—it was dark—but as I turned the corner at the top a figure darted through this door and closed it. The bolt was on my side, and I pushed it forward. It is a closet, I think." We were in the upper hall now. "If you will show me the electric switch, Miss Innes, you would better wait in your own room."

Trembling as I was, I was determined to see that door opened. I hardly knew what I feared, but so many terrible and inexplicable things had happened that suspense was worse than certainty.

"I am perfectly cool," I said, "and I am going to remain here."

The lights flashed up along that end of the corridor, throwing the doors into relief. At the intersection of the small hallway with the larger, the circular staircase wound its way up, as if it had been an afterthought of the architect. And just around the corner, in the small corridor, was the door Mr. Jamieson had indicated. I was still unfamiliar with the house, and I did not remember the door. My heart was thumping wildly in my ears, but I nodded to him to go ahead. I was perhaps eight or ten feet away—and then he threw the bolt back.

"Come out," he said quietly. There was no response. "Come—out," he repeated. Then—I think he had a revolver, but I am not sure—he stepped aside and threw the door open.

From where I stood I could not see beyond the door, but I saw Mr. Jamieson's face change and heard him mutter something, then he bolted down the stairs, three at a time. When my knees had stopped shaking, I moved forward, slowly, nervously, until I had a partial view of what was beyond the door. It seemed at first to be a closet, empty. Then I went close and examined it, to stop with a shudder. Where the floor should have been was black void and darkness, from which came the indescribable, damp smell of the cellars.

Mr. Jamieson had locked somebody in the clothes chute. As I leaned over I fancied I heard a groan—or was it the wind?

7. A SPRAINED ANKLE

I was panic-stricken. As I ran along the corridor I was confident that the mysterious intruder and probable murderer had been found, and that he lay dead or dying at the foot of the chute. I got down the staircase somehow, and through the kitchen to the basement stairs. Mr. Jamieson had been before me, and the door stood open. Liddy was standing in the middle of the kitchen, holding a frying-pan by the handle as a weapon.

"Don't go down there," she yelled, when she saw me moving toward the basement stairs. "Don't you do it, Miss Rachel. That Jamieson's down there now. There's only trouble comes of hunting ghosts; they lead you into bottomless pits and things like that. Oh, Miss Rachel, don't—" as I tried to get past her.

She was interrupted by Mr. Jamieson's reappearance. He ran up the stairs two at a time, and his face was flushed and furious.

"The whole place is locked," he said angrily. "Where's the laundry key kept?"

"It's kept in the door," Liddy snapped. "That whole end of the cellar is kept locked, so nobody can get at the clothes, and then the key's left in the door, so that unless a thief was as blind as—as some detectives, he could walk right in."

"Liddy," I said sharply, "come down with us and turn on all the lights."

She offered her resignation, as usual, on the spot, but I took her by the arm, and she came along finally. She switched on all the lights and pointed to a door just ahead.

"That's the door," she said sulkily. "The key's in it."

But the key was not in it. Mr. Jamieson shook it, but it was a heavy door, well locked. And then he stooped and began punching around the keyhole with the end of a lead-pencil. When he stood up his face was exultant.

"It's locked on the inside," he said in a low tone. "There is somebody in there."

"Lord have mercy!" gasped Liddy, and turned to run.

"Liddy," I called, "go through the house at once and see who is missing, or if any one is. We'll have to clear this thing at once. Mr. Jamieson, if you will watch here I will go to the lodge and find Warner. Thomas would be of no use. Together you may be able to force the door."

"A good idea," he assented. "But—there are windows, of course, and there is nothing to prevent whoever is in there from getting out that way."

"Then lock the door at the top of the basement stairs," I suggested, "and patrol the house from the outside."

We agreed to this, and I had a feeling that the mystery of Sunnyside was about to be solved. I ran down the steps and along the drive. Just at the corner I ran full tilt into somebody who seemed to be as much alarmed as I was. It was not until I had recoiled a step or two that I recognized Gertrude, and she me.

"Good gracious, Aunt Ray," she exclaimed, "what is the matter?"

"There's somebody locked in the laundry," I panted. "That is—unless—you didn't see any one crossing the lawn or skulking around the house, did you?"

"I think we have mystery on the brain," Gertrude said wearily. "No, I haven't seen any one, except old Thomas, who looked for all the world as if he had been ransacking the pantry. What have you locked in the laundry?"

"I can't wait to explain," I replied. "I must get Warner from the lodge. If you came out for air, you'd better put on your overshoes." And then I noticed that Gertrude was limping—

not much, but sufficiently to make her progress very slow, and seemingly painful.

"You have hurt yourself," I said sharply.

"I fell over the carriage block," she explained. "I thought perhaps I might see Halsey coming home. He—he ought to be here."

I hurried on down the drive. The lodge was some distance from the house, in a grove of trees where the drive met the county road. There were two white stone pillars to mark the entrance, but the iron gates, once closed and tended by the lodge-keeper, now stood permanently open. The day of the motor-car had come; no one had time for closed gates and lodge-keepers. The lodge at Sunnyside was merely a sort of supplementary servants' quarters: it was as convenient in its appointments as the big house and infinitely more cozy.

As I went down the drive, my thoughts were busy. Who would it be that Mr. Jamieson had trapped in the cellar? Would we find a body or some one badly injured? Scarcely either. Whoever had fallen had been able to lock the laundry door on the inside. If the fugitive had come from outside the house, how did he get in? If it was some member of the household, who could it have been? And then—a feeling of horror almost overwhelmed me. Gertrude! Gertrude and her injured ankle! Gertrude found limping slowly up the drive when I had thought she was in bed!

I tried to put the thought away, but it would not go. If Gertrude had been on the circular staircase that night, why had she fled from Mr. Jamieson? The idea, puzzling as it was, seemed borne out by this circumstance. Whoever had taken refuge at the head of the stairs could scarcely have been familiar with the house, or with the location of the chute. The mystery seemed to deepen constantly. What possible connection could there be between Halsey and Gertrude, and the murder of Arnold Armstrong? And yet, every way I turned I seemed to find something that pointed to such a connection.

At the foot of the drive the road described a long, sloping, horseshoe-shaped curve around the lodge. There were lights there, streaming cheerfully out on to the trees, and from an upper room came wavering shadows, as if some one with a lamp was moving around. I had come almost silently in my evening slippers, and I had my second collision of the evening on the road just above the house. I ran full into a man in a long coat, who was standing in the shadow beside the drive, with his back to me, watching the lighted windows.

"What the hell!" he ejaculated furiously, and turned around. When he saw me, however, he did not wait for any retort on my part. He faded away—this is not slang; he did—he absolutely disappeared in the dusk without my getting more than a glimpse of his face. I had a vague impression of unfamiliar features and of a sort of cap with a visor. Then he was gone.

I went to the lodge and rapped. It required two or three poundings to bring Thomas to the door, and he opened it only an inch or so.

"Where is Warner?" I asked.

"I—I think he's in bed, ma'm."

"Get him up," I said, "and for goodness' sake open the door, Thomas. I'll wait for Warner."

"It's kind o' close in here, ma'm," he said, obeying gingerly, and disclosing a cool and comfortable looking interior. "Perhaps you'd keer to set on the porch an' rest yo'self."

It was so evident that Thomas did not want me inside that I went in.

"Tell Warner he is needed in a hurry," I repeated, and turned into the little sitting-room. I could hear Thomas going up the stairs, could hear him rouse Warner, and the steps of the chauffeur as he hurriedly dressed. But my attention was busy with the room below.

On the center-table, open, was a sealskin traveling bag. It was filled with gold-topped bottles and brushes, and it breathed opulence, luxury, femininity from every inch of surface. How did it get there? I was still asking myself the question when Warner came running down the stairs and into the room. He was completely but somewhat incongruously dressed, and his open, boyish face looked abashed. He was a country boy, absolutely frank and reliable, of fair education and intelligence—one of the small army of American youths who turn a natural aptitude for mechanics into the special field of the automobile, and earn good salaries in a congenial occupation.

"What is it, Miss Innes?" he asked anxiously.

"There is some one locked in the laundry," I replied. "Mr. Jamieson wants you to help him break the lock. Warner, whose bag is this?"

He was in the doorway by this time, and he pretended not to hear.

"Warner," I called, "come back here. Whose bag is this?"

He stopped then, but he did not turn around.

"It's—it belongs to Thomas," he said, and fled up the drive.

To Thomas! A London bag with mirrors and cosmetic jars of which Thomas could not even have guessed the use! However, I put the bag in the back of my mind, which was fast becoming stored with anomalous and apparently irreconcilable facts, and followed Warner to the house.

Liddy had come back to the kitchen: the door to the basement stairs was double-barred, and had a table pushed against it; and beside her on the table was most of the kitchen paraphernalia.

"Did you see if there was any one missing in the house?" I asked, ignoring the array of sauce-pans rolling-pins, and the poker of the range.

"Rosie is missing," Liddy said with unction. She had objected to Rosie, the parlor maid, from the start. "Mrs. Watson went into her room, and found she had gone without her hat. People that trust themselves a dozen miles from the city, in strange houses, with servants they don't know, needn't be surprised if they wake up some morning and find their throats cut."

After which carefully veiled sarcasm Liddy relapsed into gloom. Warner came in then with a handful of small tools, and Mr. Jamieson went with him to the basement. Oddly enough, I was not alarmed. With all my heart I wished for

Halsey, but I was not frightened. At the door he was to force, Warner put down his tools and looked at it. Then he turned the handle. Without the slightest difficulty the door opened, revealing the blackness of the drying-room beyond!

Mr. Jamieson gave an exclamation of disgust.

"Gone!" he said. "Confound such careless work! I might have known."

It was true enough. We got the lights on finally and looked all through the three rooms that constituted this wing of the basement. Everything was quiet and empty. An explanation of how the fugitive had escaped injury was found in a heaped-up basket of clothes under the chute. The basket had been overturned, but that was all. Mr. Jamieson examined the windows: one was unlocked, and offered an easy escape. The window or the door? Which way had the fugitive escaped? The door seemed most probable, and I hoped it had been so. I could not have borne, just then, to think that it was my poor Gertrude we had been hounding through the darkness, and yet—I had met Gertrude not far from that very window.

I went up-stairs at last, tired and depressed. Mrs. Watson and Liddy were making tea in the kitchen. In certain walks of life the tea-pot is the refuge in times of stress, trouble or sickness: they give tea to the dying and they put it in the baby's nursing bottle. Mrs. Watson was fixing a tray to be sent in to me, and when I asked her about Rosie she confirmed her absence.

"She's not here," she said; "but I would not think much of that, Miss Innes. Rosie is a pretty young girl, and perhaps she has a sweetheart. It will be a good thing if she has. The maids stay much better when they have something like that to hold them here."

Gertrude had gone back to her room, and while I was drinking my cup of hot tea, Mr. Jamieson came in.

"We might take up the conversation where we left off an hour and a half ago," he said. "But before we go on, I want to say this: The person who escaped from the laundry was a woman with a foot of moderate size and well arched. She wore nothing but a stocking on her right foot, and, in spite of the unlocked door, she escaped by the window."

And again I thought of Gertrude's sprained ankle. Was it the right or the left?

8.   THE OTHER HALF OF THE LINE

"Miss Innes," the detective began, "what is your opinion of the figure you saw on the east veranda the night you and your maid were in the house alone?"

"It was a woman," I said positively.

"And yet your maid affirms with equal positiveness that it was a man."

"Nonsense," I broke in. "Liddy had her eyes shut—she always shuts them when she's frightened."

"And you never thought then that the intruder who came later that night might be a woman—the woman, in fact, whom you saw on the veranda?"

"I had reasons for thinking it was a man," I said remembering the pearl cuff-link.

"Now we are getting down to business. *What* were your reasons for thinking that?"

I hesitated.

"If you have any reason for believing that your midnight guest was Mr. Armstrong, other than his visit here the next night, you ought to tell me, Miss Innes. We can take nothing for granted. If, for instance, the intruder who dropped the bar and scratched the staircase—you see, I know about that—if this visitor was a woman, why should not the same woman have come back the following night, met Mr. Armstrong on the circular staircase, and in alarm shot him?"

"It was a man," I reiterated. And then, because I could think of no other reason for my statement, I told him about the pearl cuff-link. He was intensely interested.

"Will you give me the link," he said, when I finished, "or, at least, let me see it? I consider it a most important clue."

"Won't the description do?"

"Not as well as the original."

"Well, I'm very sorry," I said, as calmly as I could, "I—the thing is lost. It—it must have fallen out of a box on my dressing-table."

Whatever he thought of my explanation, and I knew he doubted it, he made no sign. He asked me to describe the link accurately, and I did so, while he glanced at a list he took from his pocket.

"One set monogram cuff-links," he read, "one set plain pearl links, one set cuff-links, woman's head set with diamonds and emeralds. There is no mention of such a link as you describe, and yet, if your theory is right, Mr. Armstrong must have taken back in his cuffs one complete cuff-link, and a half, perhaps, of the other."

The idea was new to me. If it had not been the murdered man who had entered the house that night, who had it been?

"There are a number of strange things connected with this case," the detective went on. "Miss Gertrude Innes testified that she heard some one fumbling with the lock, that the door opened, and that almost immediately the shot was fired. Now, Miss Innes, here is the strange part of that. Mr. Armstrong had no key with him. There was no key in the lock, or on the floor. In other words, the evidence points absolutely to this: Mr. Armstrong was admitted to the house from within."

"It is impossible," I broke in. "Mr. Jamieson, do you know what your words imply? Do you know that you are practically accusing Gertrude Innes of admitting that man?"

"Not quite that," he said, with his friendly smile. "In fact, Miss Innes, I am quite certain she did not. But as long as I learn only parts of the truth, from both you and her, what can I do? I know you picked up something in the flower bed: you refuse to tell me what it was. I know Miss Gertrude went back to the billiard-room to get something, she refuses to say what. You suspect what happened to the cuff-link, but you won't tell me. So far, all I am sure of is this: I do not believe Arnold Armstrong was the midnight visitor who so alarmed you by dropping—shall we say, a golf-stick? And I believe that when he did come he was admitted by some one in the house. Who knows—it may have been—Liddy!"

I stirred my tea angrily.

"I have always heard," I said dryly, "that undertakers' assistants are jovial young men. A man's sense of humor seems to be in inverse proportion to the gravity of his profession."

"A man's sense of humor is a barbarous and a cruel thing, Miss Innes," he admitted. "It is to the feminine as the hug of a bear is to the scratch of—well;—anything with claws. Is that you, Thomas? Come in."

Thomas Johnson stood in the doorway. He looked alarmed and apprehensive, and suddenly I remembered the sealskin dressing-bag in the lodge. Thomas came just inside the door and stood with his head drooping, his eyes, under their shaggy gray brows, fixed on Mr. Jamieson.

"Thomas," said the detective, not unkindly, "I sent for you to tell us what you told Sam Bohannon at the club, the day before Mr. Arnold was found here, dead. Let me see. You came here Friday night to see Miss Innes, didn't you? And came to work here Saturday morning?"

For some unexplained reason Thomas looked relieved.

"Yas, sah," he said. "You see it were like this: When Mistah Armstrong and the fam'ly went away, Mis' Watson an' me, we was lef' in charge till the place was rented. Mis' Watson, she've bin here a good while, an' she warn' skeery. So she slep' in the house. I'd bin havin' tokens—I tol' Mis' Innes some of 'em—an' I slep' in the lodge. Then one day Mis' Watson, she came to me an' she sez, sez she, 'Thomas, you'll hev to sleep up in the big house. I'm too nervous to do it any more.' But I jes' reckon to myself that ef it's too skeery fer her, it's too skeery fer me. We had it, then, sho' nuff, and it ended up with Mis' Watson stayin' in the lodge nights an' me lookin' fer work at de club."

"Did Mrs. Watson say that anything had happened to alarm her?"

"No, sah. She was jes' natchally skeered. Well, that was all, far's I know, until the night I come over to see Mis' Innes. I come across the valley, along the path from the club-house, and I goes home that way. Down in the creek bottom I almost run into a man. He wuz standin' with his back to me, an' he was workin' with one of these yere electric light things that fit in yer pocket. He was havin' trouble—one minute it'd flash out, an' the nex' it'd be gone. I hed a view of 'is white dress shirt an' tie, as I passed. I didn't see his face. But I know it warn't Mr. Arnold. It was a taller man than Mr. Arnold. Beside that, Mr. Arnold was playin' cards when I got to the club-house, same's he'd been doin' all day."

"And the next morning you came back along the path," pursued Mr. Jamieson relentlessly.

"The nex' mornin' I come back along the path an' down where I dun see the man night befoh, I picked up this here." The old man held out a tiny object and Mr. Jamieson took it. Then he held it on his extended palm for me to see. It was the other half of the pearl cuff-link!

But Mr. Jamieson was not quite through questioning him.

"And so you showed it to Sam, at the club, and asked him if he knew any one who owned such a link, and Sam said—what?"

"Wal, Sam, he 'lowed he'd seen such a pair of cuff-buttons in a shirt belongin' to Mr. Bailey—Mr. Jack Bailey, sah."

"I'll keep this link, Thomas, for a while," the detective said. "That's all I wanted to know. Good night."

As Thomas shuffled out, Mr. Jamieson watched me sharply.

"You see, Miss Innes," he said, "Mr. Bailey insists on mixing himself with this thing. If Mr. Bailey came here that Friday night expecting to meet Arnold Armstrong, and missed him—if, as I say, he had done this, might he not, seeing him enter the following night, have struck him down, as he had intended before?"

"But the motive?" I gasped.

"There could be motive proved, I think. Arnold Armstrong and John Bailey have been enemies since the latter, as cashier of the Traders' Bank, brought Arnold almost into the clutches of the law. Also, you forget that both men have been paying attention to Miss Gertrude. Bailey's flight looks bad, too."

"And you think Halsey helped him to escape?"

"Undoubtedly. Why, what could it be but flight? Miss Innes, let me reconstruct that evening, as I see it. Bailey and Armstrong had quarreled at the club. I learned this to-day. Your nephew brought Bailey over. Prompted by jealous, insane fury, Armstrong followed, coming across by the path. He entered the billiard-room wing—perhaps rapping, and being admitted by your nephew. Just inside he was shot, by some one on the circular staircase. The shot fired, your nephew and Bailey left the house at once, going toward the automobile house. They left by the lower road, which prevented them being heard, and when you and Miss Gertrude got down-stairs everything was quiet."

"But—Gertrude's story," I stammered.

"Miss Gertrude only brought forward her explanation the following morning. I do not believe it, Miss Innes. It is the story of a loving and ingenious woman."

"And—this thing to-night?"

"May upset my whole view of the case. We must give the benefit of every doubt, after all. We may, for instance, come back to the figure on the porch: if it was a woman you saw that night through the window, we might start with other premises. Or Mr. Innes' explanation may turn us in a new direction. It is possible that he shot Arnold Armstrong as a burglar and then fled, frightened at what he had done. In any case, however, I feel confident that the body was here when he left. Mr. Armstrong left the club ostensibly for a moonlight saunter, about half after eleven o'clock. It was three when the shot was fired."

I leaned back bewildered. It seemed to me that the evening had been full of significant happenings, had I only held the key. Had Gertrude been the fugitive in the clothes chute? Who was the man on the drive near the lodge, and whose gold-mounted dressing-bag had I seen in the lodge sitting-room?

It was late when Mr. Jamieson finally got up to go. I went with him to the door, and together we stood looking out over the valley. Below lay the village of Casanova, with its Old World houses, its blossoming trees and its peace. Above on the hill across the valley were the lights of the Greenwood Club. It was even possible to see the curving row of parallel lights that marked the carriage road. Rumors that I had heard about the club came back—of drinking, of high play, and once, a year ago, of a suicide under those very lights.

Mr. Jamieson left, taking a short cut to the village, and I still stood there. It must have been after eleven, and the monotonous tick of the big clock on the stairs behind me was the only sound.

Then I was conscious that some one was running up the drive. In a minute a woman darted into the area of light made by the open door, and caught me by the arm. It was Rosie—Rosie in a state of collapse from terror, and, not the least important, clutching one of my Coalport plates and a silver spoon.

She stood staring into the darkness behind, still holding the plate. I got her into the house and secured the plate; then I stood and looked down at her where she crouched tremblingly against the doorway.

"Well," I asked, "didn't your young man enjoy his meal?"

She couldn't speak. She looked at the spoon she still held— I wasn't so anxious about it: thank Heaven, it wouldn't chip—and then she stared at me.

"I appreciate your desire to have everything nice for him," I went on, "but the next time, you might take the Limoges china It's more easily duplicated and less expensive."

"I haven't a young man—not here." She had got her breath now, as I had guessed she would. "I—I have been chased by a thief, Miss Innes."

"Did he chase you out of the house and back again?" I asked.

Then Rosie began to cry—not silently, but noisily, hysterically.

I stopped her by giving her a good shake.

"What in the world is the matter with you?" I snapped. "Has the day of good common sense gone by! Sit up and tell me the whole thing." Rosie sat up then, and sniffled.

"I was coming up the drive—" she began.

"You must start with when you went *down* the drive, with my dishes and my silver," I interrupted, but, seeing more signs of hysteria, I gave in. "Very well. You were coming up the drive—"

"I had a basket of—of silver and dishes on my arm and I was carrying the plate, because—because I was afraid I'd break it. Part-way up the road a man stepped out of the bushes, and held his arm like this, spread out, so I couldn't get past. He said—he said—`Not so fast, young lady; I want you to let me see what's in that basket.'"

She got up in her excitement and took hold of my arm.

"It was like this, Miss Innes," she said, "and say you was the man. When he said that, I screamed and ducked under his arm like this. He caught at the basket and I dropped it. I ran as fast as I could, and he came after as far as the trees. Then he stopped. Oh, Miss Innes, it must have been the man that killed that Mr. Armstrong!"

"Don't be foolish," I said. "Whoever killed Mr. Armstrong would put as much space between himself and this house as he could. Go up to bed now; and mind, if I hear of this story being repeated to the other maids, I shall deduct from your wages for every broken dish I find in the drive."

I listened to Rosie as she went up-stairs, running past the shadowy places and slamming her door. Then I sat down and looked at the Coalport plate and the silver spoon. I had brought my own china and silver, and, from all appearances, I would have little enough to take back. But though I might jeer at Rosie as much as I wished, the fact remained that some one had been on the drive that night who had no business there. Although neither had Rosie, for that matter.

I could fancy Liddy's face when she missed the extra pieces of china—she had opposed Rosie from the start. If Liddy once finds a prophecy fulfilled, especially an unpleasant one, she never allows me to forget it. It seemed to me that it was absurd to leave that china dotted along the road for her to spy the next morning; so with a sudden resolution, I opened the door again and stepped out into the darkness. As the door closed behind me I half regretted my impulse; then I shut my teeth and went on.

I have never been a nervous woman, as I said before. Moreover, a minute or two in the darkness enabled me to see things fairly well. Beulah gave me rather a start by rubbing unexpectedly against my feet; then we two, side by side, went down the drive.

There were no fragments of china, but where the grove began I picked up a silver spoon. So far Rosie's story was borne out: I began to wonder if it were not indiscreet, to say the least, this midnight prowling in a neighborhood with such a deservedly bad reputation. Then I saw something gleaming, which proved to be the handle of a cup, and a step or two farther on I found a V-shaped bit of a plate. But the most surprising thing of all was to find the basket sitting comfortably beside the road, with the rest of the broken crockery piled neatly within, and a handful of small silver, spoon, forks, and the like, on top! I could only stand and stare. Then Rosie's story was true. But where had Rosie carried her basket? And why had the thief, if he were a thief, picked up the broken china out of the road and left it, with his booty?

It was with my nearest approach to a nervous collapse that I heard the familiar throbbing of an automobile engine. As it came closer I recognized the outline of the Dragon Fly, and knew that Halsey had come back.

Strange enough it must have seemed to Halsey, too, to come across me in the middle of the night, with the skirt of my gray silk gown over my shoulders to keep off the dew, holding a red and green basket under one arm and a black cat under the other. What with relief and joy, I began to cry, right there, and very nearly wiped my eyes on Beulah in the excitement.

9.   JUST LIKE A GIRL

"Aunt Ray!" Halsey said from the gloom behind the lamps. "What in the world are you doing here?"

"Taking a walk," I said, trying to be composed. I don't think the answer struck either of us as being ridiculous at the time. "Oh, Halsey, where have you been?"

"Let me take you up to the house." He was in the road, and had Beulah and the basket out of my arms in a moment. I could see the car plainly now, and Warner was at the wheel—Warner in an ulster and a pair of slippers, over Heaven knows what. Jack Bailey was not there. I got in, and we went slowly and painfully up to the house.

We did not talk. What we had to say was too important to commence there, and, besides, it took all kinds of coaxing from both men to get the Dragon Fly up the last grade. Only when we had closed the front door and stood facing each other in the hall, did Halsey say anything. He slipped his strong young arm around my shoulders and turned me so I faced the light.

"Poor Aunt Ray!" he said gently. And I nearly wept again. "I—I must see Gertrude, too; we will have a three-cornered talk."

And then Gertrude herself came down the stairs. She had not been to bed, evidently: she still wore the white negligee she had worn earlier in the evening, and she limped somewhat. During her slow progress down the stairs I had time to notice one thing: Mr. Jamieson had said the woman who escaped from the cellar had worn no shoe on her right foot. Gertrude's right ankle was the one she had sprained!

The meeting between brother and sister was tense, but without tears. Halsey kissed her tenderly, and I noticed evidences of strain and anxiety in both young faces.

"Is everything—right?" she asked.

"Right as can be," with forced cheerfulness.

I lighted the living-room and we went in there. Only a half-hour before I had sat with Mr. Jamieson in that very room, listening while he overtly accused both Gertrude and Halsey of at least a knowledge of the death of Arnold Armstrong. Now Halsey was here to speak for himself: I should learn everything that had puzzled me.

"I saw it in the paper to-night for the first time," he was saying. "It knocked me dumb. When I think of this houseful of women, and a thing like that occurring!"

Gertrude's face was still set and white. "That isn't all, Halsey," she said. "You and—and Jack left almost at the time it happened. The detective here thinks that you—that we—know something about it."

"The devil he does!" Halsey's eyes were fairly starting from his head. "I beg your pardon, Aunt Ray, but—the fellow's a lunatic."

"Tell me everything, won't you, Halsey?" I begged. "Tell me where you went that night, or rather morning, and why you went as you did. This has been a terrible forty-eight hours for all of us."

He stood staring at me, and I could see the horror of the situation dawning in his face.

"I can't tell you where I went, Aunt Ray," he said, after a moment. "As to why, you will learn that soon enough. But Gertrude knows that Jack and I left the house before this thing—this horrible murder—occurred."

"Mr. Jamieson does not believe me," Gertrude said drearily. "Halsey, if the worst comes, if they should arrest you, you must—tell."

"I shall tell nothing," he said with a new sternness in his voice. "Aunt Ray, it was necessary for Jack and me to leave that night. I can not tell you why—just yet. As to where we went, if I have to depend on that as an alibi, I shall not tell. The whole thing is an absurdity, a trumped-up charge that can not possibly be serious."

"Has Mr. Bailey gone back to the city," I demanded, "or to the club?"

"Neither," defiantly; "at the present moment I do not know where he is."

"Halsey," I asked gravely, leaning forward, "have you the slightest suspicion who killed Arnold Armstrong? The police think he was admitted from within, and that he was shot down from above, by someone on the circular staircase."

"I know nothing of it," he maintained; but I fancied I caught a sudden glance at Gertrude, a flash of something that died as it came.

As quietly, as calmly as I could, I went over the whole story, from the night Liddy and I had been alone up to the strange experience of Rosie and her pursuer. The basket still stood on the table, a mute witness to this last mystifying occurrence.

"There is something else," I said hesitatingly, at the last. "Halsey, I have never told this even to Gertrude, but the morning after the crime, I found, in a tulip bed, a revolver. It—it was yours, Halsey."

For an appreciable moment Halsey stared at me. Then he turned to Gertrude.

"My revolver, Trude!" he exclaimed. "Why, Jack took my revolver with him, didn't he?"

"Oh, for Heaven's sake don't say that," I implored. "The detective thinks possibly Jack Bailey came back, and—and the thing happened then."

"He didn't come back," Halsey said sternly. "Gertrude, when you brought down a revolver that night for Jack to take with him, what one did you bring? Mine?"

Gertrude was defiant now.

"No. Yours was loaded, and I was afraid of what Jack might do. I gave him one I have had for a year or two. It was empty."

Halsey threw up both hands despairingly.

"If that isn't like a girl!" he said. "Why didn't you do what I asked you to, Gertrude? You send Bailey off with an empty gun, and throw mine in a tulip bed, of all places on earth! Mine was a thirty-eight caliber. The inquest will show, of course, that the bullet that killed Armstrong was a thirty-eight. Then where shall I be?"

"You forget," I broke in, "that I have the revolver, and that no one knows about it."

But Gertrude had risen angrily.

"I can not stand it; it is always with me," she cried. "Halsey, I did not throw your revolver into the tulip bed. I—think—you—did it—yourself!"

They stared at each other across the big library table, with young eyes all at once hard, suspicious. And then Gertrude held out both hands to him appealingly.

"We must not," she said brokenly. "Just now, with so much at stake, it—is shameful. I know you are as ignorant as I am. Make me believe it, Halsey."

Halsey soothed her as best he could, and the breach seemed healed. But long after I went to bed he sat downstairs in the living-room alone, and I knew he was going over the case as he had learned it. Some things were clear to him that were dark to me. He knew, and Gertrude, too, why Jack Bailey and he had gone away that night, as they did. He knew where they had been for the last forty-eight hours, and why Jack Bailey had not returned with him. It seemed to me that without fuller confidence from both the children—they are always children to me—I should never be able to learn anything.

As I was finally getting ready for bed, Halsey came upstairs and knocked at my door. When I had got into a negligee—I used to say wrapper before Gertrude came back from school—I let him in. He stood in the doorway a moment, and then he went into agonies of silent mirth. I sat down on the side of the bed and waited in severe silence for him to stop, but he only seemed to grow worse.

When he had recovered he took me by the elbow and pulled me in front of the mirror.

"'How to be beautiful,'" he quoted. "'Advice to maids and matrons,' by Beatrice Fairfax!" And then I saw myself. I had neglected to remove my wrinkle eradicators, and I presume my appearance was odd. I believe that it is a woman's duty to care for her looks, but it is much like telling a necessary falsehood—one must not be found out. By the time I got them off Halsey was serious again, and I listened to his story.

"Aunt Ray," he began, extinguishing his cigarette on the back of my ivory hair-brush, "I would give a lot to tell you the whole thing. But—I can't, for a day or so, anyhow. But one thing I might have told you a long time ago. If you had known it, you would not have suspected me for a moment of—of having anything to do with the attack on Arnold Armstrong. Goodness knows what I might do to a fellow like that, if there was enough provocation, and I had a gun in my hand—under ordinary circumstances. But—I care a great deal about Louise Armstrong, Aunt Ray. I hope to marry her some day. Is it likely I would kill her brother?"

"Her stepbrother," I corrected. "No, of course, it isn't likely, or possible. Why didn't you tell me, Halsey?"

"Well, there were two reasons," he said slowly.

"One was that you had a girl already picked out for me—"

"Nonsense," I broke in, and felt myself growing red. I had, indeed, one of the—but no matter.

"And the second reason," he pursued, "was that the Armstrongs would have none of me."

I sat bolt upright at that and gasped.

"The Armstrongs!" I repeated. "With old Peter Armstrong driving a stage across the mountains while your grandfather was war governor—"

"Well, of course, the war governor's dead, and out of the matrimonial market," Halsey interrupted. "And the present Innes admits himself he isn't good enough for—for Louise."

"Exactly," I said despairingly, "and, of course, you are taken at your own valuation. The Inneses are not always so self-depreciatory."

"Not always, no," he said, looking at me with his boyish smile. "Fortunately, Louise doesn't agree with her family. She's willing to take me, war governor or no, provided her mother consents. She isn't overly-fond of her stepfather, but she adores her mother. And now, can't you see where this thing puts me? Down and out, with all of them."

"But the whole thing is absurd," I argued. "And besides, Gertrude's sworn statement that you left before Arnold Armstrong came would clear you at once."

Halsey got up and began to pace the room, and the air of cheerfulness dropped like a mask.

"She can't swear it," he said finally. "Gertrude's story was true as far as it went, but she didn't tell everything. Arnold Armstrong came here at two-thirty—came into the billiard-room and left in five minutes. He came to bring—something."

"Halsey," I cried, "you *must* tell me the whole truth. Every time I see a way for you to escape you block it yourself with this wall of mystery. What did he bring?"

"A telegram—for Bailey," he said. "It came by special messenger from town, and was—most important. Bailey had started for here, and the messenger had gone back to the city. The steward gave it to Arnold, who had been drinking all day and couldn't sleep, and was going for a stroll in the direction of Sunnyside."

"And he brought it?"

"Yes."

"What was in the telegram?"

"I can tell you—as soon as certain things are made public. It is only a matter of days now," gloomily.

"And Gertrude's story of a telephone message?"

"Poor Trude!" he half whispered. "Poor loyal little girl! Aunt Ray, there was no such message. No doubt your detective already knows that and discredits all Gertrude told him."

"And when she went back, it was to get—the telegram?"

"Probably," Halsey said slowly. "When you get to thinking about it, Aunt Ray, it looks bad for all three of us, doesn't it? And yet—I will take my oath none of us even inadvertently killed that poor devil."

I looked at the closed door into Gertrude's dressing-room, and lowered my voice.

"The same horrible thought keeps recurring to me," I whispered. "Halsey, Gertrude probably had your revolver: she must have examined it, anyhow, that night. After you—and Jack had gone, what if that ruffian came back, and she—and she—"

I couldn't finish. Halsey stood looking at me with shut lips.

"She might have heard him fumbling at the door—he had no key, the police say—and thinking it was you, or Jack, she admitted him. When she saw her mistake she ran up the stairs, a step or two, and turning, like an animal at bay, she fired."

Halsey had his hand over my lips before I finished, and in that position we stared each at the other, our stricken glances crossing.

"The revolver—my revolver—thrown into the tulip bed!" he muttered to himself. "Thrown perhaps from an upper window: you say it was buried deep. Her prostration ever since, her—Aunt Ray, you don't think it was Gertrude who fell down the clothes chute?"

I could only nod my head in a hopeless affirmative.

10. THE TRADERS BANK

The morning after Halsey's return was Tuesday. Arnold Armstrong had been found dead at the foot of the circular staircase at three o'clock on Sunday morning. The funeral services were to be held on Tuesday, and the interment of the body was to be deferred until the Armstrongs arrived from California. No one, I think, was very sorry that Arnold Armstrong was dead, but the manner of his death aroused some sympathy and an enormous amount of curiosity. Mrs. Ogden Fitzhugh, a cousin, took charge of the arrangements, and everything, I believe, was as quiet as possible. I gave Thomas Johnson and Mrs. Watson permission to go into town to pay their last respects to the dead man, but for some reason they did not care to go.

Halsey spent part of the day with Mr. Jamieson, but he said nothing of what happened. He looked grave and anxious, and he had a long conversation with Gertrude late in the afternoon.

Tuesday evening found us quiet, with the quiet that precedes an explosion. Gertrude and Halsey were both gloomy and distraught, and as Liddy had already discovered that some of the china was broken—it is impossible to have any secrets from an old servant—I was not in a pleasant humor myself. Warner brought up the afternoon mail and the evening papers at seven—I was curious to know what the papers said of the murder. We had turned away at least a dozen reporters. But I read over the head-line that ran half-way across the top of the *Gazette* twice before I comprehended it. Halsey had opened the *Chronicle* and was staring at it fixedly.

"The Traders' Bank closes its doors!" was what I read, and then I put down the paper and looked across the table.

"Did you know of this?" I asked Halsey.

"I expected it. But not so soon," he replied.

"And you?" to Gertrude.

"Jack—told us—something," Gertrude said faintly. "Oh, Halsey, what can he do now?"

"Jack!" I said scornfully. "Your Jack's flight is easy enough to explain now. And you helped him, both of you, to get away! You get that from your mother; it isn't an Innes trait. Do you know that every dollar you have, both of you, is in that bank?"

Gertrude tried to speak, but Halsey stopped her.

"That isn't all, Gertrude," he said quietly; "Jack is—under arrest."

"Under arrest!" Gertrude screamed, and tore the paper out of his hand. She glanced at the heading, then she crumpled the newspaper into a ball and flung it to the floor. While Halsey, looking stricken and white, was trying to smooth it out and read it, Gertrude had dropped her head on the table and was sobbing stormily.

I have the clipping somewhere, but just now I can remember only the essentials.

On the afternoon before, Monday, while the Traders' Bank was in the rush of closing hour, between two and three, Mr. Jacob Trautman, President of the Pearl Brewing Company, came into the bank to lift a loan. As security for the loan he had deposited some three hundred International Steamship Company 5's, in total value three hundred thousand dollars. Mr. Trautman went to the loan clerk and, after certain formalities had been gone through, the loan clerk went to the vault. Mr. Trautman, who was a large and genial German, waited for a time, whistling under his breath. The loan clerk did not come back. After an interval, Mr. Trautman saw the loan clerk emerge from the vault and go to the assistant cashier: the two went hurriedly to the vault. A lapse of another ten minutes, and the assistant cashier came out and approached Mr. Trautman. He was noticeably white and trembling. Mr. Trautman was told that through an oversight the bonds had been misplaced, and was asked to return the following morning, when everything would be made all right.

Mr. Trautman, however, was a shrewd business man, and he did not like the appearance of things. He left the bank apparently satisfied, and within thirty minutes he had called up three different members of the Traders' Board of Directors. At three-thirty there was a hastily convened board meeting, with some stormy scenes, and late in the afternoon a national bank examiner was in possession of the books. The bank had not opened for business on Tuesday.

At twelve-thirty o'clock the Saturday before, as soon as the business of the day was closed, Mr. John Bailey, the cashier of the defunct bank, had taken his hat and departed. During the afternoon he had called up Mr. Aronson, a member of the board, and said he was ill, and might not be at the bank for a day or two. As Bailey was highly thought of, Mr. Aronson merely expressed a regret. From that time until

Monday night, when Mr. Bailey had surrendered to the police, little was known of his movements. Some time after one on Saturday he had entered the Western Union office at Cherry and White Streets and had sent two telegrams. He was at the Greenwood Country Club on Saturday night, and appeared unlike himself. It was reported that he would be released under enormous bond, some time that day, Tuesday.

The article closed by saying that while the officers of the bank refused to talk until the examiner had finished his work, it was known that securities aggregating a million and a quarter were missing. Then there was a diatribe on the possibility of such an occurrence; on the folly of a one-man bank, and of a Board of Directors that met only to lunch together and to listen to a brief report from the cashier, and on the poor policy of a government that arranges a three or four-day examination twice a year. The mystery, it insinuated, had not been cleared by the arrest of the cashier. Before now minor officials had been used to cloak the misdeeds of men higher up. Inseparable as the words "speculation" and "peculation" have grown to be, John Bailey was not known to be in the stock market. His only words, after his surrender, had been "Send for Mr. Armstrong at once." The telegraph message which had finally reached the President of the Traders' Bank, in an interior town in California, had been responded to by a telegram from Doctor Walker, the young physician who was traveling with the Armstrong family, saying that Paul Armstrong was very ill and unable to travel.

That was how things stood that Tuesday evening. The Traders' Bank had suspended payment, and John Bailey was under arrest, charged with wrecking it; Paul Armstrong lay very ill in California, and his only son had been murdered two days before. I sat dazed and bewildered. The children's money was gone: that was bad enough, though I had plenty, if they would let me share. But Gertrude's grief was beyond any power of mine to comfort; the man she had chosen stood accused of a colossal embezzlement—and even worse. For in the instant that I sat there I seemed to see the coils closing around John Bailey as the murderer of Arnold Armstrong.

Gertrude lifted her head at last and stared across the table at Halsey.

"Why did he do it?" she wailed. "Couldn't you stop him, Halsey? It was suicidal to go back!"

Halsey was looking steadily through the windows of the breakfast-room, but it was evident he saw nothing.

"It was the only thing he could do, Trude," he said at last. "Aunt Ray, when I found Jack at the Greenwood Club last Saturday night, he was frantic. I can not talk until Jack tells me I may, but—he is absolutely innocent of all this, believe me. I thought, Trude and I thought, we were helping him, but it was the wrong way. He came back. Isn't that the act of an innocent man?"

"Then why did he leave at all?" I asked, unconvinced. "What innocent man would run away from here at three o'clock in the morning? Doesn't it look rather as though he thought it impossible to escape?"

Gertrude rose angrily. "You are not even just!" she flamed. "You don't know anything about it, and you condemn him!"

"I know that we have all lost a great deal of money," I said. "I shall believe Mr. Bailey innocent the moment he is shown to be. You profess to know the truth, but you can not tell me! What am I to think?"

Halsey leaned over and patted my hand.

"You must take us on faith," he said. "Jack Bailey hasn't a penny that doesn't belong to him; the guilty man will be known in a day or so."

"I shall believe that when it is proved," I said grimly. "In the meantime, I take no one on faith. The Inneses never do."

Gertrude, who had been standing aloof at a window, turned suddenly. "But when the bonds are offered for sale, Halsey, won't the thief be detected at once?"

Halsey turned with a superior smile.

"It wouldn't be done that way," he said. "They would be taken out of the vault by some one who had access to it, and used as collateral for a loan in another bank. It would be possible to realize eighty per cent. of their face value."

"In cash?"

"In cash."

"But the man who did it—he would be known?"

"Yes. I tell you both, as sure as I stand here, I believe that Paul Armstrong looted his own bank. I believe he has a million at least, as the result, and that he will never come back. I'm worse than a pauper now. I can't ask Louise to share nothing a year with me and when I think of this disgrace for her, I'm crazy."

The most ordinary events of life seemed pregnant with possibilities that day, and when Halsey was called to the telephone, I ceased all pretense at eating. When he came back from the telephone his face showed that something had occurred. He waited, however, until Thomas left the dining-room: then he told us.

"Paul Armstrong is dead," he announced gravely. "He died this morning in California. Whatever he did, he is beyond the law now."

Gertrude turned pale.

"And the only man who could have cleared Jack can never do it!" she said despairingly.

"Also," I replied coldly, "Mr. Armstrong is for ever beyond the power of defending himself. When your Jack comes to me, with some two hundred thousand dollars in his hands, which is about what you have lost, I shall believe him innocent."

Halsey threw his cigarette away and turned on me.

"There you go!" he exclaimed. "If he was the thief, he could return the money, of course. If he is innocent, he probably hasn't a tenth of that amount in the world. In his hands! That's like a woman."

Gertrude, who had been pale and despairing during the early part of the conversation, had flushed an indignant red. She got up and drew herself to her slender height, looking down at me with the scorn of the young and positive.

"You are the only mother I ever had," she said tensely. "I have given you all I would have given my mother, had she lived—my love, my trust. And now, when I need you most, you fail me. I tell you, John Bailey is a good man, an honest man. If you say he is not, you—you—"

"Gertrude," Halsey broke in sharply. She dropped beside the table and, burying her face in her arms broke into a storm of tears.

"I love him—love him," she sobbed, in a surrender that was totally unlike her. "Oh, I never thought it would be like this. I can't bear it. I can't."

Halsey and I stood helpless before the storm. I would have tried to comfort her, but she had put me away, and there was something aloof in her grief, something new and strange. At last, when her sorrow had subsided to the dry shaking sobs of a tired child, without raising her head she put out one groping hand.

"Aunt Ray!" she whispered. In a moment I was on my knees beside her, her arm around my neck, her cheek against my hair.

"Where am I in this?" Halsey said suddenly and tried to put his arms around us both. It was a welcome distraction, and Gertrude was soon herself again. The little storm had cleared the air. Nevertheless, my opinion remained unchanged. There was much to be cleared up before I would consent to any renewal of my acquaintance with

John Bailey. And Halsey and Gertrude knew it, knowing me.

11. HALSEY MAKES A CAPTURE

It was about half-past eight when we left the dining-room and still engrossed with one subject, the failure of the bank and its attendant evils Halsey and I went out into the grounds for a stroll Gertrude followed us shortly. "The light was thickening," to appropriate Shakespeare's description of twilight, and once again the tree-toads and the crickets were making the night throb with their tiny life. It was almost oppressively lonely, in spite of its beauty, and I felt a sickening pang of homesickness for my city at night—for the clatter of horses' feet on cemented paving, for the lights, the voices, the sound of children playing. The country after dark oppresses me. The stars, quite eclipsed in the city by the electric lights, here become insistent, assertive. Whether I want to or not, I find myself looking for the few I know by name, and feeling ridiculously new and small by contrast—always an unpleasant sensation.

After Gertrude joined us, we avoided any further mention of the murder. To Halsey, as to me, there was ever present, I am sure, the thought of our conversation of the night before. As we strolled back and forth along the drive, Mr. Jamieson emerged from the shadow of the trees.

"Good evening," he said, managing to include Gertrude in his bow.

Gertrude had never been even ordinarily courteous to him, and she nodded coldly. Halsey, however, was more cordial, although we were all constrained enough. He and Gertrude went on together, leaving the detective to walk with me. As soon as they were out of earshot, he turned to me.

"Do you know, Miss Innes," he said, "the deeper I go into this thing, the more strange it seems to me. I am very sorry for Miss Gertrude. It looks as if Bailey, whom she has tried so hard to save, is worse than a rascal; and after her plucky fight for him, it seems hard."

I looked through the dusk to where Gertrude's light dinner dress gleamed among the trees. She *had* made a plucky fight, poor child. Whatever she might have been driven to do, I could find nothing but a deep sympathy for her. If she had only come to me with the whole truth then!

"Miss Innes," Mr. Jamieson was saying, "in the last three days, have you seen a—any suspicious figures around the grounds? Any—woman?"

"No," I replied. "I have a houseful of maids that will bear watching, one and all. But there has been no strange woman near the house or Liddy would have seen her, you may be sure. She has a telescopic eye."

Mr. Jamieson looked thoughtful.

"It may not amount to anything," he said slowly. "It is difficult to get any perspective on things around here, because every one down in the village is sure he saw the murderer, either before or since the crime. And half of them will stretch a point or two as to facts, to be obliging. But the man who drives the hack down there tells a story that may possibly prove to be important."

"I have heard it, I think. Was it the one the parlor maid brought up yesterday, about a ghost wringing its hands on the roof? Or perhaps it's the one the milk-boy heard: a tramp washing a dirty shirt, presumably bloody, in the creek below the bridge?"

I could see the gleam of Mr. Jamieson's teeth, as he smiled.

"Neither," he said. "But Matthew Geist, which is our friend's name, claims that on Saturday night, at nine-thirty, a veiled lady—"

"I knew it would be a veiled lady," I broke in.

"A veiled lady," he persisted, "who was apparently young and beautiful, engaged his hack and asked to be driven to Sunnyside. Near the gate, however, she made him stop, in spite of his remonstrances, saying she preferred to walk to the house. She paid him, and he left her there. Now, Miss Innes, you had no such visitor, I believe?"

"None," I said decidedly.

"Geist thought it might be a maid, as you had got a supply that day. But he said her getting out near the gate puzzled him. Anyhow, we have now one veiled lady, who, with the ghostly intruder of Friday night, makes two assets that I hardly know what to do with."

"It is mystifying," I admitted, "although I can think of one possible explanation. The path from the Greenwood Club to the village enters the road near the lodge gate. A woman who wished to reach the Country Club, unperceived, might choose such a method. There are plenty of women there."

I think this gave him something to ponder, for in a short time he said good night and left. But I myself was far from satisfied. I was determined, however, on one thing. If my suspicions—for I had suspicions—were true, I would make my own investigations, and Mr. Jamieson should learn only what was good for him to know.

We went back to the house, and Gertrude, who was more like herself since her talk with Halsey, sat down at the mahogany desk in the living-room to write a letter. Halsey prowled up and down the entire east wing, now in the card-room, now in the billiard-room, and now and then blowing his clouds of tobacco smoke among the pink and gold hangings of the drawing-room. After a little I joined him in the billiard-room, and together we went over the details of the discovery of the body.

The card-room was quite dark. Where we sat, in the billiard-room, only one of the side brackets was lighted, and we spoke in subdued tones, as the hour and the subject seemed to demand. When I spoke of the figure Liddy and I had seen on the porch through the card-room window Friday night, Halsey sauntered into the darkened room, and together we stood there, much as Liddy and I had done that other night.

The window was the same grayish rectangle in the blackness as before. A few feet away in the hall was the spot where the body of Arnold Armstrong had been found. I was a bit nervous, and I put my hand on Halsey's sleeve. Suddenly, from the top of the staircase above us came the sound of a cautious footstep. At first I was not sure, but Halsey's attitude told me he had heard and was listening.

The step, slow, measured, infinitely cautious, was nearer now. Halsey tried to loosen my fingers, but I was in a paralysis of fright.

The swish of a body against the curving rail, as if for guidance, was plain enough, and now whoever it was had reached the foot of the staircase and had caught a glimpse of our rigid silhouettes against the billiard-room doorway. Halsey threw me off then and strode forward.

"Who is it?" he called imperiously, and took a half dozen rapid strides toward the foot of the staircase. Then I heard him mutter something; there was the crash of a falling body, the slam of the outer door, and, for an instant, quiet. I screamed, I think. Then I remember turning on the lights and finding Halsey, white with fury, trying to untangle himself from something warm and fleecy. He had cut his forehead a little on the lowest step of the stairs, and he was rather a ghastly sight.

He flung the white object at me, and, jerking open the outer door, raced into the darkness.

Gertrude had come on hearing the noise, and now we stood, staring at each other over—of all things on earth—a white silk and wool blanket, exquisitely fine! It was the most unghostly thing in the world, with its lavender border and its faint scent. Gertrude was the first to speak.

"Somebody—had it?" she asked.

"Yes. Halsey tried to stop whoever it was and fell. Gertrude, that blanket is not mine. I have never seen before."

She held it up and looked at it: then she went to the door on to the veranda and threw it open. Perhaps a hundred feet from the house were two figures, that moved slowly toward us as we looked.

When they came within range of the light, I recognized Halsey, and with him Mrs. Watson, the housekeeper.

12.   ONE MYSTERY FOR ANOTHER

The most commonplace incident takes on a new appearance if the attendant circumstances are unusual. There was no reason on earth why Mrs. Watson should not have carried a blanket down the east wing staircase, if she so desired. But to take a blanket down at eleven o'clock at night, with every precaution as to noise, and, when discovered, to fling it at Halsey and bolt—Halsey's word, and a good one—into the grounds,—this made the incident more than significant.

They moved slowly across the lawn and up the steps. Halsey was talking quietly, and Mrs. Watson was looking down and listening. She was a woman of a certain amount of dignity, most efficient, so far as I could see, although Liddy would have found fault if she dared. But just now Mrs. Watson's face was an enigma. She was defiant, I think, under her mask of submission, and she still showed the effect of nervous shock.

"Mrs. Watson," I said severely, "will you be so good as to explain this rather unusual occurrence?"

"I don't think it so unusual, Miss Innes." Her voice was deep and very clear: just now it was somewhat tremulous. "I was taking a blanket down to Thomas, who is—not well to-night, and I used this staircase, as being nearer the path to the lodge When—Mr. Innes called and then rushed at me, I—I was alarmed, and flung the blanket at him."

Halsey was examining the cut on his forehead in a small mirror on the wall. It was not much of an injury, but it had bled freely, and his appearance was rather terrifying.

"Thomas ill?" he said, over his shoulder. "Why, *I* thought I saw Thomas out there as you made that cyclonic break out of the door and over the porch."

I could see that under pretense of examining his injury he was watching her through the mirror.

"Is this one of the servants' blankets, Mrs. Watson?" I asked, holding up its luxurious folds to the light.

"Everything else is locked away," she replied. Which was true enough, no doubt. I had rented the house without bed furnishings.

"If Thomas is ill," Halsey said, "some member of the family ought to go down to see him. You needn't bother, Mrs. Watson. I will take the blanket."

She drew herself up quickly, as if in protest, but she found nothing to say. She stood smoothing the folds of her dead black dress, her face as white as chalk above it. Then she seemed to make up her mind.

"Very well, Mr. Innes," she said. "Perhaps you would better go. I have done all I could."

And then she turned and went up the circular staircase, moving slowly and with a certain dignity. Below, the three of us stared at one another across the intervening white blanket.

"Upon my word," Halsey broke out, "this place is a walking nightmare. I have the feeling that we three outsiders who have paid our money for the privilege of staying in this spook-factory, are living on the very top of things. We're on the lid, so to speak. Now and then we get a sight of the things inside, but we are not a part of them."

"Do you suppose," Gertrude asked doubtfully, "that she really meant that blanket for Thomas?"

"Thomas was standing beside that magnolia tree," Halsey replied, "when I ran after Mrs. Watson. It's down to this, Aunt Ray. Rosie's basket and Mrs. Watson's blanket can only mean one thing: there is somebody hiding or being hidden in the lodge. It wouldn't surprise me if we hold the key to the whole situation now. Anyhow, I'm going to the lodge to investigate."

Gertrude wanted to go, too, but she looked so shaken that I insisted she should not. I sent for Liddy to help her to bed, and then Halsey and I started for the lodge. The grass was heavy with dew, and, man-like, Halsey chose the shortest way across the lawn. Half-way, however, he stopped.

"We'd better go by the drive," he said. "This isn't a lawn; it's a field. Where's the gardener these days?"

"There isn't any," I said meekly. "We have been thankful enough, so far, to have our meals prepared and served and the beds aired. The gardener who belongs here is working at the club."

"Remind me to-morrow to send out a man from town," he said. "I know the very fellow."

I record this scrap of conversation, just as I have tried to put down anything and everything that had a bearing on what followed, because the gardener Halsey sent the next day played an important part in the events of the next few weeks—events that culminated, as you know, by stirring the country profoundly. At that time, however, I was busy trying to keep my skirts dry, and paid little or no attention to what seemed then a most trivial remark.

Along the drive I showed Halsey where I had found Rosie's basket with the bits of broken china piled inside. He was rather skeptical.

"Warner probably," he said when I had finished. "Began it as a joke on Rosie, and ended by picking up the broken china out of the road, knowing it would play hob with the tires of the car." Which shows how near one can come to the truth, and yet miss it altogether.

At the lodge everything was quiet. There was a light in the sitting-room down-stairs, and a faint gleam, as if from a shaded lamp, in one of the upper rooms. Halsey stopped and examined the lodge with calculating eyes.

"I don't know, Aunt Ray," he said dubiously; "this is hardly a woman's affair. If there's a scrap of any kind, you hike for the timber." Which was Halsey's solicitous care for me, put into vernacular.

"I shall stay right here," I said, and crossing the small veranda, now shaded and fragrant with honeysuckle, I hammered the knocker on the door.

Thomas opened the door himself—Thomas, fully dressed and in his customary health. I had the blanket over my arm.

"I brought the blanket, Thomas," I said; "I am sorry you are so ill."

The old man stood staring at me and then at the blanket. His confusion under other circumstances would have been ludicrous.

"What! Not ill?" Halsey said from the step. "Thomas, I'm afraid you've been malingering."

Thomas seemed to have been debating something with himself. Now he stepped out on the porch and closed the door gently behind him.

"I reckon you bettah come in, Mis' Innes," he said, speaking cautiously. "It's got so I dunno what to do, and it's boun' to come out some time er ruther."

He threw the door open then, and I stepped inside, Halsey close behind. In the sitting-room the old negro turned with quiet dignity to Halsey.

"You bettah sit down, sah," he said. "It's a place for a woman, sah."

Things were not turning out the way Halsey expected. He sat down on the center-table, with his hands thrust in his pockets, and watched me as I followed Thomas up the narrow stairs. At the top a woman was standing, and a second glance showed me it was Rosie.

She shrank back a little, but I said nothing. And then Thomas motioned to a partly open door, and I went in.

The lodge boasted three bedrooms up-stairs, all comfortably furnished. In this one, the largest and airiest, a night lamp was burning, and by its light I could make out a plain white metal bed. A girl was asleep there—or in a half stupor, for she muttered something now and then. Rosie had taken her courage in her hands, and coming in had turned up the light. It was only then that I knew. Fever-flushed, ill as she was, I recognized Louise Armstrong.

I stood gazing down at her in a stupor of amazement. Louise here, hiding at the lodge, ill and alone! Rosie came up to the bed and smoothed the white counterpane.

"I am afraid she is worse to-night," she ventured at last. I put my hand on the sick girl's forehead. It was burning with fever, and I turned to where Thomas lingered in the hallway.

"Will you tell me what you mean, Thomas Johnson, by not telling me this before?" I demanded indignantly.

Thomas quailed.

"Mis' Louise wouldn' let me," he said earnestly. "I wanted to. She ought to 'a' had a doctor the night she came, but she wouldn' hear to it. Is she—is she very bad, Mis' Innes?"

"Bad enough," I said coldly. "Send Mr. Innes up."

Halsey came up the stairs slowly, looking rather interested and inclined to be amused. For a moment he could not see anything distinctly in the darkened room; he stopped, glanced at Rosie and at me, and then his eyes fell on the restless head on the pillow.

I think he felt who it was before he really saw her; he crossed the room in a couple of strides and bent over the bed.

"Louise!" he said softly; but she did not reply, and her eyes showed no recognition. Halsey was young, and illness was new to him. He straightened himself slowly, still watching her, and caught my arm.

"She's dying, Aunt Ray!" he said huskily. "Dying! Why, she doesn't know me!"

"Fudge!" I snapped, being apt to grow irritable when my sympathies are aroused. "She's doing nothing of the sort,— and don't pinch my arm. If you want something to do, go and choke Thomas."

But at that moment Louise roused from her stupor to cough, and at the end of the paroxysm, as Rosie laid her back, exhausted, she knew us. That was all Halsey wanted; to him consciousness was recovery. He dropped on his knees beside the bed, and tried to tell her she was all right, and we would bring her around in a hurry, and how beautiful she looked—only to break down utterly and have to stop. And at that I came to my senses, and put him out.

"This instant!" I ordered, as he hesitated. "And send Rosie here."

He did not go far. He sat on the top step of the stairs, only leaving to telephone for a doctor, and getting in everybody's way in his eagerness to fetch and carry. I got him away finally, by sending him to fix up the car as a sort of ambulance, in case the doctor would allow the sick girl to be moved. He sent Gertrude down to the lodge loaded with all manner of impossible things, including an armful of Turkish towels and a box of mustard plasters, and as the two girls had known each other somewhat before, Louise brightened perceptibly when she saw her.

When the doctor from Englewood—the Casanova doctor, Doctor Walker, being away—had started for Sunnyside, and I had got Thomas to stop trying to explain what he did not understand himself, I had a long talk with the old man, and this is what I learned.

On Saturday evening before, about ten o'clock, he had been reading in the sitting-room down-stairs, when some one rapped at the door. The old man was alone, Warner not having arrived, and at first he was uncertain about opening the door. He did so finally, and was amazed at being confronted by Louise Armstrong. Thomas was an old family servant, having been with the present Mrs. Armstrong since she was a child, and he was overwhelmed at seeing Louise. He saw that she was excited and tired, and he drew her into the sitting-room and made her sit down. After a while he went to the house and brought Mrs. Watson, and they talked until late. The old man said Louise was in trouble, and seemed frightened. Mrs. Watson made some tea and took it to the lodge, but Louise made them both promise to keep her presence a secret. She had not known that Sunnyside was rented, and whatever her trouble was, this complicated things. She seemed puzzled. Her stepfather and her mother were still in California—that was all she would say about them. Why she had run away no one could imagine. Mr. Arnold Armstrong was at the Greenwood

Club, and at last Thomas, not knowing what else to do, went over there along the path. It was almost midnight. Part-way over he met Armstrong himself and brought him to the lodge. Mrs. Watson had gone to the house for some bed-linen, it having been arranged that under the circumstances Louise would be better at the lodge until morning. Arnold Armstrong and Louise had a long conference, during which he was heard to storm and become very violent. When he left it was after two. He had gone up to the house—Thomas did not know why—and at three o'clock he was shot at the foot of the circular staircase.

The following morning Louise had been ill. She had asked for Arnold, and was told he had left town. Thomas had not the moral courage to tell her of the crime. She refused a doctor, and shrank morbidly from having her presence known. Mrs. Watson and Thomas had had their hands full, and at last Rosie had been enlisted to help them. She carried necessary provisions—little enough—to the lodge, and helped to keep the secret.

Thomas told me quite frankly that he had been anxious to keep Louise's presence hidden for this reason: they had all seen Arnold Armstrong that night, and he, himself, for one, was known to have had no very friendly feeling for the dead man. As to the reason for Louise's flight from California, or why she had not gone to the Fitzhughs', or to some of her people in town, he had no more information than I had. With the death of her stepfather and the prospect of the immediate return of the family, things had become more and more impossible. I gathered that Thomas was as relieved as I at the turn events had taken. No, she did not know of either of the deaths in the family.

Taken all around, I had only substituted one mystery for another.

If I knew now why Rosie had taken the basket of dishes, I did not know who had spoken to her and followed her along the drive. If I knew that Louise was in the lodge, I did not know why she was there. If I knew that Arnold Armstrong had spent some time in the lodge the night before he was murdered, I was no nearer the solution of the crime. Who was the midnight intruder who had so alarmed Liddy and myself? Who had fallen down the clothes chute? Was Gertrude's lover a villain or a victim? Time was to answer all these things.

13. LOUISE

The doctor from Englewood came very soon, and I went up to see the sick girl with him. Halsey had gone to supervise the fitting of the car with blankets and pillows, and Gertrude was opening and airing Louise's own rooms at the house. Her private sitting-room, bedroom and dressing-room were as they had been when we came. They occupied the end of the east wing, beyond the circular staircase, and we had not even opened them.

The girl herself was too ill to notice what was being done. When, with the help of the doctor, who was a fatherly man with a family of girls at home, we got her to the house and up the stairs into bed, she dropped into a feverish sleep, which lasted until morning. Doctor Stewart—that was the

Englewood doctor—stayed almost all night, giving the medicine himself, and watching her closely. Afterward he told me that she had had a narrow escape from pneumonia, and that the cerebral symptoms had been rather alarming. I said I was glad it wasn't an "itis" of some kind, anyhow, and he smiled solemnly.

He left after breakfast, saying that he thought the worst of the danger was over, and that she must be kept very quiet.

"The shock of two deaths, I suppose, has done this," he remarked, picking up his case. "It has been very deplorable."

I hastened to set him right.

"She does not know of either, Doctor," I said. "Please do not mention them to her."

He looked as surprised as a medical man ever does.

"I do not know the family," he said, preparing to get into his top buggy. "Young Walker, down in Casanova, has been attending them. I understand he is going to marry this young lady."

"You have been misinformed," I said stiffly. "Miss Armstrong is going to marry my nephew."

The doctor smiled as he picked up the reins.

"Young ladies are changeable these days," he said. "We thought the wedding was to occur soon. Well, I will stop in this afternoon to see how my patient is getting along."

He drove away then, and I stood looking after him. He was a doctor of the old school, of the class of family practitioner that is fast dying out; a loyal and honorable gentleman who was at once physician and confidential adviser to his patients. When I was a girl we called in the doctor alike when we had measles, or when mother's sister died in the far West. He cut out redundant tonsils and brought the babies with the same air of inspiring self-confidence. Nowadays it requires a different specialist for each of these occurrences. When the babies cried, old Doctor Wainwright gave them peppermint and dropped warm sweet oil in their ears with sublime faith that if it was not colic it was earache. When, at the end of a year, father met him driving in his high side-bar buggy with the white mare ambling along, and asked for a bill, the doctor used to go home, estimate what his services were worth for that period, divide it in half—I don't think he kept any books—and send father a statement, in a cramped hand, on a sheet of ruled white paper. He was an honored guest at all the weddings, christenings, and funerals—yes, funerals—for every one knew he had done his best, and there was no gainsaying the ways of Providence.

Ah, well, Doctor Wainwright is gone, and I am an elderly woman with an increasing tendency to live in the past. The contrast between my old doctor at home and the Casanova doctor, Frank Walker, always rouses me to wrath and digression.

Some time about noon of that day, Wednesday, Mrs. Ogden Fitzhugh telephoned me. I have the barest acquaintance with her—she managed to be put on the governing board of the Old Ladies' Home and ruins their digestions by sending them ice-cream and cake on every holiday. Beyond that, and her reputation at bridge, which is insufferably bad—she is the worst player at the bridge club—I know little of her. It was she who had taken charge of Arnold Armstrong's funeral, however, and I went at once to the telephone.

"Yes," I said, "this is Miss Innes."

"Miss Innes," she said volubly, "I have just received a very strange telegram from my cousin, Mrs. Armstrong. Her husband died yesterday, in California and—wait, I will read you the message."

I knew what was coming, and I made up my mind at once. If Louise Armstrong had a good and sufficient reason for leaving her people and coming home, a reason, moreover, that kept her from going at once to Mrs. Ogden Fitzhugh, and that brought her to the lodge at Sunnyside instead, it was not my intention to betray her. Louise herself must notify her people. I do not justify myself now, but remember, I was in a peculiar position toward the Armstrong family. I was connected most unpleasantly with a cold-blooded crime, and my niece and nephew were practically beggared, either directly or indirectly, through the head of the family.

Mrs. Fitzhugh had found the message.

"`Paul died yesterday. Heart disease,'" she read. "`Wire at once if Louise is with you.' You see, Miss Innes, Louise must have started east, and Fanny is alarmed about her."

"Yes," I said.

"Louise is not here," Mrs. Fitzhugh went on, "and none of her friends—the few who are still in town—has seen her. I called you because Sunnyside was not rented when she went away, and Louise might have gone there."

"I am sorry, Mrs. Fitzhugh, but I can not help you," I said, and was immediately filled with compunction. Suppose Louise grew worse? Who was I to play Providence in this case? The anxious mother certainly had a right to know that her daughter was in good hands. So I broke in on Mrs. Fitzhugh's voluble excuses for disturbing me.

"Mrs. Fitzhugh," I said. "I was going to let you think I knew nothing about Louise Armstrong, but I have changed my mind. Louise is here, with me." There was a clatter of ejaculations at the other end of the wire. "She is ill, and not able to be moved. Moreover, she is unable to see any one. I wish you would wire her mother that she is with me, and tell her not to worry. No, I do not know why she came east."

"But my dear Miss Innes!" Mrs. Fitzhugh began. I cut in ruthlessly.

"I will send for you as soon as she can see you," I said. "No, she is not in a critical state now, but the doctor says she must have absolute quiet."

When I had hung up the receiver, I sat down to think. So Louise had fled from her people in California, and had come east alone! It was not a new idea, but why had she done it? It occurred to me that Doctor Walker might be concerned in it, might possibly have bothered her with unwelcome attentions; but it seemed to me that Louise was hardly a girl to take refuge in flight under such circumstances. She had always been high-spirited, with the well-poised head and buoyant step of the outdoors girl. It must have been much more in keeping with Louise's character, as I knew it, to resent vigorously any unwelcome attentions from Doctor Walker. It was the suitor whom I should have expected to see in headlong flight, not the lady in the case.

The puzzle was no clearer at the end of the half-hour. I picked up the morning papers, which were still full of the looting of the Traders' Bank, the interest at fever height again, on account of Paul Armstrong's death. The bank examiners were working on the books, and said nothing for publication: John Bailey had been released on bond. The body of Paul Armstrong would arrive Sunday and would be buried from the Armstrong town house. There were rumors that the dead man's estate had been a comparatively small one. The last paragraph was the important one.

Walter P. Broadhurst, of the Marine Bank, had produced two hundred American Traction bonds, which had been placed as security with the Marine Bank for a loan of one hundred and sixty thousand dollars, made to Paul Armstrong, just before his California trip. The bonds were a part of the missing traction bonds from the Traders' Bank! While this involved the late president of the wrecked bank, to my mind it by no means cleared its cashier.

The gardener mentioned by Halsey came out about two o'clock in the afternoon, and walked up from the station. I was favorably impressed by him. His references were good—he had been employed by the Brays' until they went to Europe, and he looked young and vigorous. He asked for one assistant, and I was glad enough to get off so easily. He was a pleasant-faced young fellow, with black hair and blue eyes, and his name was Alexander Graham. I have been particular about Alex, because, as I said before, he played an important part later.

That afternoon I had a new insight into the character of the dead banker. I had my first conversation with Louise. She sent for me, and against my better judgment I went. There were so many things she could not be told, in her weakened condition, that I dreaded the interview. It was much easier than I expected, however, because she asked no questions.

Gertrude had gone to bed, having been up almost all night, and Halsey was absent on one of those mysterious absences of his that grew more and more frequent as time went on, until it culminated in the event of the night of June the tenth. Liddy was in attendance in the sick-room. There being little or nothing to do, she seemed to spend her time smoothing the wrinkles from the counterpane. Louise lay under a field of virgin white, folded back at an angle of geometrical exactness, and necessitating a readjustment every time the sick girl turned.

Liddy heard my approach and came out to meet me. She seemed to be in a perpetual state of goose-flesh, and she had got in the habit of looking past me when she talked, as if she saw things. It had the effect of making me look over my shoulder to see what she was staring at, and was intensely irritating.

"She's awake," Liddy said, looking uneasily down the circular staircase, which was beside me. "She was talkin' in her sleep something awful—about dead men and coffins."

"Liddy," I said sternly, "did you breathe a word about everything not being right here?"

Liddy's gaze had wandered to the door of the chute, now bolted securely.

"Not a word," she said, "beyond asking her a question or two, which there was no harm in. She says there never was a ghost known here."

I glared at her, speechless, and closing the door into Louise's boudoir, to Liddy's great disappointment, I went on to the bedroom beyond.

Whatever Paul Armstrong had been, he had been lavish with his stepdaughter. Gertrude's rooms at home were always beautiful apartments, but the three rooms in the east wing at Sunnyside, set apart for the daughter of the house, were much more splendid.

From the walls to the rugs on the floor, from the furniture to the appointments of the bath, with its pool sunk in the floor instead of the customary unlovely tub, everything was luxurious. In the bedroom Louise was watching for me. It was easy to see that she was much improved; the flush was going, and the peculiar gasping breathing of the night before was now a comfortable and easy respiration.

She held out her hand and I took it between both of mine.

"What can I say to you, Miss Innes?" she said slowly. "To have come like this—"

I thought she was going to break down, but she did not.

"You are not to think of anything but of getting well," I said, patting her hand. "When you are better, I am going to scold you for not coming here at once. This is your home, my dear, and of all people in the world, Halsey's old aunt ought to make you welcome."

She smiled a little, sadly, I thought.

"I ought not to see Halsey," she said. "Miss Innes, there are a great many things you will never understand, I am afraid. I am an impostor on your sympathy, because I—I stay here and let you lavish care on me, and all the time I know you are going to despise me."

"Nonsense!" I said briskly. "Why, what would Halsey do to me if I even ventured such a thing? He is so big and masterful that if I dared to be anything but rapturous over you, he would throw me out of a window. Indeed, he would be quite capable of it."

She seemed scarcely to hear my facetious tone. She had eloquent brown eyes—the Inneses are fair, and are prone to a grayish-green optic that is better for use than appearance—and they seemed now to be clouded with trouble.

"Poor Halsey!" she said softly. "Miss Innes, I can not marry him, and I am afraid to tell him. I am a coward—a coward!"

I sat beside the bed and stared at her. She was too ill to argue with, and, besides, sick people take queer fancies.

"We will talk about that when you are stronger," I said gently.

"But there are some things I must tell you," she insisted. "You must wonder how I came here, and why I stayed hidden at the lodge. Dear old Thomas has been almost crazy, Miss Innes. I did not know that Sunnyside was rented. I knew my mother wished to rent it, without telling my—stepfather, but the news must have reached her after I left. When I started east, I had only one idea—to be alone with my thoughts for a time, to bury myself here. Then, I—must have taken a cold on the train."

"You came east in clothing suitable for California," I said, "and, like all young girls nowadays, I don't suppose you wear flannels." But she was not listening.

"Miss Innes," she said, "has my stepbrother Arnold gone away?"

"What do you mean?" I asked, startled. But Louise was literal.

"He didn't come back that night," she said, "and it was so important that I should see him."

"I believe he has gone away," I replied uncertainly. "Isn't it something that we could attend to instead?"

But she shook her head. "I must do it myself," she said dully. "My mother must have rented Sunnyside without telling my stepfather, and—Miss Innes, did you ever hear of any one being wretchedly poor in the midst of luxury?

"Did you ever long, and long, for money—money to use without question, money that no one would take you to task about? My mother and I have been surrounded for years with every indulgence everything that would make a display. But we have never had any money, Miss Innes; that must have been why mother rented this house. My stepfather pays out bills. It's the most maddening, humiliating existence in the world. I would love honest poverty better."

"Never mind," I said; "when you and Halsey are married you can be as honest as you like, and you will certainly be poor."

Halsey came to the door at that moment and I could hear him coaxing Liddy for admission to the sick room.

"Shall I bring him in?" I asked Louise, uncertain what to do. The girl seemed to shrink back among her pillows at the sound of his voice. I was vaguely irritated with her; there are few young fellows like Halsey—straightforward, honest, and willing to sacrifice everything for the one woman. I knew one once, more than thirty years ago, who was like that: he died a long time ago. And sometimes I take out his picture, with its cane and its queer silk hat, and look at it. But of late years it has grown too painful: he is always a boy—and I am an old woman. I would not bring him back if I could.

Perhaps it was some such memory that made me call out sharply.

"Come in, Halsey." And then I took my sewing and went into the boudoir beyond, to play propriety. I did not try to hear what they said, but every word came through the open door with curious distinctness. Halsey had evidently gone over to the bed and I suppose he kissed her. There was silence for a moment, as if words were superfluous things.

"I have been almost wild, sweetheart,"—Halsey's voice. "Why didn't you trust me, and send for me before?"

"It was because I couldn't trust myself," she said in a low tone. "I am too weak to struggle to-day; oh, Halsey, how I have wanted to see you!"

There was something I did not hear, then Halsey again.

"We could go away," he was saying. "What does it matter about any one in the world but just the two of us? To be always together, like this, hand in hand; Louise—don't tell me it isn't going to be. I won't believe you."

"You don't know; you don't know," Louise repeated dully. "Halsey, I care—you know that—but—not enough to marry you."

"That is not true, Louise," he said sternly. "You can not look at me with your honest eyes and say that."

"I can not marry you," she repeated miserably. "It's bad enough, isn't it? Don't make it worse. Some day, before long, you will be glad."

"Then it is because you have never loved me." There were depths of hurt pride in his voice. "You saw how much I loved you, and you let me think you cared—for a while. No—that isn't like you, Louise. There is something you haven't told me. Is it—because there is some one else?"

"Yes," almost inaudibly.

"Louise! Oh, I don't believe it."

"It is true," she said sadly. "Halsey, you must not try to see me again. As soon as I can, I am going away from here—where you are all so much kinder than I deserve. And whatever you hear about me, try to think as well of me as you can. I am going to marry—another man. How you must hate me—hate me!"

I could hear Halsey cross the room to the window. Then, after a pause, he went back to her again. I could hardly sit still; I wanted to go in and give her a good shaking.

"Then it's all over," he was saying with a long breath. "The plans we made together, the hopes, the—all of it—over! Well, I'll not be a baby, and I'll give you up the minute you say `I don't love you and I do love—some one else'!"

"I can not say that," she breathed, "but, very soon, I shall marry—the other man."

I could hear Halsey's low triumphant laugh.

"I defy him," he said. "Sweetheart, as long as you care for me, I am not afraid."

The wind slammed the door between the two rooms just then, and I could hear nothing more, although I moved my chair quite close. After a discreet interval, I went into the other room, and found Louise alone. She was staring with sad eyes at the cherub painted on the ceiling over the bed, and because she looked tired I did not disturb her.

14. AN EGG-NOG AND A TELEGRAM

We had discovered Louise at the lodge Tuesday night. It was Wednesday I had my interview with her. Thursday and Friday were uneventful, save as they marked improvement in our patient. Gertrude spent almost all the time with her, and the two had grown to be great friends. But certain things hung over me constantly; the coroner's inquest on the death of Arnold Armstrong, to be held Saturday, and the arrival of Mrs. Armstrong and young Doctor Walker, bringing the body of the dead president of the Traders' Bank. We had not told Louise of either death.

Then, too, I was anxious about the children. With their mother's inheritance swept away in the wreck of the bank, and with their love affairs in a disastrous condition, things could scarcely be worse. Added to that, the cook and Liddy had a flare-up over the proper way to make beef-tea for Louise, and, of course, the cook left.

Mrs. Watson had been glad enough, I think, to turn Louise over to our care, and Thomas went upstairs night and morning to greet his young mistress from the doorway. Poor Thomas! He had the faculty—found still in some old negroes, who cling to the traditions of slavery days—of making his employer's interest his. It was always "we" with Thomas; I miss him sorely; pipe-smoking, obsequious, not over reliable, kindly old man!

On Thursday Mr. Harton, the Armstrongs' legal adviser, called up from town. He had been advised, he said, that Mrs. Armstrong was coming east with her husband's body and would arrive Monday. He came with some hesitation, he went on, to the fact that he had been further instructed to ask me to relinquish my lease on Sunnyside, as it was Mrs. Armstrong's desire to come directly there.

I was aghast.

"Here!" I said. "Surely you are mistaken, Mr. Harton. I should think, after—what happened here only a few days ago, she would never wish to come back."

"Nevertheless," he replied, "she is most anxious to come. This is what she says. `Use every possible means to have Sunnyside vacated. Must go there at once.'"

"Mr. Harton," I said testily, "I am not going to do anything of the kind. I and mine have suffered enough at the hands of this family. I rented the house at an exorbitant figure and I have moved out here for the summer. My city home is dismantled and in the hands of decorators. I have been here one week, during which I have had not a single night of uninterrupted sleep, and I intend to stay until I have recuperated. Moreover, if Mr. Armstrong died insolvent, as I believe was the case, his widow ought to be glad to be rid of so expensive a piece of property."

The lawyer cleared his throat.

"I am very sorry you have made this decision," he said. "Miss Innes, Mrs. Fitzhugh tells me Louise Armstrong is with you."

"She is."

"Has she been informed of this—double bereavement?"

"Not yet," I said. "She has been very ill; perhaps to-night she can be told."

"It is very sad; very sad," he said. "I have a telegram for her, Mrs. Innes. Shall I send it out?"

"Better open it and read it to me," I suggested. "If it is important, that will save time."

There was a pause while Mr. Harton opened the telegram. Then he read it slowly, judicially.

"`Watch for Nina Carrington. Home Monday. Signed F. L. W.'"

"Hum!" I said. "`Watch for Nina Carrington. Home Monday.' Very well, Mr. Harton, I will tell her, but she is not in condition to watch for any one."

"Well, Miss Innes, if you decide to—er—relinquish the lease, let me know," the lawyer said.

"I shall not relinquish it," I replied, and I imagined his irritation from the way he hung up the receiver.

I wrote the telegram down word for word, afraid to trust my memory, and decided to ask Doctor Stewart how soon Louise might be told the truth. The closing of the Traders' Bank I considered unnecessary for her to know, but the death of her stepfather and stepbrother must be broken to her soon, or she might hear it in some unexpected and shocking manner.

Doctor Stewart came about four o'clock, bringing his leather satchel into the house with a great deal of care, and opening it at the foot of the stairs to show me a dozen big yellow eggs nesting among the bottles.

"Real eggs," he said proudly. "None of your anemic store eggs, but the real thing—some of them still warm. Feel them! Egg-nog for Miss Louise."

He was beaming with satisfaction, and before he left, he insisted on going back to the pantry and making an egg-nog with his own hands. Somehow, all the time he was doing it, I had a vision of Doctor Willoughby, my nerve specialist in the city, trying to make an egg-nog. I wondered if he ever prescribed anything so plebeian[2]—and so delicious. And while Doctor Stewart whisked the eggs he talked.

"I said to Mrs. Stewart," he confided, a little red in the face from the exertion, "after I went home the other day, that you would think me an old gossip, for saying what I did about Walker and Miss Louise."

"Nothing of the sort," I protested.

"The fact is," he went on, evidently justifying himself, "I got that piece of information just as we get a lot of things, through the kitchen end of the house. Young Walker's chauffeur—Walker's more fashionable than I am, and he goes around the country in a Stanhope car—well, his chauffeur comes to see our servant girl, and he told her the whole thing. I thought it was probable, because Walker spent a lot of time up here last summer, when the family was here, and besides, Riggs, that's Walker's man, had a very pat little story about the doctor's building a house on this property, just at the foot of the hill. The sugar, please."

The egg-nog was finished. Drop by drop the liquor had cooked the egg, and now, with a final whisk, a last toss in the shaker, it was ready, a symphony in gold and white. The doctor sniffed it.

"Real eggs, real milk, and a touch of real Kentucky whisky," he said.

---

[2] Common, ordinary; in ancient Rome citizens were classified as "plebeian" or "patrician" based on social class.

He insisted on carrying it up himself, but at the foot of the stairs he paused.

"Riggs said the plans were drawn for the house," he said, harking back to the old subject. "Drawn by Huston in town. So I naturally believed him."

When the doctor came down, I was ready with a question.

"Doctor," I asked, "is there any one in the neighborhood named Carrington? Nina Carrington?"

"Carrington?" He wrinkled his forehead. "Carrington? No, I don't remember any such family. There used to be Covingtons down the creek."

"The name was Carrington," I said, and the subject lapsed.

Gertrude and Halsey went for a long walk that afternoon, and Louise slept. Time hung heavy on my hands, and I did as I had fallen into a habit of doing lately—I sat down and thought things over. One result of my meditations was that I got up suddenly and went to the telephone. I had taken the most intense dislike to this Doctor Walker, whom I had never seen, and who was being talked of in the countryside as the fiancé of Louise Armstrong.

I knew Sam Huston well. There had been a time, when Sam was a good deal younger than he is now, before he had married Anne Endicott, when I knew him even better. So now I felt no hesitation in calling him over the telephone. But when his office boy had given way to his confidential clerk, and that functionary had condescended to connect his employer's desk telephone, I was somewhat at a loss as to how to begin.

"Why, how are you, Rachel?" Sam said sonorously. "Going to build that house at Rock View?" It was a twenty-year-old joke of his.

"Sometime, perhaps," I said. "Just now I want to ask you a question about something which is none of my business."

"I see you haven't changed an iota in a quarter of a century, Rachel." This was intended to be another jest. "Ask ahead: everything but my domestic affairs is at your service."

"Try to be serious," I said. "And tell me this: has your firm made any plans for a house recently, for a Doctor Walker, at Casanova?"

"Yes, we have."

"Where was it to be built? I have a reason for asking."

"It was to be, I believe, on the Armstrong place. Mr. Armstrong himself consulted me, and the inference was—in fact, I am quite certain—the house was to be occupied by Mr. Armstrong's daughter, who was engaged to marry Doctor Walker."

When the architect had inquired for the different members of my family, and had finally rung off, I was certain of one thing. Louise Armstrong was in love with Halsey, and the man she was going to marry was Doctor Walker. Moreover, this decision was not new; marriage had been contemplated for some time. There must certainly be some explanation—but what was it?

That day I repeated to Louise the telegram Mr. Warton had opened.

She seemed to understand, but an unhappier face I have never seen. She looked like a criminal whose reprieve is over, and the day of execution approaching.

15.   LIDDY GIVES THE ALARM

The next day, Friday, Gertrude broke the news of her stepfather's death to Louise. She did it as gently as she could, telling her first that he was very ill, and finally that he was dead. Louise received the news in the most unexpected manner, and when Gertrude came out to tell me how she had stood it, I think she was almost shocked.

"She just lay and stared at me, Aunt Ray," she said. "Do you know, I believe she is glad, glad! And she is too honest to pretend anything else. What sort of man was Mr. Paul Armstrong, anyhow?"

"He was a bully as well as a rascal, Gertrude," I said. "But I am convinced of one thing; Louise will send for Halsey now, and they will make it all up."

For Louise had steadily refused to see Halsey all that day, and the boy was frantic.

We had a quiet hour, Halsey and I, that evening, and I told him several things; about the request that we give up the lease to Sunnyside, about the telegram to Louise, about the rumors of an approaching marriage between the girl and Doctor Walker, and, last of all, my own interview with her the day before.

He sat back in a big chair, with his face in the shadow, and my heart fairly ached for him. He was so big and so boyish! When I had finished he drew a long breath.

"Whatever Louise does," he said, "nothing will convince me, Aunt Ray, that she doesn't care for me. And up to two months ago, when she and her mother went west, I was the happiest fellow on earth. Then something made a difference: she wrote me that her people were opposed to the marriage; that her feeling for me was what it had always been, but that something had happened which had changed her ideas as to the future. I was not to write until she wrote me, and whatever occurred, I was to think the best I could of her. It sounded like a puzzle. When I saw her yesterday, it was the same thing, only, perhaps, worse."

"Halsey," I asked, "have you any idea of the nature of the interview between Louise Armstrong and Arnold the night he was murdered?"

"It was stormy. Thomas says once or twice he almost broke into the room, he was so alarmed for Louise."

"Another thing, Halsey," I said, "have you ever heard Louise mention a woman named Carrington, Nina Carrington?"

"Never," he said positively.

For try as we would, our thoughts always came back to that fatal Saturday night, and the murder. Every conversational path led to it, and we all felt that Jamieson was tightening the threads of evidence around John Bailey. The detective's absence was hardly reassuring; he must have had something to work on in town, or he would have returned.

The papers reported that the cashier of the Traders' Bank was ill in his apartments at the Knickerbocker—a condition not surprising, considering everything. The guilt of the defunct president was no longer in doubt; the missing bonds had been advertised and some of them discovered. In every instance they had been used as collateral for large loans, and the belief was current that not less than a million and a half dollars had been realized. Every one connected with the bank had been placed under arrest, and released on heavy bond.

Was he alone in his guilt, or was the cashier his accomplice? Where was the money? The estate of the dead man was comparatively small—a city house on a fashionable street, Sunnyside, a large estate largely mortgaged, an insurance of fifty thousand dollars, and some personal property—this was all.

The rest lost in speculation probably, the papers said. There was one thing which looked uncomfortable for Jack Bailey: he and Paul Armstrong together had promoted a railroad company in New Mexico, and it was rumored that together they had sunk large sums of money there. The business alliance between the two men added to the belief that Bailey knew something of the looting. His unexplained absence from the bank on Monday lent color to the suspicion against him. The strange thing seemed to be his surrendering himself on the point of departure. To me, it seemed the shrewd calculation of a clever rascal. I was not actively antagonistic to Gertrude's lover, but I meant to be convinced, one way or the other. I took no one on faith.

That night the Sunnyside ghost began to walk again. Liddy had been sleeping in Louise's dressing-room on a couch, and the approach of dusk was a signal for her to barricade the entire suite. Situated as it was, beyond the circular staircase, nothing but an extremity of excitement would have made her pass it after dark. I confess myself that the place seemed to me to have a sinister appearance, but we kept that wing well lighted, and until the lights went out at midnight it was really cheerful, if one did not know its history.

On Friday night, then, I had gone to bed, resolved to go at once to sleep. Thoughts that insisted on obtruding themselves I pushed resolutely to the back of my mind, and I systematically relaxed every muscle. I fell asleep soon, and was dreaming that Doctor Walker was building his new house immediately in front of my windows: I could hear the thump-thump of the hammers, and then I waked to a knowledge that somebody was pounding on my door.

I was up at once, and with the sound of my footstep on the floor the low knocking ceased, to be followed immediately by sibilant whispering through the keyhole.

"Miss Rachel! Miss Rachel!" somebody was saying, over and over.

"Is that you, Liddy?" I asked, my hand on the knob.

"For the love of mercy, let me in!" she said in a low tone.

She was leaning against the door, for when I opened it, she fell in. She was greenish-white, and she had a red and black barred flannel petticoat over her shoulders.

"Listen," she said, standing in the middle of the floor and holding on to me. "Oh, Miss Rachel, it's the ghost of that dead man hammering to get in!"

Sure enough, there was a dull thud—thud—thud from some place near. It was muffled: one rather felt than heard it, and it was impossible to locate. One moment it seemed to come, three taps and a pause, from the floor under us: the next, thud—thud—thud—it came apparently from the wall.

"It's not a ghost," I said decidedly. "If it was a ghost it wouldn't rap: it would come through the keyhole." Liddy looked at the keyhole. "But it sounds very much as though some one is trying to break into the house."

Liddy was shivering violently. I told her to get me my slippers and she brought me a pair of kid gloves, so I found my things myself, and prepared to call Halsey. As before, the night alarm had found the electric lights gone: the hall, save for its night lamp, was in darkness, as I went across to Halsey's room. I hardly know what I feared, but it was a relief to find him there, very sound asleep, and with his door unlocked.

"Wake up, Halsey," I said, shaking him.

He stirred a little. Liddy was half in and half out of the door, afraid as usual to be left alone, and not quite daring to enter. Her scruples seemed to fade, however, all at once. She gave a suppressed yell, bolted into the room, and stood tightly clutching the foot-board of the bed. Halsey was gradually waking.

"I've seen it," Liddy wailed. "A woman in white down the hall!"

I paid no attention.

"Halsey," I persevered, "some one is breaking into the house. Get up, won't you?"

"It isn't our house," he said sleepily. And then he roused to the exigency of the occasion. "All right, Aunt Ray," he said, still yawning. "If you'll let me get into something—"

It was all I could do to get Liddy out of the room. The demands of the occasion had no influence on her: she had seen the ghost, she persisted, and she wasn't going into the hall. But I got her over to my room at last, more dead than alive, and made her lie down on the bed.

The tappings, which seemed to have ceased for a while, had commenced again, but they were fainter. Halsey came over in a few minutes, and stood listening and trying to locate the sound.

"Give me my revolver, Aunt Ray," he said; and I got it—the one I had found in the tulip bed—and gave it to him. He saw Liddy there and divined at once that Louise was alone.

"You let me attend to this fellow, whoever it is, Aunt Ray, and go to Louise, will you? She may be awake and alarmed."

So in spite of her protests, I left Liddy alone and went back to the east wing. Perhaps I went a little faster past the yawning blackness of the circular staircase; and I could hear Halsey creaking cautiously down the main staircase. The rapping, or pounding, had ceased, and the silence was almost painful. And then suddenly, from apparently under my very feet, there rose a woman's scream, a cry of terror that broke off as suddenly as it came. I stood frozen and still. Every drop of blood in my body seemed to leave the surface and gather around my heart. In the dead silence that followed it throbbed as if it would burst. More dead than alive, I stumbled into Louise's bedroom. She was not there!

16.   IN THE EARLY MORNING

I stood looking at the empty bed. The coverings had been thrown back, and Louise's pink silk dressing-gown was gone from the foot, where it had lain. The night lamp burned dimly, revealing the emptiness of the place. I picked it up, but my hand shook so that I put it down again, and got somehow to the door.

There were voices in the hall and Gertrude came running toward me.

"What is it?" she cried. "What was that sound? Where is Louise?"

"She is not in her room," I said stupidly. "I think—it was she—who screamed."

Liddy had joined us now, carrying a light. We stood huddled together at the head of the circular staircase, looking down into its shadows. There was nothing to be seen, and it was absolutely quiet down there. Then we heard Halsey running up the main staircase. He came quickly down the hall to where we were standing.

"There's no one trying to get in. I thought I heard some one shriek. Who was it?"

Our stricken faces told him the truth.

"Some one screamed down there," I said. "And—and Louise is not in her room."

With a jerk Halsey took the light from Liddy and ran down the circular staircase. I followed him, more slowly. My nerves seemed to be in a state of paralysis: I could scarcely step. At the foot of the stairs Halsey gave an exclamation and put down the light.

"Aunt Ray," he called sharply.

At the foot of the staircase, huddled in a heap, her head on the lower stair, was Louise Armstrong. She lay limp and white, her dressing-gown dragging loose from one sleeve of her night-dress, and the heavy braid of her dark hair stretching its length a couple of steps above her head, as if she had slipped down.

She was not dead: Halsey put her down on the floor, and began to rub her cold hands, while Gertrude and Liddy ran for stimulants. As for me, I sat there at the foot of that ghostly staircase—sat, because my knees wouldn't hold me—and wondered where it would all end. Louise was still unconscious, but she was breathing better, and I suggested that we get her back to bed before she came to. There was something grisly and horrible to me, seeing her there in almost the same attitude and in the same place where we had found her brother's body. And to add to the similarity, just then the hall clock, far off, struck faintly three o'clock.

It was four before Louise was able to talk, and the first rays of dawn were coming through her windows, which faced the east, before she could tell us coherently what had occurred. I give it as she told it. She lay propped in bed, and Halsey sat beside her, unrebuffed, and held her hand while she talked.

"I was not sleeping well," she began, "partly, I think, because I had slept during the afternoon. Liddy brought me some hot milk at ten o'clock and I slept until twelve. Then I wakened and—I got to thinking about things, and worrying, so I could not go to sleep.

"I was wondering why I had not heard from Arnold since the—since I saw him that night at the lodge. I was afraid he was ill, because—he was to have done something for me, and he had not come back. It must have been three when I heard some one rapping. I sat up and listened, to be quite sure, and the rapping kept up. It was cautious, and I was about to call Liddy.

"Then suddenly I thought I knew what it was. The east entrance and the circular staircase were always used by Arnold when he was out late, and sometimes, when he forgot his key, he would rap and I would go down and let him in. I thought he had come back to see me—I didn't think about the time, for his hours were always erratic. But I was afraid I was too weak to get down the stairs.

"The knocking kept up, and just as I was about to call Liddy, she ran through the room and out into the hall. I got up then, feeling weak and dizzy, and put on my dressing-gown. If it was Arnold, I knew I must see him.

"It was very dark everywhere, but, of course, I knew my way. I felt along for the stair-rail, and went down as quickly as I could. The knocking had stopped, and I was afraid I was too late. I got to the foot of the staircase and over to the door on to the east veranda. I had never thought of anything but that it was Arnold, until I reached the door. It was unlocked and opened about an inch. Everything was black: it was perfectly dark outside. I felt very queer and shaky. Then I thought perhaps Arnold had used his key; he did—strange things sometimes, and I turned around. Just as I reached the foot of the staircase I thought I heard some one coming. My nerves were going anyhow, there in the dark, and I could scarcely stand. I got up as far as the third or fourth step; then I felt that some one was coming toward me on the staircase. The next instant a hand met mine on the stair-rail. Some one brushed past me, and I screamed. Then I must have fainted."

That was Louise's story. There could be no doubt of its truth, and the thing that made it inexpressibly awful to me was that the poor girl had crept down to answer the summons of a brother who would never need her kindly offices again. Twice now, without apparent cause, some one had entered the house by means of the east entrance: had apparently gone his way unhindered through the house, and gone out again as he had entered. Had this unknown visitor been there a third time, the night Arnold Armstrong was murdered? Or a fourth, the time Mr. Jamieson had locked some one in the clothes chute?

Sleep was impossible, I think, for any of us. We dispersed finally to bathe and dress, leaving Louise little the worse for her experience. But I determined that before the day was over she must know the true state of affairs. Another decision I made, and I put it into execution immediately after breakfast. I had one of the unused bedrooms in the east wing, back along the small corridor, prepared for occupancy, and from that time on, Alex, the gardener, slept there. One man in that barn of a house was an absurdity, with things happening all the time, and I must say that Alex was as unobjectionable as any one could possibly have been.

The next morning, also, Halsey and I made an exhaustive examination of the circular staircase, the small entry at its foot, and the card-room opening from it. There was no evidence of anything unusual the night before, and had we not ourselves heard the rapping noises, I should have felt that Louise's imagination had run away with her. The outer door was closed and locked, and the staircase curved above us, for all the world like any other staircase.

Halsey, who had never taken seriously my account of the night Liddy and I were there alone, was grave enough now. He examined the paneling of the wainscoting above and below the stairs, evidently looking for a secret door, and suddenly there flashed into my mind the recollection of a scrap of paper that Mr. Jamieson had found among Arnold Armstrong's effects. As nearly as possible I repeated its contents to him, while Halsey took them down in a notebook.

"I wish you had told me that before," he said, as he put the memorandum carefully away. We found nothing at all in the house, and I expected little from any examination of the porch and grounds. But as we opened the outer door something fell into the entry with a clatter. It was a cue from the billiard-room.

Halsey picked it up with an exclamation.

"That's careless enough," he said. "Some of the servants have been amusing themselves."

I was far from convinced. Not one of the servants would go into that wing at night unless driven by dire necessity. And a billiard cue! As a weapon of either offense or defense it was an absurdity, unless one accepted Liddy's hypothesis of a ghost, and even then, as Halsey pointed out, a billiard-playing ghost would be a very modern evolution of an ancient institution.

That afternoon we, Gertrude, Halsey and I, attended the coroner's inquest in town. Doctor Stewart had been summoned also, it transpiring that in that early Sunday morning, when Gertrude and I had gone to our rooms, he had been called to view the body. We went, the four of us, in the machine, preferring the execrable roads to the matinee train, with half of Casanova staring at us. And on the way we decided to say nothing of Louise and her interview with her stepbrother the night he died. The girl was in trouble enough as it was.

17. A HINT OF SCANDAL

In giving the gist of what happened at the inquest, I have only one excuse—to recall to the reader the events of the night of Arnold Armstrong's murder. Many things had occurred which were not brought out at the inquest and some things were told there that were new to me. Altogether, it was a gloomy affair, and the six men in the corner, who constituted the coroner's jury, were evidently the merest puppets in the hands of that all-powerful gentleman, the coroner.

Gertrude and I sat well back, with our veils down. There were a number of people I knew: Barbara Fitzhugh, in extravagant mourning—she always went into black on the slightest provocation, because it was becoming—and Mr. Jarvis, the man who had come over from the Greenwood Club the night of the murder. Mr. Harton was there, too, looking impatient as the inquest dragged, but alive to every particle of evidence. From a corner Mr. Jamieson was watching the proceedings intently.

Doctor Stewart was called first. His evidence was told briefly, and amounted to this: on the Sunday morning previous, at a quarter before five, he had been called to the telephone. The message was from a Mr. Jarvis, who asked him to come at once to Sunnyside, as there had been an accident there, and Mr. Arnold Armstrong had been shot. He had dressed hastily, gathered up some instruments, and driven to Sunnyside.

He was met by Mr. Jarvis, who took him at once to the east wing. There, just as he had fallen, was the body of

Arnold Armstrong. There was no need of the instruments: the man was dead. In answer to the coroner's question—no, the body had not been moved, save to turn it over. It lay at the foot of the circular staircase. Yes, he believed death had been instantaneous. The body was still somewhat warm and rigor mortis had not set in. It occurred late in cases of sudden death. No, he believed the probability of suicide might be eliminated; the wounds could have been self-inflicted, but with difficulty, and there had been no weapon found.

The doctor's examination was over, but he hesitated and cleared his throat.

"Mr. Coroner," he said, "at the risk of taking up valuable time, I would like to speak of an incident that may or may not throw some light on this matter."

The audience was alert at once.

"Kindly proceed, Doctor," the coroner said.

"My home is in Englewood, two miles from Casanova," the doctor began. "In the absence of Doctor Walker, a number of Casanova people have been consulting me. A month ago—five weeks, to be exact—a woman whom I had never seen came to my office. She was in deep mourning and kept her veil down, and she brought for examination a child, a boy of six. The little fellow was ill; it looked like typhoid, and the mother was frantic. She wanted a permit to admit the youngster to the Children's Hospital in town here, where I am a member of the staff, and I gave her one. The incident would have escaped me, but for a curious thing. Two days before Mr. Armstrong was shot, I was sent for to go to the Country Club: some one had been struck with a golf-ball that had gone wild. It was late when I left—I was on foot, and about a mile from the club, on the Claysburg road, I met two people. They were disputing violently, and I had no difficulty in recognizing Mr. Armstrong. The woman, beyond doubt, was the one who had consulted me about the child."

At this hint of scandal, Mrs. Ogden Fitzhugh sat up very straight. Jamieson was looking slightly skeptical, and the coroner made a note.

"The Children's Hospital, you say, Doctor?" he asked.

"Yes. But the child, who was entered as Lucien Wallace, was taken away by his mother two weeks ago. I have tried to trace them and failed."

All at once I remembered the telegram sent to Louise by some one signed F. L. W.—presumably Doctor Walker. Could this veiled woman be the Nina Carrington of the message? But it was only idle speculation. I had no way of finding out, and the inquest was proceeding.

The report of the coroner's physician came next. The post-mortem examination showed that the bullet had entered the chest in the fourth left intercostal space and had taken an oblique course downward and backward, piercing both the heart and lungs. The left lung was collapsed, and the exit point of the ball had been found in the muscles of the back to the left of the spinal column. It was improbable that such a wound had been self-inflicted, and its oblique downward course pointed to the fact that the shot had been fired from above. In other words, as the murdered man had been found dead at the foot of a staircase, it was probable that the shot had been fired by some one higher up on the stairs. There were no marks of powder. The bullet, a thirty-eight caliber, had been found in the dead man's clothing, and was shown to the jury.

Mr. Jarvis was called next, but his testimony amounted to little.

He had been summoned by telephone to Sunnyside, had come over at once with the steward and Mr. Winthrop, at present out of town. They had been admitted by the housekeeper, and had found the body lying at the foot of the staircase. He had made a search for a weapon, but there was none around. The outer entry door in the east wing had been unfastened and was open about an inch.

I had been growing more and more nervous. When the coroner called Mr. John Bailey, the room was filled with suppressed excitement. Mr. Jamieson went forward and spoke a few words to the coroner, who nodded. Then Halsey was called.

"Mr. Innes," the coroner said, "will you tell under what circumstances you saw Mr. Arnold Armstrong the night he died?"

"I saw him first at the Country Club," Halsey said quietly. He was rather pale, but very composed. "I stopped there with my automobile for gasoline. Mr. Armstrong had been playing cards. When I saw him there, he was coming out of the card-room, talking to Mr. John Bailey."

"The nature of the discussion—was it amicable?"

Halsey hesitated.

"They were having a dispute," he said. "I asked Mr. Bailey to leave the club with me and come to Sunnyside over Sunday."

"Isn't it a fact, Mr. Innes, that you took Mr. Bailey away from the club-house because you were afraid there would be blows?"

"The situation was unpleasant," Halsey said evasively.

"At that time had you any suspicion that the Traders' Bank had been wrecked?"

"No."

"What occurred next?"

"Mr. Bailey and I talked in the billiard-room until two-thirty."

"And Mr. Arnold Armstrong came there, while you were talking?"

"Yes. He came about half-past two. He rapped at the east door, and I admitted him."

The silence in the room was intense. Mr. Jamieson's eyes never left Halsey's face.

"Will you tell us the nature of his errand?"

"He brought a telegram that had come to the club for Mr. Bailey."

"He was sober?"

"Perfectly, at that time. Not earlier."

"Was not his apparent friendliness a change from his former attitude?"

"Yes. I did not understand it."

"How long did he stay?"

"About five minutes. Then he left, by the east entrance."

"What occurred then?"

"We talked for a few minutes, discussing a plan Mr. Bailey had in mind. Then I went to the stables, where I kept my car, and got it out."

"Leaving Mr. Bailey alone in the billiard-room?"

Halsey hesitated.

"My sister was there."

Mrs. Ogden Fitzhugh had the courage to turn and eye Gertrude through her lorgnon[3].

"And then?"

"I took the car along the lower road, not to disturb the household. Mr. Bailey came down across the lawn, through the hedge, and got into the car on the road."

"Then you know nothing of Mr. Armstrong's movements after he left the house?"

"Nothing. I read of his death Monday evening for the first time."

"Mr. Bailey did not see him on his way across the lawn?"

---

[3] Variant of *lorgnette*, a pair of eyeglasses or opera glasses with a handle rather than ear pieces.

"I think not. If he had seen him he would have spoken of it."

"Thank you. That is all. Miss Gertrude Innes."

Gertrude's replies were fully as concise as Halsey's. Mrs. Fitzhugh subjected her to a close inspection, commencing with her hat and ending with her shoes. I flatter myself she found nothing wrong with either her gown or her manner, but poor Gertrude's testimony was the reverse of comforting. She had been summoned, she said, by her brother, after Mr. Armstrong had gone.

She had waited in the billiard-room with Mr. Bailey, until the automobile had been ready. Then she had locked the door at the foot of the staircase, and, taking a lamp, had accompanied Mr. Bailey to the main entrance of the house, and had watched him cross the lawn. Instead of going at once to her room, she had gone back to the billiard-room for something which had been left there. The card-room and billiard-room were in darkness. She had groped around, found the article she was looking for, and was on the point of returning to her room, when she had heard some one fumbling at the lock at the east outer door. She had thought it was probably her brother, and had been about to go to the door, when she heard it open. Almost immediately there was a shot, and she had run panic-stricken through the drawing-room and had roused the house.

"You heard no other sound?" the coroner asked. "There was no one with Mr. Armstrong when he entered?"

"It was perfectly dark. There were no voices and I heard nothing. There was just the opening of the door, the shot, and the sound of somebody falling."

"Then, while you went through the drawing-room and upstairs to alarm the household, the criminal, whoever it was, could have escaped by the east door?"

"Yes."

"Thank you. That will do."

I flatter myself that the coroner got little enough out of me. I saw Mr. Jamieson smiling to himself, and the coroner gave me up, after a time. I admitted I had found the body, said I had not known who it was until Mr. Jarvis told me, and ended by looking up at Barbara Fitzhugh and saying that in renting the house I had not expected to be involved in any family scandal. At which she turned purple.

The verdict was that Arnold Armstrong had met his death at the hands of a person or persons unknown, and we all prepared to leave. Barbara Fitzhugh flounced out without waiting to speak to me, but Mr. Harton came up, as I knew he would.

"You have decided to give up the house, I hope, Miss Innes," he said. "Mrs. Armstrong has wired me again."

"I am not going to give it up," I maintained, "until I understand some things that are puzzling me. The day that the murderer is discovered, I will leave."

"Then, judging by what I have heard, you will be back in the city very soon," he said. And I knew that he suspected the discredited cashier of the Traders' Bank.

Mr. Jamieson came up to me as I was about to leave the coroner's office.

"How is your patient?" he asked with his odd little smile.

"I have no patient," I replied, startled.

"I will put it in a different way, then. How is Miss Armstrong?"

"She—she is doing very well," I stammered.

"Good," cheerfully. "And our ghost? Is it laid?"

"Mr. Jamieson," I said suddenly, "I wish you would do one thing: I wish you would come to Sunnyside and spend a few days there. The ghost is not laid. I want you to spend one night at least watching the circular staircase. The murder of Arnold Armstrong was a beginning, not an end."

He looked serious.

"Perhaps I can do it," he said. "I have been doing something else, but—well, I will come out to-night."

We were very silent during the trip back to Sunnyside. I watched Gertrude closely and somewhat sadly. To me there was one glaring flaw in her story, and it seemed to stand out for every one to see. Arnold Armstrong had had no key, and yet she said she had locked the east door. He must have been admitted from within the house; over and over I repeated it to myself.

That night, as gently as I could, I told Louise the story of her stepbrother's death. She sat in her big, pillow-filled chair, and heard me through without interruption. It was clear that she was shocked beyond words: if I had hoped to learn anything from her expression, I had failed. She was as much in the dark as we were.

18.   A HOLE IN THE WALL

My taking the detective out to Sunnyside raised an unexpected storm of protest from Gertrude and Halsey. I was not prepared for it, and I scarcely knew how to account for it. To me Mr. Jamieson was far less formidable under my eyes where I knew what he was doing, than he was in the city, twisting circumstances and motives to suit himself and learning what he wished to know, about events at Sunnyside, in some occult way. I was glad enough to have him there, when excitements began to come thick and fast.

A new element was about to enter into affairs: Monday, or Tuesday at the latest, would find Doctor Walker back in his green and white house in the village, and Louise's attitude to him in the immediate future would signify Halsey's happiness or wretchedness, as it might turn out. Then, too, the return of her mother would mean, of course, that she would have to leave us, and I had become greatly attached to her.

From the day Mr. Jamieson came to Sunnyside there was a subtle change in Gertrude's manner to me. It was elusive, difficult to analyze, but it was there. She was no longer frank with me, although I think her affection never wavered. At the time I laid the change to the fact that I had forbidden all communication with John Bailey, and had refused to acknowledge any engagement between the two. Gertrude spent much of her time wandering through the grounds, or taking long cross-country walks. Halsey played golf at the Country Club day after day, and after Louise left, as she did the following week, Mr. Jamieson and I were much together. He played a fair game of cribbage, but he cheated at solitaire.

The night the detective arrived, Saturday, I had a talk with him.

I told him of the experience Louise Armstrong had had the night before, on the circular staircase, and about the man who had so frightened Rosie on the drive. I saw that he thought the information was important, and to my suggestion that we put an additional lock on the east wing door he opposed a strong negative.

"I think it probable," he said, "that our visitor will be back again, and the thing to do is to leave things exactly as they are, to avoid rousing suspicion. Then I can watch for at least a part of each night and probably Mr. Innes will help us out. I would say as little to Thomas as possible. The old man knows more than he is willing to admit."

I suggested that Alex, the gardener, would probably be willing to help, and Mr. Jamieson undertook to make the arrangement. For one night, however, Mr. Jamieson preferred to watch alone. Apparently nothing occurred. The detective sat in absolute darkness on the lower step of the stairs, dozing, he said afterwards, now and then. Nothing could pass him in either direction, and the door in the morning remained as securely fastened as it had been the night before. And yet one of the most inexplicable occurrences of the whole affair took place that very night.

Liddy came to my room on Sunday morning with a face as long as the moral law. She laid out my things as usual, but I missed her customary garrulousness. I was not regaled with the new cook's extravagance as to eggs, and she even forbore to mention "that Jamieson," on whose arrival she had looked with silent disfavor.

"What's the matter, Liddy?" I asked at last. "Didn't you sleep last night?"

"No, ma'm," she said stiffly.

"Did you have two cups of coffee at your dinner?" I inquired.

"No, ma'm," indignantly.

I sat up and almost upset my hot water—I always take a cup of hot water with a pinch of salt, before I get up. It tones the stomach.

"Liddy Allen," I said, "stop combing that switch and tell me what is wrong with you."

Liddy heaved a sigh.

"Girl and woman," she said, "I've been with you twenty-five years, Miss Rachel, through good temper and bad—" the idea! and what I have taken from her in the way of sulks!—"but I guess I can't stand it any longer. My trunk's packed."

"Who packed it?" I asked, expecting from her tone to be told she had wakened to find it done by some ghostly hand.

"I did; Miss Rachel, you won't believe me when I tell you this house is haunted. Who was it fell down the clothes chute? Who was it scared Miss Louise almost into her grave?"

"I'm doing my best to find out," I said. "What in the world are you driving at?" She drew a long breath.

"There is a hole in the trunk-room wall, dug out since last night. It's big enough to put your head in, and the plaster's all over the place."

"Nonsense!" I said. "Plaster is always falling."

But Liddy clenched that.

"Just ask Alex," she said. "When he put the new cook's trunk there last night the wall was as smooth as this. This morning it's dug out, and there's plaster on the cook's trunk. Miss Rachel, you can get a dozen detectives and put one on every stair in the house, and you'll never catch anything. There's some things you can't handcuff."

Liddy was right. As soon as I could, I went up to the trunk-room, which was directly over my bedroom. The plan of the upper story of the house was like that of the second floor, in the main. One end, however, over the east wing, had been left only roughly finished, the intention having been to convert it into a ball-room at some future time. The maids' rooms, trunk-room, and various store-rooms, including a large airy linen-room, opened from a long corridor, like that on the second floor. And in the trunk-room, as Liddy had said, was a fresh break in the plaster.

Not only in the plaster, but through the lathing, the aperture extended. I reached into the opening, and three feet away, perhaps, I could touch the bricks of the partition wall. For some reason, the architect, in building the house, had left a space there that struck me, even in the surprise of the discovery, as an excellent place for a conflagration to gain headway.

"You are sure the hole was not here yesterday?" I asked Liddy, whose expression was a mixture of satisfaction and alarm. In answer she pointed to the new cook's trunk—that necessary adjunct of the migratory domestic. The top was covered with fine white plaster, as was the floor. But there were no large pieces of mortar lying around—no bits of lathing. When I mentioned this to Liddy she merely raised her eyebrows. Being quite confident that the gap was of unholy origin, she did not concern herself with such trifles as a bit of mortar and lath. No doubt they were even then heaped neatly on a gravestone in the Casanova churchyard!

I brought Mr. Jamieson up to see the hole in the wall, directly after breakfast. His expression was very odd when he looked at it, and the first thing he did was to try to discover what object, if any, such a hole could have. He got a piece of candle, and by enlarging the aperture a little was able to examine what lay beyond. The result was nil. The trunk-room, although heated by steam heat, like the rest of the house, boasted of a fireplace and mantel as well. The opening had been made between the flue and the outer wall of the house. There was revealed, however, on inspection, only the brick of the chimney on one side and the outer wall of the house on the other; in depth the space extended only to the flooring. The breach had been made about four feet from the floor, and inside were all the missing bits of plaster. It had been a methodical ghost.

It was very much of a disappointment. I had expected a secret room, at the very least, and I think even Mr. Jamieson had fancied he might at last have a clue to the mystery. There was evidently nothing more to be discovered: Liddy reported that everything was serene among the servants, and that none of them had been disturbed by the noise. The maddening thing, however, was that the nightly visitor had evidently more than one way of gaining access to the house, and we made arrangements to redouble our vigilance as to windows and doors that night.

Halsey was inclined to pooh-pooh the whole affair. He said a break in the plaster might have occurred months ago and gone unnoticed, and that the dust had probably been stirred up the day before. After all, we had to let it go at that, but we put in an uncomfortable Sunday. Gertrude went to church, and Halsey took a long walk in the morning. Louise was able to sit up, and she allowed Halsey and Liddy to assist her down-stairs late in the afternoon. The east veranda was shady, green with vines and palms, cheerful with cushions and lounging chairs. We put Louise in a steamer chair, and she sat there passively enough, her hands clasped in her lap.

We were very silent. Halsey sat on the rail with a pipe, openly watching Louise, as she looked broodingly across the valley to the hills. There was something baffling in the girl's eyes; and gradually Halsey's boyish features lost their glow at seeing her about again, and settled into grim lines. He was like his father just then.

We sat until late afternoon, Halsey growing more and more moody. Shortly before six, he got up and went into the house, and in a few minutes he came out and called me to the telephone. It was Anna Whitcomb, in town, and she kept me for twenty minutes, telling me the children had had the measles, and how Madame Sweeny had botched her new gown.

When I finished, Liddy was behind me, her mouth a thin line.

"I wish you would try to look cheerful, Liddy," I groaned, "your face would sour milk." But Liddy seldom replied to my gibes. She folded her lips a little tighter.

"He called her up," she said oracularly, "he called her up, and asked her to keep you at the telephone, so he could talk to Miss Louise. *A thankless child is sharper than a serpent's tooth.*"

"Nonsense!" I said bruskly. "I might have known enough to leave them. It's a long time since you and I were in love, Liddy, and—we forget."

Liddy sniffed.

"No man ever made a fool of me," she replied virtuously.

"Well, something did," I retorted.

19. CONCERNING THOMAS

"Mr. Jamieson," I said, when we found ourselves alone after dinner that night, "the inquest yesterday seemed to me the merest recapitulation of things that were already known. It developed nothing new beyond the story of Doctor Stewart's, and that was volunteered."

"An inquest is only a necessary formality, Miss Innes," he replied. "Unless a crime is committed in the open, the inquest does nothing beyond getting evidence from witnesses while events are still in their minds. The police step in later. You and I both know how many important things never transpired. For instance: the dead man had no key, and yet Miss Gertrude testified to a fumbling at the lock, and then the opening of the door. The piece of evidence you mention, Doctor Stewart's story, is one of those things we have to take cautiously: the doctor has a patient who wears black and does not raise her veil. Why, it is the typical mysterious lady! Then the good doctor comes across Arnold Armstrong, who was a graceless scamp—*de mortuis*[4]—what's the rest of it?—and he is quarreling with a lady in black. Behold, says the doctor, they are one and the same."

"Why was Mr. Bailey not present at the inquest?"

The detective's expression was peculiar.

"Because his physician testified that he is ill, and unable to leave his bed."

"Ill!" I exclaimed. "Why, neither Halsey nor Gertrude has told me that."

"There are more things than that, Miss Innes, that are puzzling. Bailey gives the impression that he knew nothing of the crash at the bank until he read it in the paper

---

[4] Latin, *De mortuis nil nisi bonum dicendum est*—Of the dead nothing but good is to be said—the modern expression is "speak no ill of the dead."

Monday night, and that he went back and surrendered himself immediately. I do not believe it. Jonas, the watchman at the Traders' Bank, tells a different story. He says that on the Thursday night before, about eight-thirty, Bailey went back to the bank. Jonas admitted him, and he says the cashier was in a state almost of collapse. Bailey worked until midnight, then he closed the vault and went away. The occurrence was so unusual that the watchman pondered over it an the rest of the night. What did Bailey do when he went back to the Knickerbocker apartments that night? He packed a suit-case ready for instant departure. But he held off too long; he waited for something. My personal opinion is that he waited to see Miss Gertrude before flying from the country. Then, when he had shot down Arnold Armstrong that night, he had to choose between two evils. He did the thing that would immediately turn public opinion in his favor, and surrendered himself, as an innocent man. The strongest thing against him is his preparation for flight, and his deciding to come back after the murder of Arnold Armstrong. He was shrewd enough to disarm suspicion as to the graver charge?"

The evening dragged along slowly. Mrs. Watson came to my bedroom before I went to bed and asked if I had any arnica. She showed me a badly swollen hand, with reddish streaks running toward the elbow; she said it was the hand she had hurt the night of the murder a week before, and that she had not slept well since. It looked to me as if it might be serious, and I told her to let Doctor Stewart see it.

The next morning Mrs. Watson went up to town on the eleven o'clock train, and was admitted to the Charity

Hospital. She was suffering from blood-poisoning. I fully meant to go up and see her there, but other things drove her entirely from my mind. I telephoned to the hospital that day, however, and ordered a private room for her, and whatever comforts she might be allowed.

Mrs. Armstrong arrived Monday evening with her husband's body, and the services were set for the next day. The house on Chestnut Street, in town, had been opened, and Tuesday morning Louise left us to go home. She sent for me before she went, and I saw she had been crying.

"How can I thank you, Miss Innes?" she said. "You have taken me on faith, and—you have not asked me any questions. Some time, perhaps, I can tell you; and when that time comes, you will all despise me,—Halsey, too."

I tried to tell her how glad I was to have had her but there was something else she wanted to say. She said it finally, when she had bade a constrained good-by to Halsey and the car was waiting at the door.

"Miss Innes," she said in a low tone, "if they—if there is any attempt made to—to have you give up the house, do it, if you possibly can. I am afraid—to have you stay."

That was all. Gertrude went into town with her and saw her safely home. She reported a decided coolness in the greeting between Louise and her mother, and that Doctor Walker was there, apparently in charge of the arrangements for the funeral. Halsey disappeared shortly after Louise left and came home about nine that night, muddy and tired. As for Thomas, he went around dejected and sad, and I saw the detective watching him closely at dinner. Even now I wonder—what did Thomas know? What did he suspect?

At ten o'clock the household had settled down for the night. Liddy, who was taking Mrs. Watson's place, had finished examining the tea-towels and the corners of the shelves in the cooling-room, and had gone to bed. Alex, the gardener, had gone heavily up the circular staircase to his room, and Mr. Jamieson was examining the locks of the windows. Halsey dropped into a chair in the living-room, and stared moodily ahead. Once he roused.

"What sort of a looking chap is that Walker, Gertrude?" he asked!

"Rather tall, very dark, smooth-shaven. Not bad looking," Gertrude said, putting down the book she had been pretending to read. Halsey kicked a taboret[5] viciously.

"Lovely place this village must be in the winter," he said irrelevantly. "A girl would be buried alive here."

It was then some one rapped at the knocker on the heavy front door. Halsey got up leisurely and opened it, admitting Warner. He was out of breath from running, and he looked half abashed.

"I am sorry to disturb you," he said. "But I didn't know what else to do. It's about Thomas."

"What about Thomas?" I asked. Mr. Jamieson had come into the hall and we all stared at Warner.

---

[5] Taboret (also tabouret) can mean either of two different pieces of furniture, a cabinet or a stool.

"He's acting queer," Warner explained. "He's sitting down there on the edge of the porch, and he says he has seen a ghost. The old man looks bad, too; he can scarcely speak."

"He's as full of superstition as an egg is of meat," I said. "Halsey, bring some whisky and we will all go down."

No one moved to get the whisky, from which I judged there were three pocket flasks ready for emergency. Gertrude threw a shawl around my shoulders, and we all started down over the hill: I had made so many nocturnal excursions around the place that I knew my way perfectly. But Thomas was not on the veranda, nor was he inside the house. The men exchanged significant glances, and Warner got a lantern.

"He can't have gone far," he said. "He was trembling so that he couldn't stand, when I left."

Jamieson and Halsey together made the round of the lodge, occasionally calling the old man by name. But there was no response. No Thomas came, bowing and showing his white teeth through the darkness. I began to be vaguely uneasy, for the first time. Gertrude, who was never nervous in the dark, went alone down the drive to the gate, and stood there, looking along the yellowish line of the road, while I waited on the tiny veranda.

Warner was puzzled. He came around to the edge of the veranda and stood looking at it as if it ought to know and explain.

"He might have stumbled into the house," he said, "but he could not have climbed the stairs. Anyhow, he's not inside or outside, that I can see." The other members of the party

146

had come back now, and no one had found any trace of the old man. His pipe, still warm, rested on the edge of the rail, and inside on the table his old gray hat showed that its owner had not gone far.

He was not far, after all. From the table my eyes traveled around the room, and stopped at the door of a closet. I hardly know what impulse moved me, but I went in and turned the knob. It burst open with the impetus of a weight behind it, and something fell partly forward in a heap on the floor. It was Thomas—Thomas without a mark of injury on him, and dead.

20. DOCTOR WALKER'S WARNING

Warner was on his knees in a moment, fumbling at the old man's collar to loosen it, but Halsey caught his hand.

"Let him alone?" he said. "You can't help him; he is dead."

We stood there, each avoiding the other's eyes; we spoke low and reverently in the presence of death, and we tacitly avoided any mention of the suspicion that was in every mind. When Mr. Jamieson had finished his cursory examination, he got up and dusted the knees of his trousers.

"There is no sign of injury," he said, and I know I, for one, drew a long breath of relief. "From what Warner says and from his hiding in the closet, I should say he was scared to death. Fright and a weak heart, together."

"But what could have done it?" Gertrude asked. "He was all right this evening at dinner. Warner, what did he say when you found him on the porch?"

Warner looked shaken: his honest, boyish face was colorless.

"Just what I told you, Miss Innes. He'd been reading the paper down-stairs; I had put up the car, and, feeling sleepy, I came down to the lodge to go to bed. As I went up-stairs, Thomas put down the paper and, taking his pipe, went out on the porch. Then I heard an exclamation from him."

"What did he say?" demanded Jamieson.

"I couldn't hear, but his voice was strange; it sounded startled. I waited for him to call out again, but he did not, so I went down-stairs. He was sitting on the porch step, looking straight ahead, as if he saw something among the trees across the road. And he kept mumbling about having seen a ghost. He looked queer, and I tried to get him inside, but he wouldn't move. Then I thought I'd better go up to the house."

"Didn't he say anything else you could understand?" I asked.

"He said something about the grave giving up its dead."

Mr. Jamieson was going through the old man's pockets, and Gertrude was composing his arms, folding them across his white shirt-bosom, always so spotless.

Mr. Jamieson looked up at me.

"What was that you said to me, Miss Innes, about the murder at the house being a beginning and not an end? By jove, I believe you were right!"

In the course of his investigations the detective had come to the inner pocket of the dead butler's black coat. Here he found some things that interested him. One was a small flat key, with a red cord tied to it, and the other was a bit of white paper, on which was written something in Thomas' cramped hand. Mr. Jamieson read it: then he gave it to me. It was an address in fresh ink—

LUCIEN WALLACE, 14 Elm Street, Richfield.

As the card went around, I think both the detective and I watched for any possible effect it might have, but, beyond perplexity, there seemed to be none.

"Richfield!" Gertrude exclaimed. "Why, Elm Street is the main street; don't you remember, Halsey?"

"Lucien Wallace!" Halsey said. "That is the child Stewart spoke of at the inquest."

Warner, with his mechanic's instinct, had reached for the key. What he said was not a surprise.

"Yale lock," he said. "Probably a key to the east entry."

There was no reason why Thomas, an old and trusted servant, should not have had a key to that particular door, although the servants' entry was in the west wing. But I had not known of this key, and it opened up a new field of conjecture. Just now, however, there were many things to be attended to, and, leaving Warner with the body, we all went back to the house. Mr. Jamieson walked with me, while Halsey and Gertrude followed.

"I suppose I shall have to notify the Armstrongs," I said. "They will know if Thomas had any people and how to reach them. Of course, I expect to defray the expenses of the funeral, but his relatives must be found. What do you think frightened him, Mr. Jamieson?"

"It is hard to say," he replied slowly, "but I think we may be certain it was fright, and that he was hiding from something. I am sorry in more than one way: I have always believed that Thomas knew something, or suspected something, that he would not tell. Do you know how much money there was in that worn-out wallet of his? Nearly a hundred dollars! Almost two months' wages—and yet those darkies seldom have a penny. Well—what Thomas knew will be buried with him."

Halsey suggested that the grounds be searched, but Mr. Jamieson vetoed the suggestion.

"You would find nothing," he said. "A person clever enough to get into Sunnyside and tear a hole in the wall, while I watched down-stairs, is not to be found by going around the shrubbery with a lantern."

With the death of Thomas, I felt that a climax had come in affairs at Sunnyside. The night that followed was quiet enough. Halsey watched at the foot of the staircase, and a complicated system of bolts on the other doors seemed to be effectual.

Once in the night I wakened and thought I heard the tapping again. But all was quiet, and I had reached the stage where I refused to be disturbed for minor occurrences.

The Armstrongs were notified of Thomas' death, and I had my first interview with Doctor Walker as a result. He came up early the next morning, just as we finished breakfast, in a professional looking car with a black hood. I found him striding up and down the living-room, and, in spite of my preconceived dislike, I had to admit that the man was presentable. A big fellow he was, tall and dark, as Gertrude had said, smooth-shaven and erect, with prominent features and a square jaw. He was painfully spruce in his appearance, and his manner was almost obtrusively polite.

"I must make a double excuse for this early visit, Miss Innes," he said as he sat down. The chair was lower than he expected, and his dignity required collecting before he went on. "My professional duties are urgent and long neglected, and"—a fall to the every-day manner—"something must be done about that body."

"Yes," I said, sitting on the edge of my chair. "I merely wished the address of Thomas' people. You might have telephoned, if you were busy."

He smiled.

"I wished to see you about something else," he said. "As for Thomas, it is Mrs. Armstrong's wish that you would allow her to attend to the expense. About his relatives, I have already notified his brother, in the village. It was heart disease, I think. Thomas always had a bad heart."

"Heart disease and fright," I said, still on the edge of my chair. But the doctor had no intention of leaving.

"I understand you have a ghost up here, and that you have the house filled with detectives to exorcise it," he said.

For some reason I felt I was being "pumped," as Halsey says. "You have been misinformed," I replied.

"What, no ghost, no detectives!" he said, still with his smile. "What a disappointment to the village!"

I resented his attempt at playfulness. It had been anything but a joke to us.

"Doctor Walker," I said tartly, "I fail to see any humor in the situation. Since I came here, one man has been shot, and another one has died from shock. There have been intruders in the house, and strange noises. If that is funny, there is something wrong with my sense of humor."

"You miss the point," he said, still good-naturedly. "The thing that is funny, to me, is that you insist on remaining here, under the circumstances. I should think nothing would keep you."

"You are mistaken. Everything that occurs only confirms my resolution to stay until the mystery is cleared."

"I have a message for you, Miss Innes," he said, rising at last. "Mrs. Armstrong asked me to thank you for your kindness to Louise, whose whim, occurring at the time it did, put her to great inconvenience. Also—and this is a delicate matter—she asked me to appeal to your natural sympathy for her, at this time, and to ask you if you will not reconsider your decision about the house. Sunnyside is her home; she loves it dearly, and just now she wishes to retire here for quiet and peace."

"She must have had a change of heart," I said, ungraciously enough. "Louise told me her mother despised the place. Besides, this is no place for quiet and peace just now. Anyhow, doctor, while I don't care to force an issue, I shall certainly remain here, for a time at least."

"For how long?" he asked.

"My lease is for six months. I shall stay until some explanation is found for certain things. My own family is implicated now, and I shall do everything to clear the mystery of Arnold Armstrong's murder."

The doctor stood looking down, slapping his gloves thoughtfully against the palm of a well-looked-after hand.

"You say there have been intruders in the house?" he asked. "You are sure of that, Miss Innes?"

"Certain."

"In what part?"

"In the east wing."

"Can you tell me when these intrusions occurred, and what the purpose seemed to be? Was it robbery?"

"No," I said decidedly. "As to time, once on Friday night a week ago, again the following night, when Arnold Armstrong was murdered, and again last Friday night."

The doctor looked serious. He seemed to be debating some question in his mind, and to reach a decision.

"Miss Innes," he said, "I am in a peculiar position; I understand your attitude, of course; but—do you think you are wise? Ever since you have come here there have been hostile demonstrations against you and your family. I'm not a croaker, but—take a warning. Leave before anything occurs that will cause you a lifelong regret."

"I am willing to take the responsibility," I said coldly.

I think he gave me up then as a poor proposition. He asked to be shown where Arnold Armstrong's body had been found, and I took him there. He scrutinized the whole place carefully, examining the stairs and the lock. When he had taken a formal farewell I was confident of one thing. Doctor Walker would do anything he could to get me away from Sunnyside.

21. FOURTEEN ELM STREET

It was Monday evening when we found the body of poor old Thomas. Monday night had been uneventful; things were quiet at the house and the peculiar circumstances of the old man's death had been carefully kept from the servants. Rosie took charge of the dining-room and pantry, in the absence of a butler, and, except for the warning of the Casanova doctor, everything breathed of peace.

Affairs at the Traders' Bank were progressing slowly. The failure had hit small stock-holders very hard, the minister of the little Methodist chapel in Casanova among them. He had received as a legacy from an uncle a few shares of stock in the Traders' Bank, and now his joy was turned to bitterness: he had to sacrifice everything he had in the world, and his feeling against Paul Armstrong, dead, as he was, must have been bitter in the extreme. He was asked to officiate at the simple services when the dead banker's body was interred in Casanova churchyard, but the good man providentially took cold, and a substitute was called in.

A few days after the services he called to see me, a kind-faced little man, in a very bad frock-coat and laundered tie. I think he was uncertain as to my connection with the Armstrong family, and dubious whether I considered Mr. Armstrong's taking away a matter for condolence or congratulation. He was not long in doubt.

I liked the little man. He had known Thomas well, and had promised to officiate at the services in the rickety African Zion Church. He told me more of himself than he knew, and before he left, I astonished him—and myself, I admit—by promising a new carpet for his church. He was much affected, and I gathered that he had yearned over his ragged chapel as a mother over a half-clothed child.

"You are laying up treasure, Miss Innes," he said brokenly, "where neither moth nor rust corrupt, nor thieves break through and steal."

"It is certainly a safer place than Sunnyside," I admitted. And the thought of the carpet permitted him to smile. He stood just inside the doorway, looking from the luxury of the house to the beauty of the view.

"The rich ought to be good," he said wistfully. "They have so much that is beautiful, and beauty is ennobling. And yet—while I ought to say nothing but good of the dead—Mr. Armstrong saw nothing of this fair prospect. To him these trees and lawns were not the work of God. They were property, at so much an acre. He loved money, Miss Innes. He offered up everything to his golden calf. Not power, not ambition, was his fetish: it was money." Then he dropped his pulpit manner, and, turning to me with his engaging smile: "In spite of all this luxury," he said, "the country people here have a saying that Mr. Paul Armstrong could sit on a dollar and see all around it. Unlike the summer people, he gave neither to the poor nor to the church. He loved money for its own sake."

"And there are no pockets in shrouds!" I said cynically.

I sent him home in the car, with a bunch of hot-house roses for his wife, and he was quite overwhelmed. As for me, I had a generous glow that was cheap at the price of a church carpet. I received less gratification—and less gratitude—when I presented the new silver communion set to St. Barnabas.

I had a great many things to think about in those days. I made out a list of questions and possible answers, but I seemed only to be working around in a circle. I always ended where I began. The list was something like this:

Who had entered the house the night before the murder?

Thomas claimed it was Mr. Bailey, whom he had seen on the foot-path, and who owned the pearl cuff-link.

Why did Arnold Armstrong come back after he had left the house the night he was killed?

No answer. Was it on the mission Louise had mentioned?

Who admitted him?

Gertrude said she had locked the east entry. There was no key on the dead man or in the door. He must have been admitted from within.

Who had been locked in the clothes chute?

Some one unfamiliar with the house, evidently. Only two people missing from the household, Rosie and Gertrude. Rosie had been at the lodge. Therefore—but was it Gertrude? Might it not have been the mysterious intruder again?

Who had accosted Rosie on the drive?

Again—perhaps the nightly visitor. It seemed more likely some one who suspected a secret at the lodge. Was Louise under surveillance?

Who had passed Louise on the circular staircase?

Could it have been Thomas? The key to the east entry made this a possibility. But why was he there, if it were indeed he?

Who had made the hole in the trunk-room wall?

It was not vandalism. It had been done quietly, and with deliberate purpose. If I had only known how to read the purpose of that gaping aperture what I might have saved in anxiety and mental strain!

Why had Louise left her people and come home to hide at the lodge?

There was no answer, as yet, to this, or to the next questions.

Why did both she and Doctor Walker warn us away from the house?

Who was Lucien Wallace?

What did Thomas see in the shadows the night he died?

What was the meaning of the subtle change in Gertrude?

Was Jack Bailey an accomplice or a victim in the looting of the Traders' Bank?

What all-powerful reason made Louise determine to marry Doctor Walker?

The examiners were still working on the books of the Traders' Bank, and it was probable that several weeks would elapse before everything was cleared up. The firm of expert accountants who had examined the books some two months before testified that every bond, every piece of valuable paper, was there at that time. It had been shortly after their examination that the president, who had been in bad health, had gone to California. Mr. Bailey was still ill at the Knickerbocker, and in this, as in other ways, Gertrude's conduct puzzled me. She seemed indifferent, refused to discuss matters pertaining to the bank, and never, to my knowledge, either wrote to him or went to see him.

Gradually I came to the conclusion that Gertrude, with the rest of the world, believed her lover guilty, and—although I believed it myself, for that matter—I was irritated by her indifference. Girls in my day did not meekly accept the public's verdict as to the man they loved.

But presently something occurred that made me think that under Gertrude's surface calm there was a seething flood of emotions.

Tuesday morning the detective made a careful search of the grounds, but he found nothing. In the afternoon he disappeared, and it was late that night when he came home.

He said he would have to go back to the city the following day, and arranged with Halsey and Alex to guard the house.

Liddy came to me on Wednesday morning with her black silk apron held up like a bag, and her eyes big with virtuous wrath. It was the day of Thomas' funeral in the village, and Alex and I were in the conservatory cutting flowers for the old man's casket. Liddy is never so happy as when she is making herself wretched, and now her mouth drooped while her eyes were triumphant.

"I always said there were plenty of things going on here, right under our noses, that we couldn't see," she said, holding out her apron.

"I don't see with my nose," I remarked. "What have you got there?"

Liddy pushed aside a half-dozen geranium pots, and in the space thus cleared she dumped the contents of her apron— a handful of tiny bits of paper. Alex had stepped back, but I saw him watching her curiously.

"Wait a moment, Liddy," I said. "You have been going through the library paper-basket again!"

Liddy was arranging her bits of paper with the skill of long practice and paid no attention.

"Did it ever occur to you," I went on, putting my hand over the scraps, "that when people tear up their correspondence, it is for the express purpose of keeping it from being read?"

"If they wasn't ashamed of it they wouldn't take so much trouble, Miss Rachel," Liddy said oracularly. "More than that, with things happening every day, I consider it my duty. If you don't read and act on this, I shall give it to that Jamieson, and I'll venture he'll not go back to the city to-day."

That decided me. If the scraps had anything to do with the mystery ordinary conventions had no value. So Liddy arranged the scraps, like working out one of the puzzle-pictures children play with, and she did it with much the same eagerness. When it was finished she stepped aside while I read it.

"Wednesday night, nine o'clock. Bridge," I real aloud. Then, aware of Alex's stare, I turned on Liddy.

"Some one is to play bridge to-night at nine o'clock," I said. "Is that your business, or mine?"

Liddy was aggrieved. She was about to reply when I scooped up the pieces and left the conservatory.

"Now then," I said, when we got outside, "will you tell me why you choose to take Alex into your confidence? He's no fool. Do you suppose he thinks any one in this house is going to play bridge to-night at nine o'clock, by appointment! I suppose you have shown it in the kitchen, and instead of my being able to slip down to the bridge to-night quietly, and see who is there, the whole household will be going in a procession."

"Nobody knows it," Liddy said humbly. "I found it in the basket in Miss Gertrude's dressing-room. Look at the back of the sheet." I turned over some of the scraps, and, sure enough, it was a blank deposit slip from the Traders' Bank. So Gertrude was going to meet Jack Bailey that night by the bridge! And I had thought he was ill! It hardly seemed like

160

the action of an innocent man—this avoidance of daylight, and of his fiancée's people. I decided to make certain, however, by going to the bridge that night.

After luncheon Mr. Jamieson suggested that I go with him to Richfield, and I consented.

"I am inclined to place more faith in Doctor Stewart's story," he said, "since I found that scrap in old Thomas' pocket. It bears out the statement that the woman with the child, and the woman who quarreled with Armstrong, are the same. It looks as if Thomas had stumbled on to some affair which was more or less discreditable to the dead man, and, with a certain loyalty to the family, had kept it to himself. Then, you see, your story about the woman at the card-room window begins to mean something. It is the nearest approach to anything tangible that we have had yet."

Warner took us to Richfield in the car. It was about twenty-five miles by railroad, but by taking a series of atrociously rough short cuts we got there very quickly. It was a pretty little town, on the river, and back on the hill I could see the Mortons' big country house, where Halsey and Gertrude had been staying until the night of the murder.

Elm Street was almost the only street, and number fourteen was easily found. It was a small white house, dilapidated without having gained anything picturesque, with a low window and a porch only a foot or so above the bit of a lawn. There was a baby-carriage in the path, and from a swing at the side came the sound of conflict. Three small children were disputing vociferously, and a faded young woman with a kindly face was trying to hush the clamor. When she saw us she untied her gingham apron and came around to the porch.

"Good afternoon," I said. Jamieson lifted his hat, without speaking. "I came to inquire about a child named Lucien Wallace."

"I am glad you have come," she said. "In spite of the other children, I think the little fellow is lonely. We thought perhaps his mother would be here to-day."

Mr. Jamieson stepped forward.

"You are Mrs. Tate?" I wondered how the detective knew.

"Yes, sir."

"Mrs. Tate, we want to make some inquiries. Perhaps in the house—"

"Come right in," she said hospitably. And soon we were in the little shabby parlor, exactly like a thousand of its prototypes. Mrs. Tate sat uneasily, her hands folded in her lap.

"How long has Lucien been here?" Mr. Jamieson asked.

"Since a week ago last Friday. His mother paid one week's board in advance; the other has not been paid."

"Was he ill when he came?"

"No, sir, not what you'd call sick. He was getting better of typhoid, she said, and he's picking up fine."

"Will you tell me his mother's name and address?"

"That's the trouble," the young woman said, knitting her brows. "She gave her name as Mrs. Wallace, and said she had no address. She was looking for a boarding-house in town. She said she worked in a department store, and couldn't take care of the child properly, and he needed fresh air and milk. I had three children of my own, and one more didn't make much difference in the work, but—I wish she would pay this week's board."

"Did she say what store it was?"

"No, sir, but all the boy's clothes came from King's. He has far too fine clothes for the country."

There was a chorus of shouts and shrill yells from the front door, followed by the loud stamping of children's feet and a throaty "whoa, whoa!" Into the room came a tandem team of two chubby youngsters, a boy and a girl, harnessed with a clothes-line, and driven by a laughing boy of about seven, in tan overalls and brass buttons. The small driver caught my attention at once: he was a beautiful child, and, although he showed traces of recent severe illness, his skin had now the clear transparency of health.

"Whoa, Flinders," he shouted. "You're goin' to smash the trap."

Mr. Jamieson coaxed him over by holding out a lead-pencil, striped blue and yellow.

"Now, then," he said, when the boy had taken the lead-pencil and was testing its usefulness on the detective's cuff, "now then, I'll bet you don't know what your name is!"

"I do," said the boy. "Lucien Wallace."

"Great! And what's your mother's name?"

"Mother, of course. What's your mother's name?" And he pointed to me! I am going to stop wearing black: it doubles a woman's age.

"And where did you live before you came here?" The detective was polite enough not to smile.

"Grossmutter," he said. And I saw Mr. Jamieson's eyebrows go up.

"German," he commented. "Well, young man, you don't seem to know much about yourself."

"I've tried it all week," Mrs. Tate broke in. "The boy knows a word or two of German, but he doesn't know where he lived, or anything about himself."

Mr. Jamieson wrote something on a card and gave it to her.

"Mrs. Tate," he said, "I want you to do something. Here is some money for the telephone call. The instant the boy's mother appears here, call up that number and ask for the person whose name is there. You can run across to the drug-store on an errand and do it quietly. Just say, `The lady has come.'"

"`The lady has come,'" repeated Mrs. Tate. "Very well, sir, and I hope it will be soon. The milk-bill alone is almost double what it was."

"How much is the child's board?" I asked.

"Three dollars a week, including his washing."

"Very well," I said. "Now, Mrs. Tate, I am going to pay last week's board and a week in advance. If the mother comes, she is to know nothing of this visit—absolutely not a word, and, in return for your silence, you may use this money for—something for your own children."

Her tired, faded face lighted up, and I saw her glance at the little Tates' small feet. Shoes, I divined—the feet of the genteel poor being almost as expensive as their stomachs.

As we went back Mr. Jamieson made only one remark: I think he was laboring under the weight of a great disappointment.

"Is King's a children's outfitting place?" he asked.

"Not especially. It is a general department store."

He was silent after that, but he went to the telephone as soon as we got home, and called up King and Company, in the city.

After a time he got the general manager, and they talked for some time. When Mr. Jamieson hung up the receiver he turned to me.

"The plot thickens," he said with his ready smile. "There are four women named Wallace at King's none of them married, and none over twenty. I think I shall go up to the city to-night. I want to go to the Children's Hospital. But before I go, Miss Innes, I wish you would be more frank with me than you have been yet. I want you to show me the revolver you picked up in the tulip bed."

So he had known all along!

"It *was* a revolver, Mr. Jamieson," I admitted, cornered at last, "but I can not show it to you. It is not in my possession."

22. A LADDER OUT OF PLACE

At dinner Mr. Jamieson suggested sending a man out in his place for a couple of days, but Halsey was certain there would be nothing more, and felt that he and Alex could manage the situation. The detective went back to town early in the evening, and by nine o'clock Halsey, who had been playing golf—as a man does anything to take his mind away from trouble—was sleeping soundly on the big leather davenport in the living-room.

I sat and knitted, pretending not to notice when Gertrude got up and wandered out into the starlight. As soon as I was satisfied that she had gone, however, I went out cautiously. I had no intention of eavesdropping, but I wanted to be certain that it was Jack Bailey she was meeting. Too many things had occurred in which Gertrude was, or appeared to be, involved, to allow anything to be left in question.

I went slowly across the lawn, skirted the hedge to a break not far from the lodge, and found myself on the open road. Perhaps a hundred feet to the left the path led across the valley to the Country Club, and only a little way off was the foot-bridge over Casanova Creek. But just as I was about to turn down the path I heard steps coming toward me, and I shrank into the bushes. It was Gertrude, going back quickly toward the house.

I was surprised. I waited until she had had time to get almost to the house before I started. And then I stepped back again into the shadows. The reason why Gertrude had not kept her tryst was evident. Leaning on the parapet of the bridge in the moonlight, and smoking a pipe, was Alex, the gardener. I could have throttled Liddy for her carelessness in reading the torn note where he could hear. And I could cheerfully have choked Alex to death for his audacity.

But there was no help for it: I turned and followed Gertrude slowly back to the house.

The frequent invasions of the house had effectually prevented any relaxation after dusk. We had redoubled our vigilance as to bolts and window-locks but, as Mr. Jamieson had suggested, we allowed the door at the east entry to remain as before, locked by the Yale lock only. To provide only one possible entrance for the invader, and to keep a constant guard in the dark at the foot of the circular staircase, seemed to be the only method.

In the absence of the detective, Alex and Halsey arranged to change off, Halsey to be on duty from ten to two, and Alex from two until six. Each man was armed, and, as an additional precaution, the one off duty slept in a room near the head of the circular staircase and kept his door open, to be ready for emergency.

These arrangements were carefully kept from the servants, who were only commencing to sleep at night, and who retired, one and all, with barred doors and lamps that burned full until morning.

The house was quiet again Wednesday night. It was almost a week since Louise had encountered some one on the stairs, and it was four days since the discovery of the hole in the trunk-room wall.

Arnold Armstrong and his father rested side by side in the Casanova churchyard, and at the Zion African Church, on the hill, a new mound marked the last resting-place of poor Thomas.

Louise was with her mother in town, and, beyond a polite note of thanks to me, we had heard nothing from her. Doctor Walker had taken up his practice again, and we saw him now and then flying past along the road, always at top speed. The murder of Arnold Armstrong was still unavenged, and I remained firm in the position I had taken—to stay at Sunnyside until the thing was at least partly cleared.

And yet, for all its quiet, it was on Wednesday night that perhaps the boldest attempt was made to enter the house. On Thursday afternoon the laundress sent word she would like to speak to me, and I saw her in my private sitting-room, a small room beyond the dressing-room.

Mary Anne was embarrassed. She had rolled down her sleeves and tied a white apron around her waist, and she stood making folds in it with fingers that were red and shiny from her soap-suds.

"Well, Mary," I said encouragingly, "what's the matter? Don't dare to tell me the soap is out."

"No, ma'm, Miss Innes." She had a nervous habit of looking first at my one eye and then at the other, her own optics shifting ceaselessly, right eye, left eye, right eye, until I found myself doing the same thing. "No, ma'm. I was askin' did you want the ladder left up the clothes chute?"

"The what?" I screeched, and was sorry the next minute. Seeing her suspicions were verified, Mary Anne had gone white, and stood with her eyes shifting more wildly than ever.

"There's a ladder up the clothes chute, Miss Innes," she said. "It's up that tight I can't move it, and I didn't like to ask for help until I spoke to you."

It was useless to dissemble; Mary Anne knew now as well as I did that the ladder had no business to be there. I did the best I could, however. I put her on the defensive at once.

"Then you didn't lock the laundry last night?"

"I locked it tight, and put the key in the kitchen on its nail."

"Very well, then you forgot a window."

Mary Anne hesitated.

"Yes'm," she said at last. "I thought I locked them all, but there was one open this morning."

I went out of the room and down the hall, followed by Mary Anne. The door into the clothes chute was securely bolted, and when I opened it I saw the evidence of the woman's story. A pruning-ladder had been brought from where it had lain against the stable and now stood upright in the clothes shaft, its end resting against the wall between the first and second floors.

I turned to Mary.

"This is due to your carelessness," I said. "If we had all been murdered in our beds it would have been your fault." She shivered. "Now, not a word of this through the house, and send Alex to me."

The effect on Alex was to make him apoplectic with rage, and with it all I fancied there was an element of satisfaction. As I look back, so many things are plain to me that I wonder I could not see at the time. It is all known now, and yet the whole thing was so remarkable that perhaps my stupidity was excusable.

Alex leaned down the chute and examined the ladder carefully.

"It is caught," he said with a grim smile. "The fools, to have left a warning like that! The only trouble is, Miss Innes, they won't be apt to come back for a while."

"I shouldn't regard that in the light of a calamity," I replied.

Until late that evening Halsey and Alex worked at the chute. They forced down the ladder at last, and put a new bolt on the door. As for myself, I sat and wondered if I had a deadly enemy, intent on my destruction.

I was growing more and more nervous. Liddy had given up all pretense at bravery, and slept regularly in my dressing-room on the couch, with a prayer-book and a game knife from the kitchen under her pillow, thus preparing for both the natural and the supernatural. That was the way things stood that Thursday night, when I myself took a hand in the struggle.

23. WHILE THE STABLES BURNED

About nine o'clock that night Liddy came into the living-room and reported that one of the housemaids declared she had seen two men slip around the corner of the stable. Gertrude had been sitting staring in front of her, jumping at every sound. Now she turned on Liddy pettishly.

"I declare, Liddy," she said, "you are a bundle of nerves. What if Eliza did see some men around the stable? It may have been Warner and Alex."

"Warner is in the kitchen, miss," Liddy said with dignity. "And if you had come through what I have, you would be a bundle of nerves, too. Miss Rachel, I'd be thankful if you'd give me my month's wages to-morrow. I'll be going to my sister's."

"Very well," I said, to her evident amazement. "I will make out the check. Warner can take you down to the noon train."

Liddy's face was really funny.

"You'll have a nice time at your sister's," I went on. "Five children, hasn't she?"

"That's it," Liddy said, suddenly bursting into tears. "Send me away, after all these years, and your new shawl only half done, and nobody knowin' how to fix the water for your bath."

"It's time I learned to prepare my own bath." I was knitting complacently. But Gertrude got up and put her arms around Liddy's shaking shoulders.

"You are two big babies," she said soothingly. "Neither one of you could get along for an hour without the other. So stop quarreling and be good. Liddy, go right up and lay out Aunty's night things. She is going to bed early."

After Liddy had gone I began to think about the men at the stable, and I grew more and more anxious. Halsey was aimlessly knocking the billiard-balls around in the billiard-room, and I called to him.

"Halsey," I said when he sauntered in, "is there a policeman in Casanova?"

"Constable," he said laconically. "Veteran of the war, one arm; in office to conciliate the G. A. R. element. Why?"

"Because I am uneasy to-night." And I told him what Liddy had said. "Is there any one you can think of who could be relied on to watch the outside of the house to-night?"

"We might get Sam Bohannon from the club," he said thoughtfully. "It wouldn't be a bad scheme. He's a smart darky, and with his mouth shut and his shirt-front covered, you couldn't see him a yard off in the dark."

Halsey conferred with Alex, and the result, in an hour, was Sam. His instructions were simple. There had been numerous attempts to break into the house; it was the intention, not to drive intruders away, but to capture them. If Sam saw anything suspicious outside, he was to tap at the east entry, where Alex and Halsey were to alternate in keeping watch through the night.

It was with a comfortable feeling of security that I went to bed that night. The door between Gertrude's rooms and mine had been opened, and, with the doors into the hall bolted, we were safe enough. Although Liddy persisted in her belief that doors would prove no obstacles to our disturbers.

As before, Halsey watched the east entry from ten until two. He had an eye to comfort, and he kept vigil in a heavy oak chair, very large and deep. We went up-stairs rather early, and through the open door Gertrude and I kept up a running fire of conversation. Liddy was brushing my hair, and Gertrude was doing her own, with a long free sweep of her strong round arms.

"Did you know Mrs. Armstrong and Louise are in the village?" she called.

"No," I replied, startled. "How did you hear it?"

"I met the oldest Stewart girl to-day, the doctor's daughter, and she told me they had not gone back to town after the funeral. They went directly to that little yellow house next to Doctor Walker's, and are apparently settled there. They took the house furnished for the summer."

"Why, it's a bandbox," I said. "I can't imagine Fanny Armstrong in such a place."

"It's true, nevertheless. Ella Stewart says Mrs. Armstrong has aged terribly, and looks as if she is hardly able to walk."

I lay and thought over some of these things until midnight. The electric lights went out then, fading slowly until there was only a red-hot loop to be seen in the bulb, and then even that died away and we were embarked on the darkness of another night.

Apparently only a few minutes elapsed, during which my eyes were becoming accustomed to the darkness. Then I noticed that the windows were reflecting a faint pinkish light, Liddy noticed it at the same time, and I heard her jump up. At that moment Sam's deep voice boomed from somewhere just below.

"Fire!" he yelled. "The stable's on fire!"

I could see him in the glare dancing up and down on the drive, and a moment later Halsey joined him. Alex was awake and running down the stairs, and in five minutes from the time the fire was discovered, three of the maids were sitting on their trunks in the drive, although, excepting a few sparks, there was no fire nearer than a hundred yards.

Gertrude seldom loses her presence of mind, and she ran to the telephone. But by the time the Casanova volunteer fire department came toiling up the hill the stable was a furnace, with the Dragon Fly safe but blistered, in the road. Some gasoline exploded just as the volunteer department got to work, which shook their nerves as well as the burning building. The stable, being on a hill, was a torch to attract the population from every direction. Rumor had it that Sunnyside was burning, and it was amazing how many people threw something over their night-clothes and flew to the conflagration.

I take it Casanova has few fires, and Sunnyside was furnishing the people, in one way and another, the greatest excitement they had had for years.

The stable was off the west wing. I hardly know how I came to think of the circular staircase and the unguarded door at its foot. Liddy was putting my clothes into sheets, preparatory to tossing them out the window, when I found her, and I could hardly persuade her to stop.

"I want you to come with me, Liddy," I said. "Bring a candle and a couple of blankets."

She lagged behind considerably when she saw me making for the east wing, and at the top of the staircase she balked.

"I am not going down there," she said firmly.

"There is no one guarding the door down there," I explained. "Who knows?—this may be a scheme to draw everybody away from this end of the house, and let some one in here."

The instant I had said it I was convinced I had hit on the explanation, and that perhaps it was already too late. It seemed to me as I listened that I heard stealthy footsteps on the east porch, but there was so much shouting outside that it was impossible to tell. Liddy was on the point of retreat.

"Very well," I said, "then I shall go down alone. Run back to Mr. Halsey's room and get his revolver. Don't shoot down the stairs if you hear a noise: remember—I shall be down there. And hurry."

I put the candle on the floor at the top of the staircase and took off my bedroom slippers. Then I crept down the stairs, going very slowly, and listening with all my ears. I was keyed to such a pitch that I felt no fear: like the condemned who sleep and eat the night before execution, I was no longer able to suffer apprehension. I was past that. Just at the foot of the stairs I stubbed my toe against Halsey's big chair, and had to stand on one foot in a soundless agony until the pain subsided to a dull ache. And then—I knew I was right. Some one had put a key into the lock, and was turning it. For some reason it refused to work, and the key was withdrawn. There was a muttering of voices outside: I had only a second. Another trial, and the door would open. The candle above made a faint gleam down the well-like staircase, and at that moment, with a second, no more, to spare, I thought of a plan.

The heavy oak chair almost filled the space between the newel post and the door. With a crash I had turned it on its side, wedging it against the door, its legs against the stairs. I could hear a faint scream from Liddy, at the crash, and then she came down the stairs on a run, with the revolver held straight out in front of her.

"Thank God," she said, in a shaking voice. "I thought it was you."

I pointed to the door, and she understood.

"Call out the windows at the other end of the house," I whispered. "Run. Tell them not to wait for anything."

She went up the stairs at that, two at a time. Evidently she collided with the candle, for it went out, and I was left in darkness.

I was really astonishingly cool. I remember stepping over the chair and gluing my ear to the door, and I shall never forget feeling it give an inch or two there in the darkness, under a steady pressure from without. But the chair held, although I could hear an ominous cracking of one of the legs. And then, without the slightest warning, the card-room window broke with a crash. I had my finger on the trigger of the revolver, and as I jumped it went off, right through the door. Some one outside swore roundly, and for the first time I could hear what was said.

"Only a scratch. . . . Men are at the other end of the house. . . . Have the whole rat's nest on us." And a lot of profanity which I won't write down. The voices were at the broken window now, and although I was trembling violently, I was determined that I would hold them until help came. I moved up the stairs until I could see into the card-room, or rather through it, to the window. As I looked a small man put his leg over the sill and stepped into the room. The curtain confused him for a moment; then he turned, not toward me, but toward the billiard-room door. I fired again, and something that was glass or china crashed to the ground. Then I ran up the stairs and along the corridor to the main staircase. Gertrude was standing there, trying to locate the shots, and I must have been a peculiar figure, with my hair in crimps, my dressing-gown flying, no slippers, and a revolver clutched in my hands I had no time to talk. There was the sound of footsteps in the lower hall, and some one bounded up the stairs.

I had gone Berserk, I think. I leaned over the stair rail and fired again. Halsey, below, yelled at me.

"What are you doing up there?" he yelled. "You missed me by an inch."

And then I collapsed and fainted. When I came around Liddy was rubbing my temples with eau de quinine, and the search was in full blast.

Well, the man was gone. The stable burned to the ground, while the crowd cheered at every falling rafter, and the volunteer fire department sprayed it with a garden hose. And in the house Alex and Halsey searched every corner of the lower floor, finding no one.

The truth of my story was shown by the broken window and the overturned chair. That the unknown had got upstairs was almost impossible. He had not used the main staircase, there was no way to the upper floor in the east wing, and Liddy had been at the window, in the west wing, where the servants' stair went up. But we did not go to bed at all. Sam Bohannon and Warner helped in the search, and not a closet escaped scrutiny. Even the cellars were given a thorough overhauling, without result. The door in the east entry had a hole through it where my bullet had gone.

The hole slanted downward, and the bullet was embedded in the porch. Some reddish stains showed it had done execution.

"Somebody will walk lame," Halsey said, when he had marked the course of the bullet. "It's too low to have hit anything but a leg or foot."

From that time on I watched every person I met for a limp, and to this day the man who halts in his walk is an object of suspicion to me. But Casanova had no lame men: the nearest approach to it was an old fellow who tended the safety gates at the railroad, and he, I learned on inquiry, had two artificial legs. Our man had gone, and the large and expensive stable at Sunnyside was a heap of smoking rafters and charred boards. Warner swore the fire was incendiary, and in view of the attempt to enter the house, there seemed to be no doubt of it.

24. FLINDERS

If Halsey had only taken me fully into his confidence, through the whole affair, it would have been much simpler. If he had been altogether frank about Jack Bailey, and if the day after the fire he had told me what he suspected, there would have been no harrowing period for all of us, with the boy in danger. But young people refuse to profit by the experience of their elders, and sometimes the elders are the ones to suffer.

I was much used up the day after the fire, and Gertrude insisted on my going out. The machine was temporarily out of commission, and the carriage horses had been sent to a farm for the summer. Gertrude finally got a trap from the Casanova liveryman, and we went out. Just as we turned from the drive into the road we passed a woman. She had put down a small valise, and stood inspecting the house and grounds minutely. I should hardly have noticed her, had it not been for the fact that she had been horribly disfigured by smallpox.

"Ugh!" Gertrude said, when we had passed, "what a face! I shall dream of it to-night. Get up, Flinders."

"Flinders?" I asked. "Is that the horse's name?"

"It is." She flicked the horse's stubby mane with the whip. "He didn't look like a livery horse, and the liveryman said he had bought him from the Armstrongs when they purchased a couple of motors and cut down the stable. Nice Flinders—good old boy!"

Flinders was certainly not a common name for a horse, and yet the youngster at Richfield had named his prancing, curly-haired little horse Flinders! It set me to thinking.

At my request Halsey had already sent word of the fire to the agent from whom we had secured the house. Also, he had called Mr. Jamieson by telephone, and somewhat guardedly had told him of the previous night's events. Mr. Jamieson promised to come out that night, and to bring another man with him. I did not consider it necessary to notify Mrs. Armstrong, in the village. No doubt she knew of the fire, and in view of my refusal to give up the house, an interview would probably have been unpleasant enough. But as we passed Doctor Walker's white and green house I thought of something.

"Stop here, Gertrude," I said. "I am going to get out."

"To see Louise?" she asked.

"No, I want to ask this young Walker something."

She was curious, I knew, but I did not wait to explain. I went up the walk to the house, where a brass sign at the side announced the office, and went in. The reception-room was empty, but from the consulting-room beyond came the sound of two voices, not very amicable.

"It is an outrageous figure," some one was storming. Then the doctor's quiet tone, evidently not arguing, merely stating something. But I had not time to listen to some person probably disputing his bill, so I coughed. The voices ceased at once: a door closed somewhere, and the doctor entered from the hall of the house. He looked sufficiently surprised at seeing me.

"Good afternoon, Doctor," I said formally. "I shall not keep you from your patient. I wish merely to ask you a question."

"Won't you sit down?"

"It will not be necessary. Doctor, has any one come to you, either early this morning or to-day, to have you treat a bullet wound?"

"Nothing so startling has happened to me," he said. "A bullet wound! Things must be lively at Sunnyside."

"I didn't say it was at Sunnyside. But as it happens, it was. If any such case comes to you, will it be too much trouble for you to let me know?"

"I shall be only too happy," he said. "I understand you have had a fire up there, too. A fire and shooting in one night is rather lively for a quiet place like that."

"It is as quiet as a boiler-shop," I replied, as I turned to go.

"And you are still going to stay?"

"Until I am burned out," I responded. And then on my way down the steps, I turned around suddenly.

"Doctor," I asked at a venture, "have you ever heard of a child named Lucien Wallace?"

Clever as he was, his face changed and stiffened. He was on his guard again in a moment.

"Lucien Wallace?" he repeated. "No, I think not. There are plenty of Wallaces around, but I don't know any Lucien."

I was as certain as possible that he did. People do not lie readily to me, and this man lied beyond a doubt. But there was nothing to be gained now; his defenses were up, and I left, half irritated and wholly baffled.

Our reception was entirely different at Doctor Stewart's. Taken into the bosom of the family at once, Flinders tied outside and nibbling the grass at the roadside, Gertrude and I drank some home-made elderberry wine and told briefly of the fire. Of the more serious part of the night's experience, of course, we said nothing. But when at last we had left the family on the porch and the good doctor was untying our steed, I asked him the same question I had put to Doctor Walker.

"Shot!" he said. "Bless my soul, no. Why, what have you been doing up at the big house, Miss Innes?"

"Some one tried to enter the house during the fire, and was shot and slightly injured," I said hastily. "Please don't mention it; we wish to make as little of it as possible."

There was one other possibility, and we tried that. At Casanova station I saw the station master, and asked him if any trains left Casanova between one o'clock and daylight. There was none until six A.M. The next question required more diplomacy.

"Did you notice on the six-o'clock train any person—any man—who limped a little?" I asked. "Please try to remember: we are trying to trace a man who was seen loitering around Sunnyside last night before the fire."

He was all attention in a moment.

"I was up there myself at the fire," he said volubly. "I'm a member of the volunteer company. First big fire we've had since the summer house burned over to the club golf links. My wife was sayin' the other day, `Dave, you might as well 'a' saved the money in that there helmet and shirt.' And here last night they came in handy. Rang that bell so hard I hadn't time scarcely to get 'em on."

"And—did you see a man who limped?" Gertrude put in, as he stopped for breath.

"Not at the train, ma'm," he said. "No such person got on here to-day. But I'll tell you where I did see a man that limped. I didn't wait till the fire company left; there's a fast freight goes through at four forty-five, and I had to get down to the station. I seen there wasn't much more to do anyhow at the fire—we'd got the flames under control"—Gertrude looked at me and smiled—"so I started down the hill. There was folks here and there goin' home, and along by the path to the Country Club I seen two men. One was a short fellow. He was sitting on a big rock, his back to me, and he had something white in his hand, as if he was tying up his foot. After I'd gone on a piece I looked back, and he was hobbling on and—excuse me, miss—he was swearing something sickening."

"Did they go toward the club?" Gertrude asked suddenly, leaning forward.

"No, miss. I think they came into the village. I didn't get a look at their faces, but I know every chick and child in the place, and everybody knows me. When they didn't shout at me—in my uniform, you know—I took it they were strangers."

So all we had for our afternoon's work was this: some one had been shot by the bullet that went through the door; he had not left the village, and he had not called in a physician. Also, Doctor Walker knew who Lucien Wallace was, and his very denial made me confident that, in that one direction at least, we were on the right track.

The thought that the detective would be there that night was the most cheering thing of all, and I think even Gertrude was glad of it. Driving home that afternoon, I saw her in the clear sunlight for the first time in several days, and I was startled to see how ill she looked. She was thin and colorless, and all her bright animation was gone.

"Gertrude," I said, "I have been a very selfish old woman. You are going to leave this miserable house to-night. Annie Morton is going to Scotland next week, and you shall go right with her."

To my surprise, she flushed painfully.

"I don't want to go, Aunt Ray," she said. "Don't make me leave now."

"You are losing your health and your good looks," I said decidedly. "You should have a change."

"I shan't stir a foot." She was equally decided. Then, more lightly: "Why, you and Liddy need me to arbitrate between you every day in the week."

Perhaps I was growing suspicious of every one, but it seemed to me that Gertrude's gaiety was forced and artificial. I watched her covertly during the rest of the drive, and I did not like the two spots of crimson in her pale cheeks. But I said nothing more about sending her to Scotland: I knew she would not go.

25.   A VISIT FROM LOUISE

That day was destined to be an eventful one, for when I entered the house and found Eliza ensconced in the upper hall on a chair, with Mary Anne doing her best to stifle her with household ammonia, and Liddy rubbing her wrists—whatever good that is supposed to do—I knew that the ghost had been walking again, and this time in daylight.

Eliza was in a frenzy of fear. She clutched at my sleeve when I went close to her, and refused to let go until she had told her story. Coming just after the fire, the household was demoralized, and it was no surprise to me to find Alex and the under-gardener struggling down-stairs with a heavy trunk between them.

"I didn't want to do it, Miss Innes," Alex said. "But she was so excited, I was afraid she would do as she said—drag it down herself, and scratch the staircase."

I was trying to get my bonnet off and to keep the maids quiet at the same time. "Now, Eliza, when you have washed your face and stopped bawling," I said, "come into my sitting-room and tell me what has happened."

Liddy put away my things without speaking. The very set of her shoulders expressed disapproval.

"Well," I said, when the silence became uncomfortable, "things seem to be warming up."

Silence from Liddy, and a long sigh.

"If Eliza goes, I don't know where to look for another cook." More silence.

"Rosie is probably a good cook." Sniff.

"Liddy," I said at last, "don't dare to deny that you are having the time of your life. You positively gloat in this excitement. You never looked better. It's my opinion all this running around, and getting jolted out of a rut, has stirred up that torpid liver of yours."

"It's not myself I'm thinking about," she said, goaded into speech. "Maybe my liver was torpid, and maybe it wasn't; but I know this: I've got some feelings left, and to see you standing at the foot of that staircase shootin' through the door—I'll never be the same woman again."

"Well, I'm glad of that—anything for a change," I said. And in came Eliza, flanked by Rosie and Mary Anne.

Her story, broken with sobs and corrections from the other two, was this: At two o'clock (two-fifteen, Rosie insisted) she had gone up-stairs to get a picture from her room to show Mary Anne. (A picture of a *lady*, Mary Anne interposed.) She went up the servants' staircase and along the corridor to her room, which lay between the trunk-room and the unfinished ball-room. She heard a sound as she went down the corridor, like some one moving furniture, but she was not nervous. She thought it might be men examining the house after the fire the night before, but she looked in the trunk-room and saw nobody.

She went into her room quietly. The noise had ceased, and everything was quiet. Then she sat down on the side of her bed, and, feeling faint—she was subject to spells—("I told you that when I came, didn't I, Rosie?" "Yes'm, indeed she did!")—she put her head down on her pillow and—

"Took a nap. All right!" I said. "Go on."

"When I came to, Miss Innes, sure as I'm sittin' here, I thought I'd die. Somethin' hit me on the face, and I set up, sudden. And then I seen the plaster drop, droppin' from a little hole in the wall. And the first thing I knew, an iron bar that long" (fully two yards by her measure) "shot through that hole and tumbled on the bed. If I'd been still sleeping" ("Fainting," corrected Rosie) "I'd 'a' been hit on the head and killed!"

"I wisht you'd heard her scream," put in Mary Anne. "And her face as white as a pillow-slip when she tumbled down the stairs."

"No doubt there is some natural explanation for it, Eliza," I said. "You may have dreamed it, in your `fainting' attack. But if it is true, the metal rod and the hole in the wall will show it."

Eliza looked a little bit sheepish.

"The hole's there all right, Miss Innes," she said. "But the bar was gone when Mary Anne and Rosie went up to pack my trunk."

"That wasn't all," Liddy's voice came funereally from a corner. "Eliza said that from the hole in the wall a burning eye looked down at her!"

"The wall must be at least six inches thick," I said with asperity. "Unless the person who drilled the hole carried his eyes on the ends of a stick, Eliza couldn't possibly have seen them."

But the fact remained, and a visit to Eliza's room proved it. I might jeer all I wished: some one had drilled a hole in the unfinished wall of the ball-room, passing between the bricks of the partition, and shooting through the unresisting plaster of Eliza's room with such force as to send the rod flying on to her bed. I had gone up-stairs alone, and I confess the thing puzzled me: in two or three places in the wall small apertures had been made, none of them of any depth. Not the least mysterious thing was the disappearance of the iron implement that had been used.

I remembered a story I read once about an impish dwarf that lived in the spaces between the double walls of an ancient castle. I wondered vaguely if my original idea of a secret entrance to a hidden chamber could be right, after all, and if we were housing some erratic guest, who played pranks on us in the dark, and destroyed the walls that he might listen, hidden safely away, to our amazed investigations.

Mary Anne and Eliza left that afternoon, but Rosie decided to stay. It was about five o'clock when the hack came from the station to get them, and, to my amazement, it had an occupant. Matthew Geist, the driver, asked for me, and explained his errand with pride.

"I've brought you a cook, Miss Innes," he said. "When the message came to come up for two girls and their trunks, I supposed there was something doing, and as this here woman had been looking for work in the village, I thought I'd bring her along."

Already I had acquired the true suburbanite ability to take servants on faith; I no longer demanded written and unimpeachable references. I, Rachel Innes, have learned not to mind if the cook sits down comfortably in my sitting-room when she is taking the orders for the day, and I am grateful if the silver is not cleaned with scouring soap. And so that day I merely told Liddy to send the new applicant in. When she came, however, I could hardly restrain a gasp of surprise. It was the woman with the pitted face.

She stood somewhat awkwardly just inside the door, and she had an air of self-confidence that was inspiring. Yes, she could cook; was not a fancy cook, but could make good soups and desserts if there was any one to take charge of the salads. And so, in the end, I took her. As Halsey said, when we told him, it didn't matter much about the cook's face, if it was clean.

I have spoken of Halsey's restlessness. On that day it seemed to be more than ever a resistless impulse that kept him out until after luncheon. I think he hoped constantly that he might meet Louise driving over the hills in her runabout: possibly he did meet her occasionally, but from his continued gloom I felt sure the situation between them was unchanged.

Part of the afternoon I believe he read—Gertrude and I were out, as I have said, and at dinner we both noticed that something had occurred to distract him. He was disagreeable, which is unlike him, nervous, looking at his watch every few minutes, and he ate almost nothing. He asked twice during the meal on what train Mr. Jamieson and the other detective were coming, and had long periods of abstraction during which he dug his fork into my damask cloth and did not hear when he was spoken to. He refused dessert, and left the table early, excusing himself on the ground that he wanted to see Alex.

Alex, however, was not to be found. It was after eight when Halsey ordered the car, and started down the hill at a pace that, even for him, was unusually reckless. Shortly after, Alex reported that he was ready to go over the house, preparatory to closing it for the night. Sam Bohannon came at a quarter before nine, and began his patrol of the grounds, and with the arrival of the two detectives to look forward to, I was not especially apprehensive.

At half-past nine I heard the sound of a horse driven furiously up the drive. It came to a stop in front of the house, and immediately after there were hurried steps on the veranda. Our nerves were not what they should have been, and Gertrude, always apprehensive lately, was at the door almost instantly. A moment later Louise had burst into the room and stood there bareheaded and breathing hard!

"Where is Halsey?" she demanded. Above her plain black gown her eyes looked big and somber, and the rapid drive had brought no color to her face. I got up and drew forward a chair.

"He has not come back," I said quietly. "Sit down, child; you are not strong enough for this kind of thing."

I don't think she even heard me.

"He has not come back?" she asked, looking from me to Gertrude. "Do you know where he went? Where can I find him?"

"For Heaven's sake, Louise," Gertrude burst out, "tell us what is wrong. Halsey is not here. He has gone to the station for Mr. Jamieson. What has happened?"

"To the station, Gertrude? You are sure?"

"Yes," I said. "Listen. There is the whistle of the train now."

She relaxed a little at our matter-of-fact tone, and allowed herself to sink into a chair.

"Perhaps I was wrong," she said heavily. "He—will be here in a few moments if—everything is right."

We sat there, the three of us, without attempt at conversation. Both Gertrude and I recognized the futility of asking Louise any questions: her reticence was a part of a role she had assumed. Our ears were strained for the first throb of the motor as it turned into the drive and commenced the climb to the house. Ten minutes passed, fifteen, twenty. I saw Louise's hands grow rigid as they clutched the arms of her chair. I watched Gertrude's bright color slowly ebbing away, and around my own heart I seemed to feel the grasp of a giant hand.

Twenty-five minutes, and then a sound. But it was not the chug of the motor: it was the unmistakable rumble of the Casanova hack. Gertrude drew aside the curtain and peered into the darkness.

"It's the hack, I am sure," she said, evidently relieved. "Something has gone wrong with the car, and no wonder—the way Halsey went down the hill."

It seemed a long time before the creaking vehicle came to a stop at the door. Louise rose and stood watching, her hand to her throat. And then Gertrude opened the door, admitting Mr. Jamieson and a stocky, middle-aged man. Halsey was not with them. When the door had closed and Louise realized that Halsey had not come, her expression changed. From tense watchfulness to relief, and now again to absolute despair, her face was an open page.

"Halsey?" I asked unceremoniously, ignoring the stranger. "Did he not meet you?"

"No." Mr. Jamieson looked slightly surprised. "I rather expected the car, but we got up all right."

"You didn't see him at all?" Louise demanded breathlessly.

Mr. Jamieson knew her at once, although he had not seen her before. She had kept to her rooms until the morning she left.

"No, Miss Armstrong," he said. "I saw nothing of him. What is wrong?"

"Then we shall have to find him," she asserted. "Every instant is precious. Mr. Jamieson, I have reason for believing that he is in danger, but I don't know what it is. Only—he must be found."

The stocky man had said nothing. Now, however, he went quickly toward the door.

"I'll catch the hack down the road and hold it," he said. "Is the gentleman down in the town?"

"Mr. Jamieson," Louise said impulsively, "I can use the hack. Take my horse and trap outside and drive like mad. Try to find the Dragon Fly—it ought to be easy to trace. I can think of no other way. Only, don't lose a moment."

The new detective had gone, and a moment later Jamieson went rapidly down the drive, the cob's feet striking fire at every step. Louise stood looking after them. When she turned around she faced Gertrude, who stood indignant, almost tragic, in the hall.

"You *know* what threatens Halsey, Louise," she said accusingly. "I believe you know this whole horrible thing, this mystery that we are struggling with. If anything happens to Halsey, I shall never forgive you."

Louise only raised her hands despairingly and dropped them again.

"He is as dear to me as he is to you," she said sadly. "I tried to warn him."

"Nonsense!" I said, as briskly as I could. "We are making a lot of trouble out of something perhaps very small. Halsey was probably late—he is always late. Any moment we may hear the car coming up the road."

But it did not come. After a half-hour of suspense, Louise went out quietly, and did not come back. I hardly knew she was gone until I heard the station hack moving off. At eleven o'clock the telephone rang. It was Mr. Jamieson.

"I have found the Dragon Fly, Miss Innes," he said. "It has collided with a freight car on the siding above the station. No, Mr. Innes was not there, but we shall probably find him. Send Warner for the car."

But they did not find him. At four o'clock the next morning we were still waiting for news, while Alex watched the house and Sam the grounds. At daylight I dropped into exhausted sleep. Halsey had not come back, and there was no word from the detective.

26. HALSEY'S DISAPPEARANCE

Nothing that had gone before had been as bad as this. The murder and Thomas' sudden death we had been able to view in a detached sort of way. But with Halsey's disappearance everything was altered. Our little circle, intact until now, was broken. We were no longer onlookers who saw a battle passing around them. We were the center of action. Of course, there was no time then to voice such an idea. My mind seemed able to hold only one thought: that Halsey had been foully dealt with, and that every minute lost might be fatal.

Mr. Jamieson came back about eight o'clock the next morning: he was covered with mud, and his hat was gone. Altogether, we were a sad-looking trio that gathered around a breakfast that no one could eat. Over a cup of black coffee the detective told us what he had learned of Halsey's movements the night before. Up to a certain point the car had made it easy enough to follow him. And I gathered that Mr. Burns, the other detective, had followed a similar car for miles at dawn, only to find it was a touring car on an endurance run.

"He left here about ten minutes after eight," Mr. Jamieson said. "He went alone, and at eight twenty he stopped at Doctor Walker's. I went to the doctor's about midnight, but he had been called out on a case, and had not come back at four o'clock. From the doctor's it seems Mr. Innes walked across the lawn to the cottage Mrs. Armstrong and her daughter have taken. Mrs. Armstrong had retired, and he said perhaps a dozen words to Miss Louise. She will not say what they were, but the girl evidently suspects what has occurred. That is, she suspects foul play, but she doesn't know of what nature. Then, apparently, he started directly for the station. He was going very fast—the flagman at the Carol Street crossing says he saw the car pass. He knew the siren. Along somewhere in the dark stretch between Carol Street and the depot he evidently swerved suddenly—perhaps some one in the road—and went full into the side of a freight. We found it there last night."

"He might have been thrown under the train by the force of the shock," I said tremulously.

Gertrude shuddered.

"We examined every inch of track. There was—no sign."

"But surely—he can't be—gone!" I cried. "Aren't there traces in the mud—anything?"

"There is no mud—only dust. There has been no rain. And the footpath there is of cinders. Miss Innes, I am inclined to think that he has met with bad treatment, in the light of what has gone before. I do not think he has been murdered." I shrank from the word. "Burns is back in the country, on a clue we got from the night clerk at the drug-store. There will be two more men here by noon, and the city office is on the lookout."

"The creek?" Gertrude asked.

"The creek is shallow now. If it were swollen with rain, it would be different. There is hardly any water in it. Now, Miss Innes," he said, turning to me, "I must ask you some questions. Had Mr. Halsey any possible reason for going away like this, without warning?"

"None whatever."

"He went away once before," he persisted. "And you were as sure then."

"He did not leave the Dragon Fly jammed into the side of a freight car before."

"No, but he left it for repairs in a blacksmith shop, a long distance from here. Do you know if he had any enemies? Any one who might wish him out of the way?"

"Not that I know of, unless—no, I can not think of any."

"Was he in the habit of carrying money?"

"He never carried it far. No, he never had more than enough for current expenses."

Mr. Jamieson got up then and began to pace the room. It was an unwonted concession to the occasion.

"Then I think we get at it by elimination. The chances are against flight. If he was hurt, we find no trace of him. It looks almost like an abduction. This young Doctor Walker—

have you any idea why Mr. Innes should have gone there last night?"

"I can not understand it," Gertrude said thoughtfully. "I don't think he knew Doctor Walker at all, and—their relations could hardly have been cordial, under the circumstances."

Jamieson pricked up his ears, and little by little he drew from us the unfortunate story of Halsey's love affair, and the fact that Louise was going to marry Doctor Walker.

Mr. Jamieson listened attentively.

"There are some interesting developments here," he said thoughtfully. "The woman who claims to be the mother of Lucien Wallace has not come back. Your nephew has apparently been spirited away. There is an organized attempt being made to enter this house; in fact, it has been entered. Witness the incident with the cook yesterday. And I have a new piece of information."

He looked carefully away from Gertrude. "Mr. John Bailey is not at his Knickerbocker apartments, and I don't know where he is. It's a hash, that's what it is. It's a Chinese puzzle. They won't fit together, unless—unless Mr. Bailey and your nephew have again—"

And once again Gertrude surprised me. "They are not together," she said hotly. "I—know where Mr. Bailey is, and my brother is not with him."

The detective turned and looked at her keenly.

"Miss Gertrude," he said, "if you and Miss Louise would only tell me everything you know and surmise about this business, I should be able to do a great many things. I believe I could find your brother, and I might be able to— well, to do some other things." But Gertrude's glance did not falter.

"Nothing that I know could help you to find Halsey," she said stubbornly. "I know absolutely as little of his disappearance as you do, and I can only say this: I do not trust Doctor Walker. I think he hated Halsey, and he would get rid of him if he could."

"Perhaps you are right. In fact, I had some such theory myself. But Doctor Walker went out late last night to a serious case in Summitville, and is still there. Burns traced him there. We have made guarded inquiry at the Greenwood Club, and through the village. There is absolutely nothing to go on but this. On the embankment above the railroad, at the point where we found the machine, is a small house. An old woman and a daughter, who is very lame, live there. They say that they distinctly heard the shock when the Dragon Fly hit the car, and they went to the bottom of their garden and looked over. The automobile was there; they could see the lights, and they thought someone had been injured. It was very dark, but they could make out two figures, standing together. The women were curious, and, leaving the fence, they went back and by a roundabout path down to the road. When they got there the car was still standing, the headlight broken and the bonnet crushed, but there was no one to be seen."

The detective went away immediately, and to Gertrude and me was left the woman's part, to watch and wait. By luncheon nothing had been found, and I was frantic. I went up-stairs to Halsey's room finally, from sheer inability to sit across from Gertrude any longer, and meet her terror-filled eyes.

Liddy was in my dressing-room, suspiciously red-eyed, and trying to put a right sleeve in a left armhole of a new waist for me. I was too much shaken to scold.

"What name did that woman in the kitchen give?" she demanded, viciously ripping out the offending sleeve.

"Bliss. Mattie Bliss," I replied.

"Bliss. M. B. Well, that's not what she has on her suitcase. It is marked N. F. C."

The new cook and her initials troubled me not at all. I put on my bonnet and sent for what the Casanova liveryman called a "stylish turnout." Having once made up my mind to a course of action, I am not one to turn back. Warner drove me; he was plainly disgusted, and he steered the livery horse as he would the Dragon Fly, feeling uneasily with his left foot for the clutch, and working his right elbow at an imaginary horn every time a dog got in the way.

Warner had something on his mind, and after we had turned into the road, he voiced it.

"Miss Innes," he said. "I overheard a part of a conversation yesterday that I didn't understand. It wasn't my business to understand it, for that matter. But I've been thinking all day that I'd better tell you. Yesterday afternoon, while you and Miss Gertrude were out driving, I had got the car in some sort of shape again after the fire, and I went to the library to call Mr. Innes to see it. I went into the living-room, where Miss Liddy said he was, and half-way across to the library I heard him talking to some one. He seemed to be walking up and down, and he was in a rage, I can tell you."

"What did he say?"

"The first thing I heard was—excuse me, Miss Innes, but it's what he said, `The damned rascal,' he said, `I'll see him in'—well, in hell was what he said, `in hell first.' Then somebody else spoke up; it was a woman. She said, `I warned them, but they thought I would be afraid.'"

"A woman! Did you wait to see who it was?"

"I wasn't spying, Miss Innes," Warner said with dignity. "But the next thing caught my attention. She said, `I knew there was something wrong from the start. A man isn't well one day, and dead the next, without some reason.' I thought she was speaking of Thomas."

"And you don't know who it was!" I exclaimed. "Warner, you had the key to this whole occurrence in your hands, and did not use it!"

However, there was nothing to be done. I resolved to make inquiry when I got home, and in the meantime, my present errand absorbed me. This was nothing less than to see Louise Armstrong, and to attempt to drag from her what she knew, or suspected, of Halsey's disappearance. But here, as in every direction I turned, I was baffled.

A neat maid answered the bell, but she stood squarely in the doorway, and it was impossible to preserve one's dignity and pass her.

"Miss Armstrong is very ill, and unable to see any one," she said. I did not believe her.

"And Mrs. Armstrong—is she also ill?"

"She is with Miss Louise and can not be disturbed."

"Tell her it is Miss Innes, and that it is a matter of the greatest importance."

"It would be of no use, Miss Innes. My orders are positive."

At that moment a heavy step sounded on the stairs. Past the maid's white-strapped shoulder I could see a familiar thatch of gray hair, and in a moment I was face to face with Doctor Stewart. He was very grave, and his customary geniality was tinged with restraint.

"You are the very woman I want to see," he said promptly. "Send away your trap, and let me drive you home. What is this about your nephew?"

"He has disappeared, doctor. Not only that, but there is every evidence that he has been either abducted, or—" I could not finish. The doctor helped me into his capacious buggy in silence. Until we had got a little distance he did not speak; then he turned and looked at me.

"Now tell me about it," he said. He heard me through without speaking.

"And you think Louise knows something?" he said when I had finished. "I don't—in fact, I am sure of it. The best evidence of it is this: she asked me if he had been heard from, or if anything had been learned. She won't allow Walker in the room, and she made me promise to see you and tell you this: don't give up the search for him. Find him, and find him soon. He is living."

"Well," I said, "if she knows that, she knows more. She is a very cruel and ungrateful girl."

"She is a very sick girl," he said gravely. "Neither you nor I can judge her until we know everything. Both she and her mother are ghosts of their former selves. Under all this, these two sudden deaths, this bank robbery, the invasions at Sunnyside and Halsey's disappearance, there is some mystery that, mark my words, will come out some day. And when it does, we shall find Louise Armstrong a victim."

I had not noticed where we were going, but now I saw we were beside the railroad, and from a knot of men standing beside the track I divined that it was here the car had been found. The siding, however, was empty. Except a few bits of splintered wood on the ground, there was no sign of the accident.

"Where is the freight car that was rammed?" the doctor asked a bystander.

"It was taken away at daylight, when the train was moved."

There was nothing to be gained. He pointed out the house on the embankment where the old lady and her daughter had heard the crash and seen two figures beside the car. Then we drove slowly home. I had the doctor put me down at the gate, and I walked to the house—past the lodge where we had found Louise, and, later, poor Thomas; up the drive where I had seen a man watching the lodge and where, later, Rosie had been frightened; past the east entrance, where so short a time before the most obstinate effort had been made to enter the house, and where, that night two weeks ago, Liddy and I had seen the strange woman. Not far from the west wing lay the blackened ruins of the stables. I felt like a ruin myself, as I paused on the broad veranda before I entered the house.

Two private detectives had arrived in my absence, and it was a relief to turn over to them the responsibility of the house and grounds. Mr. Jamieson, they said, had arranged for more to assist in the search for the missing man, and at that time the country was being scoured in all directions.

The household staff was again depleted that afternoon. Liddy was waiting to tell me that the new cook had gone, bag and baggage, without waiting to be paid. No one had admitted the visitor whom Warner had heard in the library, unless, possibly, the missing cook. Again I was working in a circle.

27. WHO IS NINA CARRINGTON?

The four days, from Saturday to the following Tuesday, we lived, or existed, in a state of the most dreadful suspense. We ate only when Liddy brought in a tray, and then very little. The papers, of course, had got hold of the story, and we were besieged by newspaper men. From all over the country false clues came pouring in and raised hopes that crumbled again to nothing. Every morgue within a hundred miles, every hospital, had been visited, without result.

Mr. Jamieson, personally, took charge of the organized search, and every evening, no matter where he happened to be, he called us by long distance telephone. It was the same formula. "Nothing to-day. A new clue to work on. Better luck to-morrow."

And heartsick we would put up the receiver and sit down again to our vigil.

The inaction was deadly. Liddy cried all day, and, because she knew I objected to tears, sniffled audibly around the corner.

"For Heaven's sake, smile!" I snapped at her. And her ghastly attempt at a grin, with her swollen nose and red eyes, made me hysterical. I laughed and cried together, and pretty soon, like the two old fools we were, we were sitting together weeping into the same handkerchief.

Things were happening, of course, all the time, but they made little or no impression. The Charity Hospital called up Doctor Stewart and reported that Mrs. Watson was in a critical condition. I understood also that legal steps were being taken to terminate my lease at Sunnyside. Louise was out of danger, but very ill, and a trained nurse guarded her like a gorgon. There was a rumor in the village, brought up by Liddy from the butcher's, that a wedding had already taken place between Louise and Doctor Walkers and this roused me for the first time to action.

On Tuesday, then, I sent for the car, and prepared to go out. As I waited at the *porte-cochère*[6] I saw the under-gardener, an inoffensive, grayish-haired man, trimming borders near the house.

---

[6] A portico-like structure at an entrance to a building through which a carriage or motor vehicle can pass in order for the occupants to alight under cover

The day detective was watching him, sitting on the carriage block. When he saw me, he got up.

"Miss Innes," he said, taking of his hat, "do you know where Alex, the gardener, is?"

"Why, no. Isn't he here?" I asked.

"He has been gone since yesterday afternoon. Have you employed him long?"

"Only a couple of weeks."

"Is he efficient? A capable man?"

"I hardly know," I said vaguely. "The place looks all right, and I know very little about such things. I know much more about boxes of roses than bushes of them."

"This man," pointing to the assistant, "says Alex isn't a gardener. That he doesn't know anything about plants."

"That's very strange," I said, thinking hard. "Why, he came to me from the Brays, who are in Europe."

"Exactly." The detective smiled. "Every man who cuts grass isn't a gardener, Miss Innes, and just now it is our policy to believe every person around here a rascal until he proves to be the other thing."

Warner came up with the car then, and the conversation stopped. As he helped me in, however, the detective said something further.

"Not a word or sign to Alex, if he comes back," he said cautiously.

I went first to Doctor Walker's. I was tired of beating about the bush, and I felt that the key to Halsey's disappearance was here at Casanova, in spite of Mr. Jamieson's theories.

The doctor was in. He came at once to the door of his consulting-room, and there was no mask of cordiality in his manner.

"Please come in," he said curtly.

"I shall stay here, I think, doctor." I did not like his face or his manner; there was a subtle change in both. He had thrown off the air of friendliness, and I thought, too, that he looked anxious and haggard.

"Doctor Walker," I said, "I have come to you to ask some questions. I hope you will answer them. As you know, my nephew has not yet been found."

"So I understand," stiffly.

"I believe, if you would, you could help us, and that leads to one of my questions. Will you tell me what was the nature of the conversation you held with him the night he was attacked and carried off?"

"Attacked! Carried off!" he said, with pretended surprise. "Really, Miss Innes, don't you think you exaggerate? I understand it is not the first time Mr. Innes has—disappeared."

"You are quibbling, doctor. This is a matter of life and death. Will you answer my question?"

"Certainly. He said his nerves were bad, and I gave him a prescription for them. I am violating professional ethics when I tell you even as much as that."

I could not tell him he lied. I think I looked it. But I hazarded a random shot.

"I thought perhaps," I said, watching him narrowly, "that it might be about—Nina Carrington."

For a moment I thought he was going to strike me. He grew livid, and a small crooked blood-vessel in his temple swelled and throbbed curiously. Then he forced a short laugh.

"Who is Nina Carrington?" he asked.

"I am about to discover that," I replied, and he was quiet at once. It was not difficult to divine that he feared Nina Carrington a good deal more than he did the devil. Our leave-taking was brief; in fact, we merely stared at each other over the waiting-room table, with its litter of year-old magazines. Then I turned and went out.

"To Richfield," I told Warner, and on the way I thought, and thought hard.

"Nina Carrington, Nina Carrington," the roar and rush of the wheels seemed to sing the words. "Nina Carrington, N. C." And I then knew, knew as surely as if I had seen the whole thing. There had been an N. C. on the suit-case belonging to the woman with the pitted face. How simple it all seemed. Mattie Bliss had been Nina Carrington. It was she Warner had heard in the library. It was something she had told Halsey that had taken him frantically to Doctor Walker's office, and from there perhaps to his death. If we could find the woman, we might find what had become of Halsey.

We were almost at Richfield now, so I kept on. My mind was not on my errand there now. It was back with Halsey on that memorable night. What was it he had said to Louise, that had sent her up to Sunnyside, half wild with fear for him? I made up my mind, as the car drew up before the Tate cottage, that I would see Louise if I had to break into the house at night.

Almost exactly the same scene as before greeted my eyes at the cottage. Mrs. Tate, the baby-carriage in the path, the children at the swing—all were the same.

She came forward to meet me, and I noticed that some of the anxious lines had gone out of her face. She looked young, almost pretty.

"I am glad you have come back," she said. "I think I will have to be honest and give you back your money."

"Why?" I asked. "Has the mother come?"

"No, but some one came and paid the boy's board for a month. She talked to him for a long time, but when I asked him afterward he didn't know her name."

"A young woman?"

"Not very young. About forty, I suppose. She was small and fair-haired, just a little bit gray, and very sad. She was in deep mourning, and, I think, when she came, she expected to go at once. But the child, Lucien, interested her. She talked to him for a long time, and, indeed, she looked much happier when she left."

"You are sure this was not the real mother?"

"O mercy, no! Why, she didn't know which of the three was Lucien. I thought perhaps she was a friend of yours, but, of course, I didn't ask."

"She was not—pock-marked?" I asked at a venture. "No, indeed. A skin like a baby's. But perhaps you will know the initials. She gave Lucien a handkerchief and forgot it. It was very fine, black-bordered, and it had three hand-worked letters in the corner—F. B. A."

"No," I said with truth enough, "she is not a friend of mine." F. B. A. was Fanny Armstrong, without a chance of doubt!

With another warning to Mrs. Tate as to silence, we started back to Sunnyside. So Fanny Armstrong knew of Lucien Wallace, and was sufficiently interested to visit him and pay for his support. Who was the child's mother and where was she? Who was Nina Carrington? Did either of them know where Halsey was or what had happened to him?

On the way home we passed the little cemetery where Thomas had been laid to rest. I wondered if Thomas could have helped us to find Halsey, had he lived. Farther along was the more imposing burial-ground, where Arnold Armstrong and his father lay in the shadow of a tall granite shaft. Of the three, I think Thomas was the only one sincerely mourned.

28.   A TRAMP AND THE TOOTHACHE

The bitterness toward the dead president of the Traders' Bank seemed to grow with time. Never popular, his memory was execrated by people who had lost nothing, but who were filled with disgust by constantly hearing new stories of the man's grasping avarice. The Traders' had been a favorite bank for small tradespeople, and in its savings department it had solicited the smallest deposits. People who had thought to be self-supporting to the last found themselves confronting the poorhouse, their two or three hundred dollar savings wiped away. All bank failures have this element, however, and the directors were trying to promise twenty per cent on deposits.

But, like everything else those days, the bank failure was almost forgotten by Gertrude and myself. We did not mention Jack Bailey: I had found nothing to change my impression of his guilt, and Gertrude knew how I felt. As for the murder of the bank president's son, I was of two minds. One day I thought Gertrude knew or at least suspected that Jack had done it; the next I feared that it had been Gertrude herself, that night alone on the circular staircase. And then the mother of Lucien Wallace would obtrude herself, and an almost equally good case might be made against her. There were times, of course, when I was disposed to throw all those suspicions aside, and fix definitely on the unknown, whoever that might be.

I had my greatest disappointment when it came to tracing Nina Carrington. The woman had gone without leaving a trace. Marked as she was, it should have been easy to follow her, but she was not to be found. A description to one of the detectives, on my arrival at home, had started the ball rolling. But by night she had not been found. I told Gertrude, then, about the telegram to Louise when she had been ill before; about my visit to Doctor Walker, and my suspicions that Mattie Bliss and Nina Carrington were the same. She thought, as I did, that there was little doubt of it.

I said nothing to her, however, of the detective's suspicions about Alex. Little things that I had not noticed at the time now came back to me. I had an uncomfortable feeling that perhaps Alex was a spy, and that by taking him into the house I had played into the enemy's hand. But at eight o'clock that night Alex himself appeared, and with him a strange and repulsive individual. They made a queer pair, for Alex was almost as disreputable as the tramp, and he had a badly swollen eye.

Gertrude had been sitting listlessly waiting for the evening message from Mr. Jamieson, but when the singular pair came in, as they did, without ceremony, she jumped up and stood staring. Winters, the detective who watched the house at night, followed them, and kept his eyes sharply on Alex's prisoner. For that was the situation as it developed.

He was a tall lanky individual, ragged and dirty, and just now he looked both terrified and embarrassed. Alex was too much engrossed to be either, and to this day I don't think I ever asked him why he went off without permission the day before.

"Miss Innes," Alex began abruptly, "this man can tell us something very important about the disappearance of Mr. Innes. I found him trying to sell this watch."

He took a watch from his pocket and put it on the table. It was Halsey's watch. I had given it to him on his twenty-first birthday: I was dumb with apprehension.

"He says he had a pair of cuff-links also, but he sold them—"

"Fer a dollar'n half," put in the disreputable individual hoarsely, with an eye on the detective.

"He is not—dead?" I implored. The tramp cleared his throat.

"No'm," he said huskily. "He was used up pretty bad, but he weren't dead. He was comin' to hisself when I"—he stopped and looked at the detective. "I didn't steal it, Mr. Winters," he whined. "I found it in the road, honest to God, I did."

Mr. Winters paid no attention to him. He was watching Alex.

"I'd better tell what he told me," Alex broke in. "It will be quicker. When Jamieson—when Mr. Jamieson calls up we can start him right. Mr. Winters, I found this man trying to sell that watch on Fifth Street. He offered it to me for three dollars."

"How did you know the watch?" Winters snapped at him.

"I had seen it before, many times. I used it at night when I was watching at the foot of the staircase." The detective was satisfied. "When he offered the watch to me, I knew it, and I pretended I was going to buy it. We went into an alley and I got the watch." The tramp shivered. It was plain how Alex had secured the watch. "Then—I got the story from this fellow. He claims to have seen the whole affair. He says he was in an empty car—in the car the automobile struck."

The tramp broke in here, and told his story, with frequent interpretations by Alex and Mr. Winters. He used a strange medley, in which familiar words took unfamiliar meanings, but it was gradually made clear to us.

On the night in question the tramp had been "pounding his ear"—this stuck to me as being graphic—in an empty box-car along the siding at Casanova. The train was going west, and due to leave at dawn. The tramp and the "brakey" were friendly, and things going well. About ten o'clock, perhaps earlier, a terrific crash against the side of the car roused him. He tried to open the door, but could not move it. He got out of the other side, and just as he did so, he heard some one groan.

The habits of a lifetime made him cautious. He slipped on to the bumper of a car and peered through. An automobile had struck the car, and stood there on two wheels. The tail lights were burning, but the headlights were out. Two men were stooping over some one who lay on the ground. Then the taller of the two started on a dog-trot along the train looking for an empty. He found one four cars away and ran back again. The two lifted the unconscious man into the empty box-car, and, getting in themselves, stayed for three or four minutes. When they came out, after closing the sliding door, they cut up over the railroad embankment toward the town. One, the short one, seemed to limp.

The tramp was wary. He waited for ten minutes or so. Some women came down a path to the road and inspected the automobile. When they had gone, he crawled into the box-car and closed the door again. Then he lighted a match. The figure of a man, unconscious, gagged, and with his hands tied, lay far at the end.

The tramp lost no time; he went through his pockets, found a little money and the cuff-links, and took them. Then he loosened the gag—it had been cruelly tight—and went his way, again closing the door of the box-car. Outside on the road he found the watch. He got on the fast freight east, some time after, and rode into the city. He had sold the cuff-links, but on offering the watch to Alex he had been "copped."

The story, with its cold recital of villainy, was done. I hardly knew if I were more anxious, or less. That it was Halsey, there could be no doubt. How badly he was hurt, how far he had been carried, were the questions that demanded immediate answer. But it was the first real information we had had; my boy had not been murdered outright. But instead of vague terrors there was now the real fear that he might be lying in some strange hospital receiving the casual attention commonly given to the charity cases. Even this, had we known it, would have been paradise to the terrible truth. I wake yet and feel myself cold and trembling with the horror of Halsey's situation for three days after his disappearance.

Mr. Winters and Alex disposed of the tramp with a warning. It was evident he had told us all he knew. We had occasion, within a day or two, to be doubly thankful that we had given him his freedom. When Mr. Jamieson telephoned that night we had news for him; he told me what I had not realized before—that it would not be possible to find Halsey at once, even with this clue. The cars by this time, three days, might be scattered over the Union.

But he said to keep on hoping, that it was the best news we had had. And in the meantime, consumed with anxiety as we were, things were happening at the house in rapid succession.

We had one peaceful day—then Liddy took sick in the night. I went in when I heard her groaning, and found her with a hot-water bottle to her face, and her right cheek swollen until it was glassy.

"Toothache?" I asked, not too gently. "You deserve it. A woman of your age, who would rather go around with an exposed nerve in her head than have the tooth pulled! It would be over in a moment."

"So would hanging," Liddy protested, from behind the hot-water bottle.

I was hunting around for cotton and laudanum.

"You have a tooth just like it yourself, Miss Rachel," she whimpered. "And I'm sure Doctor Boyle's been trying to take it out for years."

There was no laudanum, and Liddy made a terrible fuss when I proposed carbolic acid, just because I had put too much on the cotton once and burned her mouth. I'm sure it never did her any permanent harm; indeed, the doctor said afterward that living on liquid diet had been a splendid rest for her stomach. But she would have none of the acid, and she kept me awake groaning, so at last I got up and went to Gertrude's door. To my surprise, it was locked.

I went around by the hall and into her bedroom that way. The bed was turned down, and her dressing-gown and night-dress lay ready in the little room next, but Gertrude was not there. She had not undressed.

I don't know what terrible thoughts came to me in the minute I stood there. Through the door I could hear Liddy grumbling, with a squeal now and then when the pain stabbed harder. Then, automatically, I got the laudanum and went back to her.

It was fully a half-hour before Liddy's groans subsided. At intervals I went to the door into the hall and looked out, but I saw and heard nothing suspicious. Finally, when Liddy had dropped into a doze, I even ventured as far as the head of the circular staircase, but there floated up to me only the even breathing of Winters, the night detective, sleeping just inside the entry. And then, far off, I heard the rapping noise that had lured Louise down the staircase that other night, two weeks before. It was over my head, and very faint— three or four short muffled taps, a pause, and then again, stealthily repeated.

The sound of Mr. Winters' breathing was comforting; with the thought that there was help within call, something kept me from waking him. I did not move for a moment; ridiculous things Liddy had said about a ghost—I am not at all superstitious, except, perhaps, in the middle of the night, with everything dark—things like that came back to me. Almost beside me was the clothes chute. I could feel it, but I could see nothing. As I stood, listening intently, I heard a sound near me. It was vague, indefinite. Then it ceased; there was an uneasy movement and a grunt from the foot of the circular staircase, and silence again.

I stood perfectly still, hardly daring to breathe.

Then I knew I had been right. Some one was stealthily-passing the head of the staircase and coming toward me in the dark. I leaned against the wall for support—my knees were giving way. The steps were close now, and suddenly I thought of Gertrude. Of course it was Gertrude. I put out one hand in front of me, but I touched nothing. My voice almost refused me, but I managed to gasp out, "Gertrude!"

"Good Lord!" a man's voice exclaimed, just beside me. And then I collapsed. I felt myself going, felt some one catch me, a horrible nausea—that was all I remembered.

When I came to it was dawn. I was lying on the bed in Louise's room, with the cherub on the ceiling staring down at me, and there was a blanket from my own bed thrown over me. I felt weak and dizzy, but I managed to get up and totter to the door. At the foot of the circular staircase Mr. Winters was still asleep. Hardly able to stand, I crept back to my room. The door into Gertrude's room was no longer locked: she was sleeping like a tired child. And in my dressing-room Liddy hugged a cold hot water bottle, and mumbled in her sleep.

"There's some things you can't hold with hand cuffs," she was muttering thickly.

29. A SCRAP OF PAPER

For the first time in twenty years, I kept my bed that day. Liddy was alarmed to the point of hysteria, and sent for Doctor Stewart just after breakfast. Gertrude spent the morning with me, reading something—I forget what. I was too busy with my thoughts to listen. I had said nothing to the two detectives. If Mr. Jamieson had been there, I should have told him everything, but I could not go to these strange men and tell them my niece had been missing in the middle of the night; that she had not gone to bed at all; that while I was searching for her through the house, I had met a stranger who, when I fainted, had carried me into a room and left me there, to get better or not, as it might happen.

The whole situation was terrible: had the issues been less vital, it would have been absurd. Here we were, guarded day and night by private detectives, with an extra man to watch the grounds, and yet we might as well have lived in a Japanese paper house, for all the protection we had.

And there was something else: the man I had met in the darkness had been even more startled than I, and about his voice, when he muttered his muffled exclamation, there was something vaguely familiar. All that morning, while Gertrude read aloud, and Liddy watched for the doctor, I was puzzling over that voice, without result.

And there were other things, too. I wondered what Gertrude's absence from her room had to do with it all, or if it had any connection. I tried to think that she had heard the rapping noises before I did and gone to investigate, but

I'm afraid I was a moral coward that day. I could not ask her.

Perhaps the diversion was good for me. It took my mind from Halsey, and the story we had heard the night before. The day, however, was a long vigil, with every ring of the telephone full of possibilities. Doctor Walker came up, some time just after luncheon, and asked for me.

"Go down and see him," I instructed Gertrude. "Tell him I am out—for mercy's sake don't say I'm sick. Find out what he wants, and from this time on, instruct the servants that he is not to be admitted. I loathe that man."

Gertrude came back very soon, her face rather flushed.

"He came to ask us to get out," she said, picking up her book with a jerk. "He says Louise Armstrong wants to come here, now that she is recovering."

"And what did you say?"

"I said we were very sorry we could not leave, but we would be delighted to have Louise come up here with us. He looked daggers at me. And he wanted to know if we would recommend Eliza as a cook. He has brought a patient, a man, out from town, and is increasing his establishment—that's the way he put it."

"I wish him joy of Eliza," I said tartly. "Did he ask for Halsey?"

"Yes. I told him that we were on the track last night, and that it was only a question of time. He said he was glad, although he didn't appear to be, but he said not to be too sanguine."

"Do you know what I believe?" I asked. "I believe, as firmly as I believe anything, that Doctor Walker knows something about Halsey, and that he could put his finger on him, if he wanted to."

There were several things that day that bewildered me. About three o'clock Mr. Jamieson telephoned from the Casanova station and Warner went down to meet him. I got up and dressed hastily, and the detective was shown up to my sitting-room.

"No news?" I asked, as he entered. He tried to look encouraging, without success. I noticed that he looked tired and dusty, and, although he was ordinarily impeccable in his appearance, it was clear that he was at least two days from a razor.

"It won't be long now, Miss Innes," he said. "I have come out here on a peculiar errand, which I will tell you about later. First, I want to ask some questions. Did any one come out here yesterday to repair the telephone, and examine the wires on the roof?"

"Yes," I said promptly; "but it was not the telephone. He said the wiring might have caused the fire at the stable. I went up with him myself, but he only looked around."

Mr. Jamieson smiled.

"Good for you!" he applauded. "Don't allow any one in the house that you don't trust, and don't trust anybody. All are not electricians who wear rubber gloves."

He refused to explain further, but he got a slip of paper out of his pocketbook and opened it carefully.

"Listen," he said. "You heard this before and scoffed. In the light of recent developments I want you to read it again. You are a clever woman, Miss Innes. Just as surely as I sit here, there is something in this house that is wanted very anxiously by a number of people. The lines are closing up, Miss Innes."

The paper was the one he had found among Arnold Armstrong's effects, and I read it again:

> "——by altering the plans for——rooms, may be possible. The best way, in my opinion, would be to——the plan for——in one of the——rooms—— chimney."

"I think I understand," I said slowly. "Some one is searching for the secret room, and the invaders—"

"And the holes in the plaster—"

"Have been in the progress of his—"

"Or her—investigations."

"Her?" I asked.

"Miss Innes," the detective said, getting up, "I believe that somewhere in the walls of this house is hidden some of the money, at least, from the Traders' Bank. I believe, just as surely, that young Walker brought home from California the knowledge of something of the sort and, failing in his effort to reinstall Mrs. Armstrong and her daughter here, he, or a confederate, has tried to break into the house. On two occasions I think he succeeded."

"On three, at least," I corrected. And then I told him about the night before. "I have been thinking hard," I concluded, "and I do not believe the man at the head of the circular staircase was Doctor Walker. I don't think he could have got in, and the voice was not his."

Mr. Jamieson got up and paced the floor, his hands behind him.

"There is something else that puzzles me," he said, stepping before me. "Who and what is the woman Nina Carrington? If it was she who came here as Mattie Bliss, what did she tell Halsey that sent him racing to Doctor Walker's, and then to Miss Armstrong? If we could find that woman we would have the whole thing."

"Mr. Jamieson, did you ever think that Paul Armstrong might not have died a natural death?"

"That is the thing we are going to try to find out," he replied. And then Gertrude came in, announcing a man below to see Mr. Jamieson.

"I want you present at this interview, Miss Innes," he said. "May Riggs come up? He has left Doctor Walker and he has something he wants to tell us."

Riggs came into the room diffidently, but Mr. Jamieson put him at his ease. He kept a careful eye on me, however, and slid into a chair by the door when he was asked to sit down.

"Now, Riggs," began Mr. Jamieson kindly. "You are to say what you have to say before this lady."

"You promised you'd keep it quiet, Mr. Jamieson." Riggs plainly did not trust me. There was nothing friendly in the glance he turned on me.

"Yes, yes. You will be protected. But, first of all, did you bring what you promised?"

Riggs produced a roll of papers from under his coat, and handed them over. Mr. Jamieson examined them with lively satisfaction, and passed them to me. "The blue-prints of Sunnyside," he said. "What did I tell you? Now, Riggs, we are ready."

"I'd never have come to you, Mr. Jamieson," he began, "if it hadn't been for Miss Armstrong. When Mr. Innes was spirited away, like, and Miss Louise got sick because of it, I thought things had gone far enough. I'd done some things for the doctor before that wouldn't just bear looking into, but I turned a bit squeamish."

"Did you help with that?" I asked, leaning forward.

"No, ma'm. I didn't even know of it until the next day, when it came out in the Casanova Weekly Ledger. But I know who did it, all right. I'd better start at the beginning.

"When Doctor Walker went away to California with the Armstrong family, there was talk in the town that when he came back he would be married to Miss Armstrong, and we all expected it. First thing I knew, I got a letter from him, in the west. He seemed to be excited, and he said Miss Armstrong had taken a sudden notion to go home and he sent me some money. I was to watch for her, to see if she went to Sunnyside, and wherever she was, not to lose sight of her until he got home. I traced her to the lodge, and I guess I scared you on the drive one night, Miss Innes."

"And Rosie!" I ejaculated.

Riggs grinned sheepishly.

"I only wanted to make sure Miss Louise was there. Rosie started to run, and I tried to stop her and tell her some sort of a story to account for my being there. But she wouldn't wait."

"And the broken china—in the basket?"

"Well, broken china's death to rubber tires," he said. "I hadn't any complaint against you people here, and the Dragon Fly was a good car."

So Rosie's highwayman was explained.

"Well, I telegraphed the doctor where Miss Louise was and I kept an eye on her. Just a day or so before they came home with the body, I got another letter, telling me to watch for a woman who had been pitted with smallpox. Her name was Carrington, and the doctor made things pretty strong. If I found any such woman loafing around, I was not to lose sight of her for a minute until the doctor got back.

"Well, I would have had my hands full, but the other woman didn't show up for a good while, and when she did the doctor was home."

"Riggs," I asked suddenly, "did you get into this house a day or two after I took it, at night?"

"I did not, Miss Innes. I have never been in the house before. Well, the Carrington woman didn't show up until the night Mr. Halsey disappeared. She came to the office late, and the doctor was out. She waited around, walking the floor and working herself into a passion. When the doctor didn't come back, she was in an awful way. She wanted me to hunt him, and when he didn't appear, she called him names; said he couldn't fool her. There was murder being done, and she would see him swing for it.

"She struck me as being an ugly customer, and when she left, about eleven o'clock, and went across to the Armstrong place, I was not far behind her. She walked all around the house first, looking up at the windows. Then she rang the bell, and the minute the door was opened she was through it, and into the hall."

"How long did she stay?"

"That's the queer part of it," Riggs said eagerly. "She didn't come out that night at all. I went to bed at daylight, and that was the last I heard of her until the next day, when I saw her on a truck at the station, covered with a sheet. She'd been struck by the express and you would hardly have known her—dead, of course. I think she stayed all night in the Armstrong house, and the agent said she was crossing the track to take the up-train to town when the express struck her."

"Another circle!" I exclaimed. "Then we are just where we started."

"Not so bad as that, Miss Innes," Riggs said eagerly. "Nina Carrington came from the town in California where Mr. Armstrong died. Why was the doctor so afraid of her? The Carrington woman knew something. I lived with Doctor Walker seven years, and I know him well. There are few things he is afraid of. I think he killed Mr. Armstrong out in the west somewhere, that's what I think. What else he did I don't know—but he dismissed me and pretty nearly throttled me—for telling Mr. Jamieson here about Mr.

Innes' having been at his office the night he disappeared, and about my hearing them quarreling."

"What was it Warner overheard the woman say to Mr. Innes, in the library?" the detective asked me.

"She said `I knew there was something wrong from the start. A man isn't well one day and dead the next without some reason.'"

How perfectly it all seemed to fit!

30. WHEN CHURCHYARDS YAWN

It was on Wednesday Riggs told us the story of his connection with some incidents that had been previously unexplained. Halsey had been gone since the Friday night before, and with the passage of each day I felt that his chances were lessening. I knew well enough that he might be carried thousands of miles in the box-car, locked in, perhaps, without water or food. I had read of cases where bodies had been found locked in cars on isolated sidings in the west, and my spirits went down with every hour.

His recovery was destined to be almost as sudden as his disappearance, and was due directly to the tramp Alex had brought to Sunnyside. It seems the man was grateful for his release, and when he learned some thing of Halsey's whereabouts from another member of his fraternity—for it is a fraternity—he was prompt in letting us know.

On Wednesday evening Mr. Jamieson, who had been down at the Armstrong house trying to see Louise—and failing—was met near the gate at Sunnyside by an individual precisely as repulsive and unkempt as the one Alex had captured. The man knew the detective, and he gave him a piece of dirty paper, on which was scrawled the words—"He's at City Hospital, Johnsville." The tramp who brought the paper pretended to know nothing, except this: the paper had been passed along from a "hobo" in Johnsville, who seemed to know the information would be valuable to us.

Again the long distance telephone came into requisition. Mr. Jamieson called the hospital, while we crowded around him. And when there was no longer any doubt that it was Halsey, and that he would probably recover, we all laughed and cried together. I am sure I kissed Liddy, and I have had terrible moments since when I seem to remember kissing Mr. Jamieson, too, in the excitement.

Anyhow, by eleven o'clock that night Gertrude was on her way to Johnsville, three hundred and eighty miles away, accompanied by Rosie. The domestic force was now down to Mary Anne and Liddy, with the under-gardener's wife coming every day to help out. Fortunately, Warner and the detectives were keeping bachelor hall in the lodge. Out of deference to Liddy they washed their dishes once a day, and they concocted queer messes, according to their several abilities. They had one triumph that they ate regularly for breakfast, and that clung to their clothes and their hair the rest of the day. It was bacon, hardtack and onions, fried together. They were almost pathetically grateful, however, I noticed, for an occasional broiled tenderloin.

It was not until Gertrude and Rosie had gone and Sunnyside had settled down for the night, with Winters at the foot of the staircase, that Mr. Jamieson broached a subject he had evidently planned before he came.

"Miss Innes," he said, stopping me as I was about to go to my room up-stairs, "how are your nerves tonight?"

"I have none," I said happily. "With Halsey found, my troubles have gone."

"I mean," he persisted, "do you feel as though you could go through with something rather unusual?"

"The most unusual thing I can think of would be a peaceful night. But if anything is going to occur, don't dare to let me miss it."

"Something is going to occur," he said. "And you're the only woman I can think of that I can take along." He looked at his watch. "Don't ask me any questions, Miss Innes. Put on heavy shoes, and some old dark clothes, and make up your mind not to be surprised at anything."

Liddy was sleeping the sleep of the just when I went up-stairs, and I hunted out my things cautiously. The detective was waiting in the hall, and I was astonished to see Doctor Stewart with him.

They were talking confidentially together, but when I came down they ceased. There were a few preparations to be made: the locks to be gone over, Winters to be instructed as to renewed vigilance, and then, after extinguishing the hall light, we crept, in the darkness, through the front door, and into the night.

I asked no questions. I felt that they were doing me honor in making me one of the party, and I would show them I could be as silent as they. We went across the fields, passing through the woods that reached almost to the ruins of the stable, going over stiles now and then, and sometimes stepping over low fences. Once only somebody spoke, and then it was an emphatic bit of profanity from Doctor Stewart when he ran into a wire fence.

We were joined at the end of five minutes by another man, who fell into step with the doctor silently. He carried something over his shoulder which I could not make out. In this way we walked for perhaps twenty minutes. I had lost all sense of direction: I merely stumbled along in silence, allowing Mr. Jamieson to guide me this way or that as the path demanded. I hardly know what I expected. Once, when through a miscalculation I jumped a little short over a ditch and landed above my shoe-tops in the water and ooze, I remember wondering if this were really I, and if I had ever tasted life until that summer. I walked along with the water sloshing in my boots, and I was actually cheerful. I remember whispering to Mr. Jamieson that I had never seen the stars so lovely, and that it was a mistake, when the Lord had made the night so beautiful, to sleep through it!

The doctor was puffing somewhat when we finally came to a halt. I confess that just at that minute even Sunnyside seemed a cheerful spot. We had paused at the edge of a level cleared place, bordered all around with primly trimmed evergreen trees. Between them I caught a glimpse of starlight shining down on rows of white headstones and an occasional more imposing monument, or towering shaft. In spite of myself, I drew my breath in sharply. We were on the edge of the Casanova churchyard.

I saw now both the man who had joined the party and the implements he carried. It was Alex, armed with two long-handled spades. After the first shock of surprise, I flatter myself I was both cool and quiet. We went in single file between the rows of headstones, and although, when I found myself last, I had an instinctive desire to keep looking back over my shoulder, I found that, the first uneasiness past, a cemetery at night is much the same as any other country place, filled with vague shadows and unexpected noises. Once, indeed—but Mr. Jamieson said it was an owl, and I tried to believe him.

In the shadow of the Armstrong granite shaft we stopped. I think the doctor wanted to send me back.

"It's no place for a woman," I heard him protesting angrily. But the detective said something about witnesses, and the doctor only came over and felt my pulse.

"Anyhow, I don't believe you're any worse off here than you would be in that nightmare of a house," he said finally, and put his coat on the steps of the shaft for me to sit on.

There is an air of finality about a grave: one watches the earth thrown in, with the feeling that this is the end. Whatever has gone before, whatever is to come in eternity, that particular temple of the soul has been given back to the elements from which it came. Thus, there is a sense of desecration, of a reversal of the everlasting fitness of things, in resurrecting a body from its mother clay. And yet that night, in the Casanova churchyard, I sat quietly by, and watched Alex and Mr. Jamieson steaming over their work, without a single qualm, except the fear of detection.

The doctor kept a keen lookout, but no one appeared. Once in a while he came over to me, and gave me a reassuring pat on the shoulder.

"I never expected to come to this," he said once. "There's one thing sure—I'll not be suspected of complicity. A doctor is generally supposed to be handier at burying folks than at digging them up."

The uncanny moment came when Alex and Jamieson tossed the spades on the grass, and I confess I hid my face. There was a period of stress, I think, while the heavy coffin was being raised. I felt that my composure was going, and, for fear I would shriek, I tried to think of something else— what time Gertrude would reach Halsey—anything but the grisly reality that lay just beyond me on the grass.

And then I heard a low exclamation from the detective and I felt the pressure of the doctor's fingers on my arm.

"Now, Miss Innes," he said gently. "If you will come over—"

I held on to him frantically, and somehow I got there and looked down. The lid of the casket had been raised and a silver plate on it proved we had made no mistake. But the face that showed in the light of the lantern was a face I had never seen before. The man who lay before us was not Paul Armstrong!

31. BETWEEN TWO FIREPLACES

What with the excitement of the discovery, the walk home under the stars in wet shoes and draggled skirts, and getting up-stairs and undressed without rousing Liddy, I was completely used up. What to do with my boots was the greatest puzzle of all, there being no place in the house safe from Liddy, until I decided to slip upstairs the next morning and drop them into the hole the "ghost" had made in the trunk-room wall.

I went asleep as soon as I reached this decision, and in my dreams I lived over again the events of the night. Again I saw the group around the silent figure on the grass, and again, as had happened at the grave, I heard Alex's voice, tense and triumphant:

"Then we've got them," he said. Only, in my dreams, he said it over and over until he seemed to shriek it in my ears.

I wakened early, in spite of my fatigue, and lay there thinking. Who was Alex? I no longer believed that he was a gardener. Who was the man whose body we had resurrected? And where was Paul Armstrong? Probably living safely in some extraditionless country on the fortune he had stolen. Did Louise and her mother know of the shameful and wicked deception? What had Thomas known, and Mrs. Watson? Who was Nina Carrington?

This last question, it seemed to me, was answered. In some way the woman had learned of the substitution, and had tried to use her knowledge for blackmail. Nina Carrington's own story died with her, but, however it happened, it was clear that she had carried her knowledge to Halsey the afternoon Gertrude and I were looking for clues to the man I had shot on the east veranda. Halsey had been half crazed by what he heard; it was evident that Louise was marrying Doctor Walker to keep the shameful secret, for her mother's sake. Halsey, always reckless, had gone at once to Doctor Walker and denounced him. There had been a scene, and he left on his way to the station to meet and notify Mr. Jamieson of what he had learned. The doctor was active mentally and physically. Accompanied perhaps by Riggs, who had shown himself not overscrupulous until he quarreled with his employer, he had gone across to the railroad embankment, and, by jumping in front of the car, had caused Halsey to swerve. The rest of the story we knew.

That was my reconstructed theory of that afternoon and evening: it was almost correct—not quite.

There was a telegram that morning from Gertrude.

> *"Halsey conscious and improving.*
> *Probably home in day or so.*
> *GERTRUDE."*

With Halsey found and improving in health, and with at last something to work on, I began that day, Thursday, with fresh courage. As Mr. Jamieson had said, the lines were closing up. That I was to be caught and almost finished in the closing was happily unknown to us all.

It was late when I got up. I lay in my bed, looking around the four walls of the room, and trying to imagine behind what one of them a secret chamber might lie. Certainly, in daylight, Sunnyside deserved its name: never was a house more cheery and open, less sinister in general appearance. There was not a corner apparently that was not open and above-board, and yet, somewhere behind its handsomely papered walls I believed firmly that there lay a hidden room, with all the possibilities it would involve.

I made a mental note to have the house measured during the day, to discover any discrepancy between the outer and inner walls, and I tried to recall again the exact wording of the paper Jamieson had found.

The slip had said "chimney." It was the only clue, and a house as large as Sunnyside was full of them. There was an open fireplace in my dressing-room, but none in the bedroom, and as I lay there, looking around, I thought of something that made me sit up suddenly. The trunk-room, just over my head, had an open fireplace and a brick chimney, and yet, there was nothing of the kind in my room. I got out of bed and examined the opposite wall closely. There was apparently no flue, and I knew there was none in the hall just beneath. The house was heated by steam, as I have said before. In the living-room was a huge open fireplace, but it was on the other side.

Why did the trunk-room have both a radiator and an open fireplace? Architects were not usually erratic! It was not fifteen minutes before I was up-stairs, armed with a tape-measure in lieu of a foot-rule, eager to justify Mr. Jamieson's opinion of my intelligence, and firmly resolved not to tell him of my suspicion until I had more than theory to go on. The hole in the trunk-room wall still yawned there, between the chimney and the outer wall. I examined it again, with no new result. The space between the brick wall and the plaster and lath one, however, had a new significance. The hole showed only one side of the chimney, and I determined to investigate what lay in the space on the other side of the mantel.

I worked feverishly. Liddy had gone to the village to market, it being her firm belief that the store people sent short measure unless she watched the scales, and that, since the failure of the Traders' Bank, we must watch the corners; and I knew that what I wanted to do must be done before she came back. I had no tools, but after rummaging around I found a pair of garden scissors and a hatchet, and thus armed, I set to work. The plaster came out easily: the lathing was more obstinate. It gave under the blows, only to spring back into place again, and the necessity for caution made it doubly hard.

I had a blister on my palm when at last the hatchet went through and fell with what sounded like the report of a gun to my overstrained nerves. I sat on a trunk, waiting to hear Liddy fly up the stairs, with the household behind her, like the tail of a comet. But nothing happened, and with a growing feeling of uncanniness I set to work enlarging the opening.

The result was absolutely nil. When I could hold a lighted candle in the opening, I saw precisely what I had seen on the other side of the chimney—a space between the true wall and the false one, possibly seven feet long and about three feet wide. It was in no sense of the word a secret chamber, and it was evident it had not been disturbed since the house was built. It was a supreme disappointment.

It had been Mr. Jamieson's idea that the hidden room, if there was one, would be found somewhere near the circular staircase. In fact, I knew that he had once investigated the entire length of the clothes chute, hanging to a rope, with this in view. I was reluctantly about to concede that he had been right, when my eyes fell on the mantel and fireplace. The latter had evidently never been used: it was closed with a metal fire front, and only when the front refused to move, and investigation showed that it was not intended to be moved, did my spirits revive.

I hurried into the next room. Yes, sure enough, there was a similar mantel and fireplace there, similarly closed. In both rooms the chimney flue extended well out from the wall. I measured with the tape-line, my hands trembling so that I could scarcely hold it. They extended two feet and a half into each room, which, with the three feet of space between the two partitions, made eight feet to be accounted for. Eight feet in one direction and almost seven in the other—what a chimney it was!

But I had only located the hidden room. I was not in it, and no amount of pressing on the carving of the wooden mantels, no search of the floors for loose boards, none of the customary methods availed at all. That there was a means of entrance, and probably a simple one, I could be certain. But what? What would I find if I did get in? Was the detective right, and were the bonds and money from the Traders' Bank there? Or was our whole theory wrong? Would not Paul Armstrong have taken his booty with him? If he had not, and if Doctor Walker was in the secret, he would have known how to enter the chimney room. Then— who had dug the other hole in the false partition?

32. ANNE WATSON'S STORY

Liddy discovered the fresh break in the trunk-room wall while we were at luncheon, and ran shrieking down the stairs. She maintained that, as she entered, unseen hands had been digging at the plaster; that they had stopped when she went in, and she had felt a gust of cold damp air. In support of her story she carried in my wet and muddy boots, that I had unluckily forgotten to hide, and held them out to the detective and myself.

"What did I tell you?" she said dramatically. "Look at 'em. They're yours, Miss Rachel—and covered with mud and soaked to the tops. I tell you, you can scoff all you like; something has been wearing your shoes. As sure as you sit there, there's the smell of the graveyard on them. How do we know they weren't tramping through the Casanova churchyard last night, and sitting on the graves!"

Mr. Jamieson almost choked to death. "I wouldn't be at all surprised if they were doing that very thing, Liddy," he said, when he got his breath. "They certainly look like it."

I think the detective had a plan, on which he was working, and which was meant to be a coup. But things went so fast there was no time to carry it into effect. The first thing that occurred was a message from the Charity Hospital that Mrs. Watson was dying, and had asked for me. I did not care much about going. There is a sort of melancholy pleasure to be had out of a funeral, with its pomp and ceremony, but I shrank from a death-bed. However, Liddy got out the black things and the crape veil I keep for such occasions, and I went. I left Mr. Jamieson and the day detective going over every inch of the circular staircase, pounding, probing and measuring. I was inwardly elated to think of the surprise I was going to give them that night; as it turned out, I *did* surprise them almost into spasms.

I drove from the train to the Charity Hospital, and was at once taken to a ward. There, in a gray-walled room in a high iron bed, lay Mrs. Watson. She was very weak, and she only opened her eyes and looked at me when I sat down beside her. I was conscience-stricken. We had been so engrossed that I had left this poor creature to die without even a word of sympathy.

The nurse gave her a stimulant, and in a little while she was able to talk. So broken and half-coherent, however, was her story that I shall tell it in my own way. In an hour from the time I entered the Charity Hospital, I had heard a sad and pitiful narrative, and had seen a woman slip into the unconsciousness that is only a step from death.

Briefly, then, the housekeeper's story was this:

She was almost forty years old, and had been the sister-mother of a large family of children. One by one they had died, and been buried beside their parents in a little town in the Middle West. There was only one sister left, the baby, Lucy. On her the older girl had lavished all the love of an impulsive and emotional nature. When Anne, the elder, was thirty-two and Lucy was nineteen, a young man had come to the town. He was going east, after spending the summer at a celebrated ranch in Wyoming—one of those places where wealthy men send worthless and dissipated sons, for a season of temperance, fresh air and hunting. The sisters, of course, knew nothing of this, and the young man's ardor rather carried them away. In a word, seven years before, Lucy Haswell had married a young man whose name was given as Aubrey Wallace.

Anne Haswell had married a carpenter in her native town, and was a widow. For three months everything went fairly well. Aubrey took his bride to Chicago, where they lived at a hotel. Perhaps the very unsophistication that had charmed him in Valley Mill jarred on him in the city. He had been far from a model husband, even for the three months, and when he disappeared Anne was almost thankful. It was different with the young wife, however. She drooped and fretted, and on the birth of her baby boy, she had died. Anne took the child, and named him Lucien.

Anne had had no children of her own, and on Lucien she had lavished all her aborted maternal instinct. On one thing she was determined, however: that was that Aubrey Wallace should educate his boy. It was a part of her devotion to the child that she should be ambitious for him: he must have every opportunity. And so she came east. She drifted around, doing plain sewing and keeping a home somewhere always for the boy. Finally, however, she realized that her only training had been domestic, and she put the boy in an Episcopalian home, and secured the position of housekeeper to the Armstrongs. There she found Lucien's father, this time under his own name. It was Arnold Armstrong.

I gathered that there was no particular enmity at that time in Anne's mind. She told him of the boy, and threatened exposure if he did not provide for him. Indeed, for a time, he did so. Then he realized that Lucien was the ruling passion in this lonely woman's life. He found out where the child was hidden, and threatened to take him away. Anne was frantic. The positions became reversed. Where Arnold had given money for Lucien's support, as the years went on he forced money from Anne Watson instead until she was always penniless. The lower Arnold sank in the scale, the heavier his demands became. With the rupture between him and his family, things were worse. Anne took the child from the home and hid him in a farmhouse near Casanova, on the Claysburg road. There she went sometimes to see the boy, and there he had taken fever. The people were Germans, and he called the farmer's wife Grossmutter. He had grown into a beautiful boy, and he was all Anne had to live for.

The Armstrongs left for California, and Arnold's persecutions began anew. He was furious over the child's disappearance and she was afraid he would do her some hurt. She left the big house and went down to the lodge. When I had rented Sunnyside, however, she had thought the persecutions would stop. She had applied for the position of housekeeper, and secured it.

That had been on Saturday. That night Louise arrived unexpectedly. Thomas sent for Mrs. Watson and then went for Arnold Armstrong at the Greenwood Club. Anne had been fond of Louise—she reminded her of Lucy. She did not know what the trouble was, but Louise had been in a state of terrible excitement. Mrs. Watson tried to hide from Arnold, but he was ugly. He left the lodge and went up to the house about two-thirty, was admitted at the east entrance and came out again very soon. Something had occurred, she didn't know what; but very soon Mr. Innes and another gentleman left, using the car.

Thomas and she had got Louise quiet, and a little before three, Mrs. Watson started up to the house. Thomas had a key to the east entry, and gave it to her.

On the way across the lawn she was confronted by Arnold, who for some reason was determined to get into the house. He had a golf-stick in his hand, that he had picked up somewhere, and on her refusal he had struck her with it. One hand had been badly cut, and it was that, poisoning having set in, which was killing her. She broke away in a frenzy of rage and fear, and got into the house while Gertrude and Jack Bailey were at the front door. She went up-stairs, hardly knowing what she was doing. Gertrude's door was open, and Halsey's revolver lay there on the bed. She picked it up and turning, ran part way down the circular staircase. She could hear Arnold fumbling at the lock outside. She slipped down quietly and opened the door: he was inside before she had got back to the stairs. It was quite dark, but she could see his white shirt-bosom. From the fourth step she fired. As he fell, somebody in the billiard-room screamed and ran. When the alarm was raised, she had had no time to get up-stairs: she hid in the west wing until every one was down on the lower floor. Then she slipped upstairs, and threw the revolver out of an upper window, going down again in time to admit the men from the Greenwood Club.

If Thomas had suspected, he had never told. When she found the hand Arnold had injured was growing worse, she gave the address of Lucien at Richfield to the old man, and almost a hundred dollars. The money was for Lucien's board until she recovered. She had sent for me to ask me if I would try to interest the Armstrongs in the child. When she found herself growing worse, she had written to Mrs. Armstrong, telling her nothing but that Arnold's legitimate child was at Richfield, and imploring her to recognize him. She was dying: the boy was an Armstrong, and entitled to his father's share of the estate. The papers were in her trunk at Sunnyside, with letters from the dead man that would prove what she said. She was going; she would not be judged by earthly laws; and somewhere else perhaps Lucy would plead for her. It was she who had crept down the circular staircase, drawn by a magnet, that night Mr. Jamieson had heard some one there. Pursued, she had fled madly, anywhere—through the first door she came to. She had fallen down the clothes chute, and been saved by the basket beneath. I could have cried with relief; then it had not been Gertrude, after all!

That was the story. Sad and tragic though it was, the very telling of it seemed to relieve the dying woman. She did not know that Thomas was dead, and I did not tell her. I promised to look after little Lucien, and sat with her until the intervals of consciousness grew shorter and finally ceased altogether. She died that night.

33. AT THE FOOT OF THE STAIRS

As I drove rapidly up to the house from Casanova Station in the hack, I saw the detective Burns loitering across the street from the Walker place. So Jamieson was putting the screws on—lightly now, but ready to give them a twist or two, I felt certain, very soon.

The house was quiet. Two steps of the circular staircase had been pried off, without result, and beyond a second message from Gertrude, that Halsey insisted on coming home and they would arrive that night, there was nothing new. Mr. Jamieson, having failed to locate the secret room, had gone to the village. I learned afterwards that he called at Doctor Walker's, under pretense of an attack of acute indigestion, and before he left, had inquired about the evening trains to the city. He said he had wasted a lot of time on the case, and a good bit of the mystery was in my imagination! The doctor was under the impression that the house was guarded day and night. Well, give a place a reputation like that, and you don't need a guard at all,— thus Jamieson. And sure enough, late in the afternoon, the two private detectives, accompanied by Mr. Jamieson, walked down the main street of Casanova and took a city-bound train.

That they got off at the next station and walked back again to Sunnyside at dusk, was not known at the time. Personally, I knew nothing of either move; I had other things to absorb me at that time.

Liddy brought me some tea while I rested after my trip, and on the tray was a small book from the Casanova library. It was called *The Unseen World* and had a cheerful cover on which a half-dozen sheeted figures linked hands around a headstone.

At this point in my story, Halsey always says: "Trust a woman to add two and two together, and make six." To which I retort that if two and two plus X make six, then to discover the unknown quantity is the simplest thing in the world. That a houseful of detectives missed it entirely was because they were busy trying to prove that two and two make four.

The depression due to my visit to the hospital left me at the prospect of seeing Halsey again that night. It was about five o'clock when Liddy left me for a nap before dinner, having put me into a gray silk dressing-gown and a pair of slippers. I listened to her retreating footsteps, and as soon as she was safely below stairs, I went up to the trunk-room. The place had not been disturbed, and I proceeded at once to try to discover the entrance to the hidden room. The openings on either side, as I have said, showed nothing but perhaps three feet of brick wall.

There was no sign of an entrance—no levers, no hinges, to give a hint. Either the mantel or the roof, I decided, and after a half-hour at the mantel, productive of absolutely no result, I decided to try the roof.

I am not fond of a height. The few occasions on which I have climbed a step-ladder have always left me dizzy and weak in the knees. The top of the Washington monument is as impossible to me as the elevation of the presidential chair. And yet—I climbed out on to the Sunnyside roof without a second's hesitation. Like a dog on a scent, like my bearskin progenitor, with his spear and his wild boar, to me now there was the lust of the chase, the frenzy of pursuit, the dust of battle. I got quite a little of the latter on me as I climbed from the unfinished ball-room out through a window to the roof of the east wing of the building, which was only two stories in height.

Once out there, access to the top of the main building was rendered easy—at least it looked easy—by a small vertical iron ladder, fastened to the wall outside of the ball-room, and perhaps twelve feet high. The twelve feet looked short from below, but they were difficult to climb. I gathered my silk gown around me, and succeeded finally in making the top of the ladder.

Once there, however, I was completely out of breath. I sat down, my feet on the top rung, and put my hair pins in more securely, while the wind bellowed my dressing-gown out like a sail. I had torn a great strip of the silk loose, and now I ruthlessly finished the destruction of my gown by jerking it free and tying it around my head.

From far below the smallest sounds came up with peculiar distinctness. I could hear the paper boy whistling down the drive, and I heard something else. I heard the thud of a stone, and a spit, followed by a long and startled "meow" from Beulah. I forgot my fear of a height, and advanced boldly almost to the edge of the roof.

It was half-past six by that time, and growing dusk.

"You boy, down there!" I called.

The paper boy turned and looked around. Then, seeing nobody, he raised his eyes. It was a moment before he located me: when he did, he stood for one moment as if paralyzed, then he gave a horrible yell, and dropping his papers, bolted across the lawn to the road without stopping to look around. Once he fell, and his impetus was so great that he turned an involuntary somersault. He was up and off again without any perceptible pause, and he leaped the hedge—which I am sure under ordinary stress would have been a feat for a man.

I am glad in this way to settle the Gray Lady story, which is still a choice morsel in Casanova. I believe the moral deduced by the village was that it is always unlucky to throw a stone at a black cat.

With Johnny Sweeny a cloud of dust down the road, and the dinner-hour approaching, I hurried on with my investigations. Luckily, the roof was flat, and I was able to go over every inch of it. But the result was disappointing; no trap-door revealed itself, no glass window; nothing but a couple of pipes two inches across, and standing perhaps eighteen inches high and three feet apart, with a cap to prevent rain from entering and raised to permit the passage of air. I picked up a pebble from the roof and dropped it down, listening with my ear at one of the pipes. I could hear it strike on something with a sharp, metallic sound, but it was impossible for me to tell how far it had gone.

I gave up finally and went down the ladder again, getting in through the ball-room window without being observed. I went back at once to the trunk-room, and, sitting down on a box, I gave my mind, as consistently as I could, to the problem before me. If the pipes in the roof were ventilators to the secret room, and there was no trap-door above, the entrance was probably in one of the two rooms between which it lay—unless, indeed, the room had been built, and the opening then closed with a brick and mortar wall.

The mantel fascinated me. Made of wood and carved, the more I looked the more I wondered that I had not noticed before the absurdity of such a mantel in such a place. It was covered with scrolls and panels, and finally, by the merest accident, I pushed one of the panels to the side. It moved easily, revealing a small brass knob.

It is not necessary to detail the fluctuations of hope and despair, and not a little fear of what lay beyond, with which I twisted and turned the knob. It moved, but nothing seemed to happen, and then I discovered the trouble. I pushed the knob vigorously to one side, and the whole mantel swung loose from the wall almost a foot, revealing a cavernous space beyond.

I took a long breath, closed the door from the trunk-room into the hall—thank Heaven, I did not lock it—and pulling the mantel-door wide open, I stepped into the chimney-room. I had time to get a hazy view of a small portable safe, a common wooden table and a chair—then the mantel door swung to, and clicked behind me. I stood quite still for a moment, in the darkness, unable to comprehend what had happened. Then I turned and beat furiously at the door with my fists. It was closed and locked again, and my fingers in the darkness slid over a smooth wooden surface without a sign of a knob.

I was furiously angry—at myself, at the mantel door, at everything. I did not fear suffocation; before the thought had come to me I had already seen a gleam of light from the two small ventilating pipes in the roof. They supplied air, but nothing else. The room itself was shrouded in blackness.

I sat down in the stiff-backed chair and tried to remember how many days one could live without food and water. When that grew monotonous and rather painful, I got up and, according to the time-honored rule for people shut in unknown and ink-black prisons, I felt my way around—it was small enough, goodness knows. I felt nothing but a splintery surface of boards, and in endeavoring to get back to the chair, something struck me full in the face, and fell with the noise of a thousand explosions to the ground. When I had gathered up my nerves again, I found it had been the bulb of a swinging electric light, and that had it not been for the accident, I might have starved to death in an illuminated sepulcher.

I must have dozed off. I am sure I did not faint. I was never more composed in my life. I remember planning, if I were not discovered, who would have my things. I knew Liddy would want my heliotrope poplin, and she's a fright in lavender. Once or twice I heard mice in the partitions, and so I sat on the table, with my feet on the chair. I imagined I could hear the search going on through the house, and once some one came into the trunk-room; I could distinctly hear footsteps.

"In the chimney! In the chimney!" I called with all my might, and was rewarded by a piercing shriek from Liddy and the slam of the trunk-room door.

I felt easier after that, although the room was oppressively hot and enervating. I had no doubt the search for me would now come in the right direction, and after a little, I dropped into a doze. How long I slept I do not know.

It must have been several hours, for I had been tired from a busy day, and I wakened stiff from my awkward position. I could not remember where I was for a few minutes, and my head felt heavy and congested. Gradually I roused to my surroundings, and to the fact that in spite of the ventilators, the air was bad and growing worse. I was breathing long, gasping respirations, and my face was damp and clammy. I must have been there a long time, and the searchers were probably hunting outside the house, dredging the creek, or beating the woodland. I knew that another hour or two would find me unconscious, and with my inability to cry out would go my only chance of rescue. It was the combination of bad air and heat, probably, for some inadequate ventilation was coming through the pipes. I tried to retain my consciousness by walking the length of the room and back, over and over, but I had not the strength to keep it up, so I sat down on the table again, my back against the wall.

The house was very still. Once my straining ears seemed to catch a footfall beneath me, possibly in my own room. I groped for the chair from the table, and pounded with it frantically on the floor. But nothing happened: I realized bitterly that if the sound was heard at all, no doubt it was classed with the other rappings that had so alarmed us recently.

It was impossible to judge the flight of time. I measured five minutes by counting my pulse, allowing seventy-two beats to the minute. But it took eternities, and toward the last I found it hard to count; my head was confused.

And then—I heard sounds from below me, in the house. There was a peculiar throbbing, vibrating noise that I felt rather than heard, much like the pulsing beat of fire engines in the city. For one awful moment I thought the house was on fire, and every drop of blood in my body gathered around my heart; then I knew. It was the engine of the automobile, and Halsey had come back. Hope sprang up afresh. Halsey's clear head and Gertrude's intuition might do what Liddy's hysteria and three detectives had failed in.

After a time I thought I had been right. There was certainly something going on down below; doors were slamming, people were hurrying through the halls, and certain high notes of excited voices penetrated to me shrilly. I hoped they were coming closer, but after a time the sounds died away below, and I was left to the silence and heat, to the weight of the darkness, to the oppression of walls that seemed to close in on me and stifle me.

The first warning I had was a stealthy fumbling at the lock of the mantel-door. With my mouth open to scream, I stopped. Perhaps the situation had rendered me acute, perhaps it was instinctive. Whatever it was, I sat without moving, and some one outside, in absolute stillness, ran his fingers over the carving of the mantel and—found the panel.

Now the sounds below redoubled: from the clatter and jarring I knew that several people were running up the stairs, and as the sounds approached, I could even hear what they said.

"Watch the end staircases!" Jamieson was shouting. "Damnation—there's no light here!" And then a second later. "All together now. One—two—three—"

The door into the trunk-room had been locked from the inside. At the second that it gave, opening against the wall with a crash and evidently tumbling somebody into the room, the stealthy fingers beyond the mantel-door gave the knob the proper impetus, and—the door swung open, and closed again. Only—and Liddy always screams and puts her fingers in her ears at this point—only now I was not alone in the chimney room. There was some one else in the darkness, some one who breathed hard, and who was so close I could have touched him with my hand.

I was in a paralysis of terror. Outside there were excited voices and incredulous oaths. The trunks were being jerked around in a frantic search, the windows were thrown open, only to show a sheer drop of forty feet. And the man in the room with me leaned against the mantel-door and listened. His pursuers were plainly baffled: I heard him draw a long breath, and turn to grope his way through the blackness. Then—he touched my hand, cold, clammy, death-like.

A hand in an empty room! He drew in his breath, the sharp intaking of horror that fills lungs suddenly collapsed. Beyond jerking his hand away instantly, he made no movement. I think absolute terror had him by the throat. Then he stepped back, without turning, retreating foot by foot from The Dread in the corner, and I do not think he breathed.

Then, with the relief of space between us, I screamed, ear-splittingly, madly, and they heard me outside.

"In the chimney!" I shrieked. "Behind the mantel! The mantel!"

With an oath the figure hurled itself across the room at me, and I screamed again. In his blind fury he had missed me; I heard him strike the wall. That one time I eluded him; I was across the room, and I had got the chair. He stood for a second, listening, then—he made another rush, and I struck out with my weapon. I think it stunned him, for I had a second's respite when I could hear him breathing, and some one shouted outside:

"We—Can't—get—in. How—does—it—open?"

But the man in the room had changed his tactics. I knew he was creeping on me, inch by inch, and I could not tell from where. And then—he caught me. He held his hand over my mouth, and I bit him. I was helpless, strangling,—and some one was trying to break in the mantel from outside. It began to yield somewhere, for a thin wedge of yellowish light was reflected on the opposite wall. When he saw that, my assailant dropped me with a curse; then—the opposite wall swung open noiselessly, closed again without a sound, and I was alone. The intruder was gone.

"In the next room!" I called wildly. "The next room!" But the sound of blows on the mantel drowned my voice. By the time I had made them understand, a couple of minutes had elapsed. The pursuit was taken up then, by all except Alex, who was determined to liberate me. When I stepped out into the trunk-room, a free woman again, I could hear the chase far below.

I must say, for all Alex's anxiety to set me free, he paid little enough attention to my plight. He jumped through the opening into the secret room, and picked up the portable safe.

"I am going to put this in Mr. Halsey's room, Miss Innes," he said, "and I shall send one of the detectives to guard it."

I hardly heard him. I wanted to laugh and cry in the same breath—to crawl into bed and have a cup of tea, and scold Liddy, and do any of the thousand natural things that I had never expected to do again. And the air! The touch of the cool night air on my face!

As Alex and I reached the second floor, Mr. Jamieson met us. He was grave and quiet, and he nodded comprehendingly when he saw the safe.

"Will you come with me for a moment, Miss Innes?" he asked soberly, and on my assenting, he led the way to the east wing. There were lights moving around below, and some of the maids were standing gaping down. They screamed when they saw me, and drew back to let me pass. There was a sort of hush over the scene; Alex, behind me, muttered something I could not hear, and brushed past me without ceremony. Then I realized that a man was lying doubled up at the foot of the staircase, and that Alex was stooping over him.

As I came slowly down, Winters stepped back, and Alex straightened himself, looking at me across the body with impenetrable eyes. In his hand he held a shaggy gray wig, and before me on the floor lay the man whose headstone stood in Casanova churchyard—Paul Armstrong.

Winters told the story in a dozen words. In his headlong flight down the circular staircase, with Winters just behind,

Paul Armstrong had pitched forward violently, struck his head against the door to the east veranda, and probably broken his neck. He had died as Winters reached him.

As the detective finished, I saw Halsey, pale and shaken, in the card-room doorway, and for the first time that night I lost my self-control. I put my arms around my boy, and for a moment he had to support me. A second later, over Halsey's shoulder, I saw something that turned my emotion into other channels, for, behind him, in the shadowy card-room, were Gertrude and Alex, the gardener, and—there is no use mincing matters—he was kissing her!

I was unable to speak. Twice I opened my mouth: then I turned Halsey around and pointed. They were quite unconscious of us; her head was on his shoulder, his face against her hair. As it happened, it was Mr. Jamieson who broke up the tableau.

He stepped over to Alex and touched him on the arm.

"And now," he said quietly, "how long are you and I to play *our* little comedy, Mr. Bailey?"

34. THE ODDS AND ENDS

Of Doctor Walker's sensational escape that night to South America, of the recovery of over a million dollars in cash and securities in the safe from the chimney room—the papers have kept the public well informed. Of my share in discovering the secret chamber they have been singularly silent. The inner history has never been told. Mr. Jamieson got all kinds of credit, and some of it he deserved, but if

Jack Bailey, as Alex, had not traced Halsey and insisted on the disinterring of Paul Armstrong's casket, if he had not suspected the truth from the start, where would the detective have been?

When Halsey learned the truth, he insisted on going the next morning, weak as he was, to Louise, and by night she was at Sunnyside, under Gertrude's particular care, while her mother had gone to Barbara Fitzhugh's.

What Halsey said to Mrs. Armstrong I never knew, but that he was considerate and chivalrous I feel confident. It was Halsey's way always with women.

He and Louise had no conversation together until that night. Gertrude and Alex—I mean Jack—had gone for a walk, although it was nine o'clock, and anybody but a pair of young geese would have known that dew was falling, and that it is next to impossible to get rid of a summer cold.

At half after nine, growing weary of my own company, I went down-stairs to find the young people. At the door of the living-room I paused. Gertrude and Jack had returned and were there, sitting together on a divan, with only one lamp lighted. They did not see or hear me, and I beat a hasty retreat to the library. But here again I was driven back. Louise was sitting in a deep chair, looking the happiest I had ever seen her, with Halsey on the arm of the chair, holding her close.

It was no place for an elderly spinster. I retired to my up-stairs sitting-room and got out Eliza Klinefelter's lavender slippers. Ah, well, the foster motherhood would soon have to be put away in camphor again.

The next day, by degrees, I got the whole story.

Paul Armstrong had a besetting evil—the love of money. Common enough, but he loved money, not for what it would buy, but for its own sake. An examination of the books showed no irregularities in the past year since John had been cashier, but before that, in the time of Anderson, the old cashier, who had died, much strange juggling had been done with the records. The railroad in New Mexico had apparently drained the banker's private fortune, and he determined to retrieve it by one stroke. This was nothing less than the looting of the bank's securities, turning them into money, and making his escape.

But the law has long arms. Paul Armstrong evidently studied the situation carefully. Just as the only good Indian is a dead Indian, so the only safe defaulter is a dead defaulter. He decided to die, to all appearances, and when the hue and cry subsided, he would be able to enjoy his money almost anywhere he wished.

The first necessity was an accomplice. The connivance of Doctor Walker was suggested by his love for Louise. The man was unscrupulous, and with the girl as a bait, Paul Armstrong soon had him fast. The plan was apparently the acme of simplicity: a small town in the west, an attack of heart disease, a body from a medical college dissecting-room shipped in a trunk to Doctor Walker by a colleague in San Francisco, and palmed off for the supposed dead banker. What was simpler?

The woman, Nina Carrington, was the cog that slipped. What she only suspected, what she really knew, we never learned. She was a chambermaid in the hotel at C—, and it was evidently her intention to blackmail Doctor Walker. His position at that time was uncomfortable: to pay the woman to keep quiet would be confession. He denied the whole thing, and she went to Halsey.

It was this that had taken Halsey to the doctor the night he disappeared. He accused the doctor of the deception, and, crossing the lawn, had said something cruel to Louise. Then, furious at her apparent connivance, he had started for the station. Doctor Walker and Paul Armstrong—the latter still lame where I had shot him—hurried across to the embankment, certain only of one thing. Halsey must not tell the detective what he suspected until the money had been removed from the chimney-room. They stepped into the road in front of the car to stop it, and fate played into their hands. The car struck the train, and they had only to dispose of the unconscious figure in the road. This they did as I have told. For three days Halsey lay in the box car, tied hand and foot, suffering tortures of thirst, delirious at times, and discovered by a tramp at Johnsville only in time to save his life.

To go back to Paul Armstrong. At the last moment his plans had been frustrated. Sunnyside, with its hoard in the chimney-room, had been rented without his knowledge! Attempts to dislodge me having failed, he was driven to breaking into his own house. The ladder in the chute, the burning of the stable and the entrance through the card-room window—all were in the course of a desperate attempt to get into the chimney-room.

Louise and her mother had, from the first, been the great stumbling-blocks. The plan had been to send Louise away until it was too late for her to interfere, but she came back to the hotel at C— just at the wrong time. There was a terrible scene. The girl was told that something of the kind was necessary, that the bank was about to close and her stepfather would either avoid arrest and disgrace in this way, or kill himself. Fanny Armstrong was a weakling, but Louise was more difficult to manage. She had no love for her stepfather, but her devotion to her mother was entire, self-sacrificing. Forced into acquiescence by her mother's appeals, overwhelmed by the situation, the girl consented and fled.

From somewhere in Colorado she sent an anonymous telegram to Jack Bailey at the Traders' Bank. Trapped as she was, she did not want to see an innocent man arrested. The telegram, received on Thursday, had sent the cashier to the bank that night in a frenzy.

Louise arrived at Sunnyside and found the house rented. Not knowing what to do, she sent for Arnold at the Greenwood Club, and told him a little, not all. She told him that there was something wrong, and that the bank was about to close. That his father was responsible. Of the conspiracy she said nothing. To her surprise, Arnold already knew, through Bailey that night, that things were not right. Moreover, he suspected what Louise did not, that the money was hidden at Sunnyside. He had a scrap of paper that indicated a concealed room somewhere.

His inherited cupidity was aroused. Eager to get Halsey and Jack Bailey out of the house, he went up to the east entry, and in the billiard-room gave the cashier what he had refused earlier in the evening—the address of Paul

Armstrong in California and a telegram which had been forwarded to the club for Bailey, from Doctor Walker. It was in response to one Bailey had sent, and it said that Paul Armstrong was very ill.

Bailey was almost desperate. He decided to go west and find Paul Armstrong, and to force him to disgorge. But the catastrophe at the bank occurred sooner than he had expected. On the moment of starting west, at Andrews Station, where Mr. Jamieson had located the car, he read that the bank had closed, and, going back, surrendered himself.

John Bailey had known Paul Armstrong intimately. He did not believe that the money was gone; in fact, it was hardly possible in the interval since the securities had been taken. Where was it? And from some chance remark let fall some months earlier by Arnold Armstrong at a dinner, Bailey felt sure there was a hidden room at Sunnyside. He tried to see the architect of the building, but, like the contractor, if he knew of such a room he refused any information. It was Halsey's idea that John Bailey come to the house as a gardener, and pursue his investigations as he could. His smooth upper lip had been sufficient disguise, with his change of clothes, and a hair-cut by a country barber.

So it was Alex, Jack Bailey, who had been our ghost. Not only had he alarmed Louise—and himself, he admitted—on the circular staircase, but he had dug the hole in the trunk-room wall, and later sent Eliza into hysteria. The note Liddy had found in Gertrude's scrap-basket was from him, and it was he who had startled me into unconsciousness by the clothes chute, and, with Gertrude's help, had carried me to

Louise's room. Gertrude, I learned, had watched all night beside me, in an extremity of anxiety about me.

That old Thomas had seen his master, and thought he had seen the Sunnyside ghost, there could be no doubt. Of that story of Thomas', about seeing Jack Bailey in the footpath between the club and Sunnyside, the night Liddy and I heard the noise on the circular staircase—that, too, was right. On the night before Arnold Armstrong was murdered, Jack Bailey had made his first attempt to search for the secret room. He secured Arnold's keys from his room at the club and got into the house, armed with a golf-stick for sounding the walls. He ran against the hamper at the head of the stairs, caught his cuff-link in it, and dropped the golf-stick with a crash. He was glad enough to get away without an alarm being raised, and he took the "owl" train to town.

The oddest thing to me was that Mr. Jamieson had known for some time that Alex was Jack Bailey. But the face of the pseudo-gardener was very queer indeed, when that night, in the card-room, the detective turned to him and said:

"How long are you and I going to play our little comedy, *Mr. Bailey*?"

Well, it is all over now. Paul Armstrong rests in Casanova churchyard, and this time there is no mistake. I went to the funeral, because I wanted to be sure he was really buried, and I looked at the step of the shaft where I had sat that night, and wondered if it was all real. Sunnyside is for sale—no, I shall not buy it. Little Lucien Armstrong is living with his step-grandmother, and she is recovering gradually from troubles that had extended over the entire period of her second marriage. Anne Watson lies not far from the man she killed, and who as surely caused her death. Thomas, the fourth victim of the conspiracy, is buried on the hill. With Nina Carrington, five lives were sacrificed in the course of this grim conspiracy.

There will be two weddings before long, and Liddy has asked for my heliotrope poplin to wear to the church. I knew she would. She has wanted it for three years, and she was quite ugly the time I spilled coffee on it. We are very quiet, just the two of us. Liddy still clings to her ghost theory, and points to my wet and muddy boots in the trunk-room as proof. I am gray, I admit, but I haven't felt as well in a dozen years. Sometimes, when I am bored, I ring for Liddy, and we talk things over. When Warner married Rosie, Liddy sniffed and said what I took for faithfulness in Rosie had been nothing but mawkishness. I have not yet outlived Liddy's contempt because I gave them silver knives and forks as a wedding gift.

So we sit and talk, and sometimes Liddy threatens to leave, and often I discharge her, but we stay together somehow. I am talking of renting a house next year, and Liddy says to be sure there is no ghost. To be perfectly frank, I never really lived until that summer. Time has passed since I began this story. My neighbors are packing up for another summer. Liddy is having the awnings put up, and the window boxes filled. Liddy or no Liddy, I shall advertise to-morrow for a house in the country, and I don't care if it has a Circular Staircase.

THE END

Visit the **Summit Classic Press** website at
www.summitclassicpress.com
for information about other available classic books
and our schedule of upcoming new releases.

Summit Classic Press
265 South Main St., Suite 115
Akron, Ohio 44308

Made in the USA
Lexington, KY
16 June 2016